SL BEAUMONT

Cyber Count

A Kat Munro Thriller

Contents

Other books by SL Beaumont

The Kat Munro Thrillers
  Death Count
  Cyber Count

Shadow of Doubt

The Carlswick Mysteries
  The Carlswick Affair
  The Carlswick Treasure
  The Carlswick Conspiracy
  The Carlswick Deception
  The Carlswick Mythology
  The Reluctant Witness

Chapter 1

Marshall Tyler stamped his feet to keep warm and tossed his blond curls out of his eyes. It was supposed to be spring in London, but there wasn't much evidence of that yet. He couldn't wait for summer when school would finally be done. He would decamp to his parents' holiday home on the French Riviera for the holidays, where he'd spend each day working out at the gym, working on his tan, and chasing any number of beautiful girls who flocked to the region.

He took another look at his watch, a gift from his mother, an expensive Girard-Perregaux timepiece similar to the one footballer Cristiano Ronaldo favoured. They were late. He'd give them another five minutes, and then he'd return to school and apologise to his mate Harry. Maybe he shouldn't have gone behind his back to arrange this meeting, but Marshall loved the thrill of what they'd done. Harry wanted to take it slow, but Marshall had seen the opportunity when it presented itself. Despite Harry's objections, he'd gone ahead and submitted the proposal anyway. Perhaps he was going to be a shrewd businessman like his father after all.

There was a rustle in the weeds near the abandoned building where he'd been instructed to wait. He spun around and caught a glimpse of the mangy red tail of an urban fox disappearing into the undergrowth. The single-level brick structure and surrounding security fence were marked with 'Keep Out' signs, overlaid with meaningless graffiti. Plastic bags, food containers and all manner of rubbish had blown into a pile against the wire fence at one end of the site. The lights on the estate lining the streets leading to the old substation had flickered on during the time he'd been waiting, and dusk now blanketed the city.

He looked around at the growing shadows, and a shiver ran down his spine. He couldn't wait to leave this dodgy part of London behind him. He couldn't believe, out of all the places where he could have completed his schooling, that his parents had sent him to a boarding school in the East End. It had been his father's way of providing some counterbalance to the opulent lifestyle Marshall had been born into.

They weren't coming. Marshall felt the emptiness of disappointment twist his stomach. He took one more look about him, turned his collar up and ducked back through a hole in the broken fence. When he straightened, two men were standing in front of him.

He jumped and took a step back, crashing into the fence. One of the men laughed, a harsh chesty sound. Marshall couldn't make out much of their features in the gloom, except that they were both broad-shouldered, with knitted beanies pulled down over their ears.

"Tyler?" the first one asked.

"You're just a kid." The second man sounded surprised.

Marshall nodded and swallowed, feeling a sudden dryness in his throat.

"Let's talk around the back, where we won't be overheard,"

the first man said.

Marshall hesitated, unsure whether he wanted to be out of sight of the flats. Still, it didn't seem to be a suggestion, so he ducked back through the hole in the fence and waited while the two men followed. He took a deep breath and reminded himself that he was the one in charge; he had the thing they wanted. Squaring his shoulders, he led them around the edge of the substation into an overgrown yard that led down to the railway siding.

"Do you have it?"

The two men stood blocking his exit.

"Has the money been transferred?" Marshall asked. He heard the slight tremor in his voice and hoped that the men didn't.

"Yeah."

Marshall took out his phone and tapped on the app for the bank account. The balance was unchanged from when he'd looked earlier. "It's not there," he said. "I can't give it to you until I've been paid."

The second man stepped forward and knocked the phone from Marshall's hand. The screen shattered as it landed at his feet.

"You didn't really think we'd pay your blackmail, did you?" the first man sneered. "Now give it here."

Marshall felt a frisson of fear. He opened his mouth to call for help, but the men laughed.

"No one will hear you, and if they do, no one will come to your aid, not around these parts."

Marshall took a step backwards, but the first man grabbed him while the second man landed a solid punch to his abdomen, followed by one to his jaw. Marshall's head dropped to one side, and he struggled to draw in a breath.

"Stop, I don't have it on me," he rasped. "But I can get it for you."

The man hit him once more, and Marshall felt pain radiate from the centre of his face. Blood gushed from his nose, spilling down the front of his jacket.

"We'll wait here, and you go and get it," the first man said, releasing him and pushing him towards the building. "You have thirty minutes."

"And we'll keep that fancy watch as collateral to make sure you come back." The second man reached for his arm, releasing the clasp on the strap and slipping the watch from Marshall's wrist. He held it up to his face for a closer look. "Very nice."

"No," Marshall said, making a grab for the watch. The man pulled away as Marshall's fingers grazed the back of his hand. "That was a present from my mother."

"You know what you need to do if you want it and your phone back."

Chapter 2

Kat Munro draped the towel over her shoulder and strolled towards the door behind the last member of her fitness class. She flicked off the light switch, throwing the small mirror-lined studio into darkness.

"See you next week, Kat," called a young woman in sweatpants and a singlet walking with a pronounced limp, as she crossed the foyer to the changing rooms.

"Bye." Kat stepped into the corridor, pulling the door closed behind her. The sound of laughter caught her attention, and she saw a trio of men deep in conversation in the centre of the gym's spacious reception area. Marco, the gym's super-fit owner, was talking with a young man leaning on crutches. A wide grin spread across Marco's handsome face at something that the younger man said.

Marco slapped a hand on his shoulder. "We'll have you fighting fit in no time with that attitude, Tommy," he said.

Marco's dark hair was pulled back into a ponytail held in place by a thin leather strip. He was an excellent advertisement for the benefits of looking after oneself. He didn't look anywhere close to his almost forty years of age. His smooth, olive, southern European complexion probably added to the illusion, Kat thought. It was really a shame she could only think of him as a friend now.

The group's third member looked a little out of place in street clothes and shiny black shoes. He asked a question that Kat missed, and the mood turned sombre, causing her to hesitate as she approached the group, but Marco had seen her. "Kat, *bella*, join us," he called in accented English. "I was explaining that rehab for injuries like Tommy's usually takes many months. But I've thrown out the usual recovery timeline since he's exceeding all expectations."

Tommy turned in her direction, and Kat once again saw the evidence of his injuries. One side of his body had suffered severe burns. The skin on the left side of his jaw and neck was smooth and shiny from multiple skin grafts, and one hand was red and angry looking. His left leg was missing below the knee. Despite the pain that he must have been enduring, Tommy gave her a cheerful grin.

"Hey, Kat."

"Hey, Tommy. Sounds like you've been showing off again."

Tommy laughed. "Give me an audience, and I'll perform. This is Connor; he's a journalist doing an article on me for *The Times*."

"Ooh, *The Times*, Tommy, you'll be famous," Kat said. She turned to the reporter and held out her right hand. "Kat Munro," she said.

"Connor O'Malley," the journalist replied in a lilting Irish accent as he shook her hand. He was of slight build with short reddish-blond hair. He glanced at Kat's other hand. "If you don't mind me asking, were you injured in combat too?"

Kat raised her life-like hi-tech prosthetic left hand. "Nothing as brave, just a car accident," she said.

"Marco?" a man's voice called from across the lobby.

"Excuse me," Marco said. "Looks like I'm needed. Give me a call if you need anything else, Connor. I'll leave your name at reception for that free trial."

"Thanks," Connor said as Marco strode away. "Kat, you and Tommy obviously know each other. Do you work here?"

Kat shook her head. "Not really; I run a couple of classes as part of a charity that I'm involved with, that's all. I'm actually a forensic accountant in my day job."

Connor cocked his head to one side. "Now that sounds interesting."

"Yeah, it can be."

The automatic glass doors at the entrance to the gym swished open, and a man in a leather jacket entered. "Hey, Tommy, your chariot awaits," he said.

Kat recognised the voice and snapped her head around, feeling a nervous tangle of emotions knot in her stomach. She forced a smile.

"Hi, Adam," she said, unable to keep the surprise from her voice. "I, ah, didn't realise you knew Tommy."

DS Adam Jackson looked as uncomfortable as Kat felt. He ran a hand through his thick dark hair and cleared his throat. "Kat." He gave her a single nod of greeting.

Tommy's gaze swung from Adam to Kat. "Before he became a cop, Adam was my captain on my very first tour, Kat. He's been one of my taxi drivers since I got out of the hospital."

Kat understood. In fact, she knew very well how members of the military, ex and current, looked out for one another, having had two brothers in the services.

"Connor, how's the article coming along?" Adam turned his attention to the journalist, shaking his hand.

"Good, I just about have everything I need." Connor too

looked from Adam to Kat, picking up the unspoken tension.

"How have you been, Adam?" Kat said.

"Good," he said. "You?"

"Fine." Kat glanced into his eyes. He looked tired and distracted. There was a moment of awkward silence.

"You seem to know everyone, Kat," Connor said, filling the quiet.

"Adam and I worked together on a case a few months ago," Kat said.

"Adam and Kat were held hostage," Tommy added.

Connor's eyebrows rose. "Would I know the case?" he asked.

"It's still going through the courts, so we can't say too much," Adam said, recognising the journalistic interest in Connor's otherwise innocent question.

"Sounds like there's a story there," Connor said. He handed Adam a business card. "Call me when you can talk about it, detective."

"Sure," Adam said. "Ready to go, Tommy?"

Tommy started moving towards the main doors, his crutches tapping on the wooden floor. Adam gave Kat a quick glance before following.

"I hope you didn't overdo it, mate," he said to Tommy before they were swallowed by the darkness and the doors swished shut.

Kat watched them depart.

"Well, good to meet you, Connor," she said, turning back towards the changing rooms.

"Kat, would you like to get a drink? I'd love to pick the brain of a forensic accountant."

Kat paused and looked at him for a long moment. He

was a good-looking guy, with sharp, intelligent eyes looking out from behind small oval-shaped glasses. He gave her an encouraging lopsided grin. Even though she had sworn off men again, after the disastrous encounter with Adam, one drink couldn't hurt.

"I really can't talk about that case," she said.

"I'm sure that we can find plenty of other things to talk about," he said.

Kat let the flirtatious comment pass. "When?"

"Now?"

"I can't now; I have to go and kick the crap out of Marco," she said, as the door to the main workout studio opened, and Marco stuck his head out looking for her. Spotting her, he tossed a roll of hand wrap, which Kat caught with ease in her prosthetic hand and began wrapping it around her right hand.

"Excuse me?" Connor said.

Kat laughed at his expression. "I kickbox. I train with Marco a couple of times a week."

"Now that, I'd like to see," Connor said.

"We've only just met, don't go getting ahead of yourself," she said.

Connor laughed. "In that case, give me your number, and I'll call you to arrange that drink." He pulled his phone from his pocket.

Kat reeled off her mobile number before she could second-guess herself.

"I'll be in touch," Connor said.

Kat smiled before walking to join Marco, who threw his arm around her shoulder and led her into the studio. Six men and two women were going through a warm-up routine of squats, mountain climbers and burpees. A row of six boxing bags hung from metal brackets attached to the walls on either side of the room.

"Really, *Katerina*, that skinny white boy?" he teased. "You know you only have to ask."

Kat ducked out from under his arm. "Are you trying to give me a reason to hit you?"

Marco laughed and clapped his hands. "Okay, everyone, let's get started. We'll begin with a jab, cross, round kick drill before moving on to jab, cross, jab, push kick."

Kat adjusted her dark auburn hair in its high ponytail, pulled on her boxing gloves and joined them. The class members moved in front of a bag each and went through the drills. Marco walked up and down behind them, offering advice on technique, and shouting encouragement before calling the class to the centre of the room.

"Okay, partner up," he said. "Half of you put on the arm and thigh guards. We'll swap halfway through. I want you working on your round kicks. Remember to step out, not towards your opponent. Kat, you're with me." Kat pulled on her protective headgear.

The class set to work, working in pairs. Whenever someone lost their balance and tumbled to the mat, there was laughter.

"Kat, I want you to work on your defence. The update to your prosthesis is making you pull back your left hand a fraction slower than your right arm, and it's affecting your balance."

"Yeah, but it spirals much better," Kat said, punching out to show him.

"You're right, it does," Marco said. "It's so amazing what those scientists of yours can do."

Kat bounced on her toes before stepping closer, firing a jab with her left hand, a cross with her right before shifting her bodyweight and landing a round kick with her shin on his thigh pad, with a satisfying thud. Kat hopped back, took a deep breath, and reset.

"Good," Marco encouraged as her next kick landed, and she dodged out of the way of his counterstrike.

"Was that your detective I saw arriving to pick up young Tommy?" he asked as she came at him again.

"He's not my detective," Kat said through gritted teeth.

Marco laughed, and Kat added an extra jab which caught him off guard and grazed his jaw.

"Touched a nerve, have we?"

"Nah, stop trying to distract me," she said, kicking out again.

The next thing she knew, she was sitting on the mat. She glared at Marco's outstretched hand, ignored it and leapt to her feet.

"Remember, channel your anger. You stepped towards me in your haste, you need to step out, or your opponent will land something to your head," he said.

"I'll land something to your head in a moment if you don't shut it," Kat muttered, resetting her stance before coming at him again.

Chapter 3

Adam had left his car parked by the kerb outside the entrance to the gym.

"Perk of the job, being able to park wherever you want," Tommy said, shaking his head at the police parking permit displayed on the dash of Adam's car. The gold paintwork of the restored 1976 Ford Capri gleamed under the streetlights. "Are you trying to be Bodie or Doyle?"

Tommy eased himself into the front, holding on to the door surround and lowering his body in. Adam took his crutches and tilted the driver's seat forward, laying them in back before resetting the seat and climbing in.

"Well, I have to say that was a little awkward," Tommy said.

Adam tugged at his ear. "Awkward?"

"Come on, mate," Tommy said with a laugh. "You and Kat. Don't tell me that's the first time you've seen her since…" he trailed off.

"It wasn't like that," Adam said.

"It wasn't like what? She's gorgeous, and she clearly likes you; God knows why." Tommy pulled his seatbelt on as Adam started the car and eased into the traffic. "I'll lay money on the fact that Connor will already have her phone number and be booking a fancy restaurant, as we speak."

Adam gripped the steering wheel before speaking in a low voice. "Enough, or you can walk."

Tommy held his hands up. "Okay, man, just sayin'."

"Well, don't."

They drove in silence for a couple of blocks.

"So, Nancy must be due soon," Tommy said.

"About six weeks," Adam said.

"If you don't mind me saying, you don't seem overjoyed," Tommy said.

"It's complicated, Tommy, you know that."

"Are you two back together?"

Adam shook his head. "We'll co-parent; however that's supposed to work."

"Then, what's the issue with Kat?"

"I can't be running around with her when Nancy is about to give birth to my child."

"But…"

"Tommy, I'm trying to do the right thing for everyone here," Adam said.

"Doesn't seem to me that you're doing the right thing for you or Kat."

Adam fell silent again for a moment. "Enough about me," he said. "Tell me how you're doing?"

"Great, never been better. You've heard the term 'babe magnet', well that's me now. I always thought the uniform helped," Tommy said. "But hey, I should've got some hideous scars and lost a leg sooner."

"At least your gallows humour is still intact," Adam said, glancing across at him.

"It's hanging on by a thread, mate."

"Is it really that bad?"

"I might as well be invisible as far as the opposite sex is concerned," Tommy said. "Why do you think I'm so invested in your love life?"

"Mine is a mess, you should look elsewhere for inspiration."

"Yeah, but seeing that yours is a mess doesn't make me feel quite so bad about mine," Tommy said.

"You've just got to give it time," Adam said. "Get yourself properly healed, get fit again and have your new leg fitted."

"Time," Tommy said, turning to stare out the window. "That's what the psycho-babblers keep telling me."

"Well, you know you're getting the best rehab in London, working with Marco," Adam said.

"I thought you didn't like him." Tommy gave Adam a sly look. "Or was it his relationship with Kat that you didn't like?"

"And just like that, you've pulled the conversation back to her," Adam said.

Tommy laughed. "Any word on Jake?" he asked. The car pulled out from the side road and joined the North Circular.

Adam shook his head. "Nah, but I'm convinced Webster knows more than he's letting on. He's up on so many charges that I keep hoping he'll be ready to trade some information for a reduced sentence at some point, but nothing yet."

"It's just so strange that he disappeared off the face of the earth," Tommy said. "How long has it been?"

"Almost three years."

"It would be good for Jake's family to know what happened to him, get some closure."

"Yeah, I'm certain he's dead, but there's always that glimmer of hope until there's a body."

Tommy nodded and stared out at the traffic. "That there is," he agreed.

Chapter 4

"Earth to Kat," Shamira said, waving her delicate hands in front of Kat's face. Intricate, fading henna patterns covered the backs of both hands, leftovers from a family wedding celebration at the weekend.

"Sorry, I was miles away," Kat said, shaking her head. "You were saying?"

"I was saying that he must have a hidden bank account or two. I've been trying to rebuild his income and expenditure for the last twenty-four months. I can't see where all of his money has gone," Shamira said, running her fingers through her long straight black hair in frustration. She pushed back from her desk. "Are you sure you're okay? Would you like a coffee?"

"I'm fine, but coffee would be great, thanks," Kat said.

She watched her friend stroll across the open-plan office toward the small kitchen cleverly hidden beneath the stairwell in their newly refurbished office. Forensic Accounting Associates had only been back in the building for a few weeks, following the fire which had destroyed their floor and damaged the ones immediately above and below.

Nate, the other member of Kat's team, returned from a meeting in one of the glass-fronted conference rooms on the far side of the floor and dropped onto his chair at the remaining desk in the pod of three. "You're looking pensive, mate." Nate looked the antithesis of an accountant, with his long messy blond locks and tattoos that peeked out from beneath the neck of his business shirt.

"I was just thinking what a nice job they did repairing the office," Kat said, looking across the polished wooden floors to the red brick walls of the converted grain store that was home to the firm.

Nate shivered, shaking his head. "I still get chills thinking about that day."

"I'm not surprised; you could have been killed."

"Here you go," Shamira said, returning with a small tray containing three flat whites. "I thought you'd want one, surfer boy."

"Thank you, ma'am," Nate said, helping himself to a cup. "Although there's not much chance of surfing in this weather. I have to say, it's the one thing I miss about Australia. You can surf at Bondi all year round."

Shamira pulled her chair alongside Kat's.

"So, are you going to tell us why you're so distracted today? You're not due to testify in the CIP case yet, are you?"

"No, it's nothing like that," she said.

"Well, what is it?" Shamira pressed. "We're not going to let you bottle things up again, so spill."

Kat sighed. "I bumped into Adam."

Over her head, Nate and Shamira exchanged a knowing glance.

"What was that look?" Kat demanded.

"We just know that you're still a little sensitive where he's concerned," Shamira said, her tone gentle.

Kat glared at her. "You would be too if you'd finally admitted your feelings for someone only to find out that his ex-wife was having his baby. End of story. There's nothing for me to be sensitive about."

"I think it was as much a shock for Adam as it was for you, am I right?" Shamira said.

"Doesn't change the facts."

Shamira tried to maintain a neutral expression. "And will you be seeing him again?"

Kat shook her head and took a sip of her coffee. "Not if I can help it, there's too much water under that particular bridge."

"If you say so."

"It was just a bit strange seeing him when I was least expecting it, that's all," Kat admitted. "I was unprepared, but it's good that we don't have to work with him again."

"Until the next murder," Nate said, wiggling his eyebrows.

"Ugh, you don't have to sound so excited about it," Shamira said.

"Besides, I somehow have a date tonight with a journalist that I met at the gym," Kat said before her face creased with a frown. "Although, thinking about it again, I might cancel. Now, about that missing bank account, I agree, and I think I know where some of the money might be going." Kat spun her chair back around to face her computer screens, placing her mug on the desk to one side.

"Wait, wait, you've got a date?"

"I have."

"And you've waited until now to tell me." Shamira's voice rose, and she looked a little put out.

"It's no biggie."

"Kat, you haven't dated anyone since Adam."

"She's right," Nate said.

"And I didn't really date him, if you recall. Now, moving on, please. I've found a lease on a flat in that huge apartment complex near the river at Pimlico in the name of one of our politician's companies."

Shamira peered at the screen. "Ah, he's probably got a mistress holed up there. Why are politicians such dirt-bags?"

"Whoa there, you've been listening to his soon-to-be ex-wife too much," Nate said. "There's no evidence that he's having an affair or that he's a dirt-bag. It could just be a shrewd property investment."

"Well, why didn't he declare it to his wife's lawyers, then?" Shamira said.

"I don't know, but just because Deborah Sharp runs a charity, it doesn't make her a saint," Nate said.

"Actually, Jeremy does some good for the business community," Kat said, pulling a newspaper from her bag. "There was an article in here on the number of start-up businesses that his department's programme, the Future Sustainable Business Initiative, has been assisting over the past couple of years."

"So both of their halos are shining," Nate said, turning to pick up his ringing desk phone.

Kat sat the newspaper to one side and faced her computer screen.

Shamira touched Kat's arm. "Don't cancel your date," she said.

"It's not a big deal, Shamira."

"Kat, you need to stop pushing everyone away. Life can be very lonely if you don't take risks and let people in," Shamira said.

Kat gave her an exasperated look. "I'm not lonely."

"When did you last go anywhere that wasn't work or the gym?"

"I went to the Portobello Road Market last Sunday."

"With?" Shamira asked.

"No one," Kat mumbled.

"And when did you last come out with Nate and me or anyone else? You've got to stop hiding and pushing everyone away."

"Kat, do you have a moment?"

Kat looked up to see their receptionist, a woman in her forties, standing in front of their workstations. Her short greying hair curled around her face, and she had worry lines etched into her features.

"Sure, Rosie," Kat said. "Anything to save me from this one and her incessant questions." She jumped up and followed Rosie across the floor to an empty meeting room.

Shamira pulled a face and called after her. "You'll turn into a crazy, reclusive cat lady if you're not careful."

Rosie closed the door and with a heavy sigh dropped onto a chair at one end of the meeting table. Kat slid onto the chair beside her and took in the jumble of modern and historic buildings comprising the cityscape through the floor-to-ceiling windows on one side of the small room, before turning her attention to Rosie.

"What's up?" she asked.

"My son, Harry, is missing," Rosie said, pressing her fingers against her temple as if trying to stop a headache. "He didn't come home from school yesterday."

"Oh no, I'm sorry to hear that. Have you called the police?"

"I did, but they said it wasn't high risk or something,"

Rosie said. "He's seventeen and sometimes stays over at his friends' houses or at the boarding lodge at school. He says they're doing homework, but I always suspect they're having a gaming session, so I keep hoping it's just that. But the thing is, he usually calls to let us know."

"Have you talked to his friends or the school?"

"Yes." Rosie wrung her hands. "He hasn't turned up for school today, and he's not with any of his local mates. I wouldn't normally be worried, but my husband Terry and I were looking in Harry's room last night to see if we could find the phone numbers for some of his other friends when we found a crumpled statement for a bank account with a balance of over one hundred thousand pounds."

She looked up at Kat with red-rimmed eyes. "We've no idea where he got that much money from. He was building a few websites for people, but nothing that would earn that sort of money."

Kat opened her mouth to speak, but Rosie continued.

"If I go back to the police and report him missing, then I'll have to show them, and I don't want to do that if there is some innocent explanation. He's a good boy. Do you think that you could come and take a look at his computer? He's got three screens that seem to talk to each other, but we can't even get into it."

"Sure, if you think it will help to find him. Can I bring Nate? He's the technology whizz kid," Kat said. "But if he doesn't turn up soon, you need to go back to the police."

"Thank you." Rosie looked relieved. "Could you come straight after work today?"

"Yeah, I'll check with Nate, but that should be fine. Are you okay to leave around five? I have somewhere to be later?"

"Absolutely, thank you, Kat."

Kat reached over and squeezed Rosie's hand. "Who knows? He might be home by then, and you can ask him yourself."

"I hope so. Terry has stayed home today, just in case."

Chapter 5

When the first note arrived, Adam had ignored it as coming from some nut-job who'd read in the newspaper about the high-profile CIP case he'd worked on a few months earlier. Police officers, especially those featured in news reports, seemed to become targets of people who were a little unhinged or had grudges against those in authority. But now he sat holding a second envelope addressed to 'DS Adam Jackson'. He turned it over in his hands. This one appeared to have been hand-delivered. There was no stamp or postmark to indicate that it had come via the Royal Mail or a courier. He pulled on a pair of disposable gloves and readied an evidence bag.

He searched through the drawers of his desk at one end of the open-plan CID office at the station until he found a letter opener and sliced open the top of the envelope. If it contained what he thought, then he would need to have the seal DNA tested. Maybe the sender had licked the glue strip to stick the envelope.

Setting down the letter opener, he held the envelope away from him and shook out the single folded piece of paper. He dropped the envelope into the evidence bag and put it to one side before spreading the page out on the desk. The letter was handwritten, in black ink using block capitals, on ordinary white paper.

'THEY KNOW THAT I KNEW THE AMBUSH AT HEL-MAND WOULD HAPPEN...JT'

Voices in the hallway announced the arrival of his team.

"Hey, sarge," Detective Constable Julian Talbot said, dropping his gym bag on the floor beside his chair and kicking it under the desk with his foot.

"Morning," Adam said before picking up his phone, photographing the letter and slipping it into the evidence bag with the envelope. He sealed it and filled in the details.

"What've you got there?" Julian asked. His short hair was still wet from his post-workout shower, and he wore his usual self-imposed uniform of jeans and a button-down shirt. A clipped dark brown goatee beard covered his upper lip and chin.

"Do you remember the letter I got last week, the cryptic one?" Adam said.

"Yes, the one supposedly from your mate Jake. You thought it was from one of the usual cranks."

"I've received another one," Adam said, handing the evidence bag to him.

"What happened at Helmand?" Julian asked, after reading the note.

"We were involved in an incident that killed one of my team and injured others, including me. Jake was working in military intelligence at the time, but if he'd had advance warning of an ambush he would have stopped the mission. I know that isn't from Jake. Someone is messing with me, but who and why now after all this time?"

Julian shrugged and handed the note back.

"Who's Jake?" the newest member of Adam's homicide team, Constable Eloise Salter, asked, joining the conversation. Her uniform was freshly ironed, and her tumble of wild black hair was tamed into a sleek bun. Since joining the unit, she'd impressed everyone with her quick wit and no-nonsense approach.

Adam looked pained for a moment. "Jake Truro is my best mate who's been missing for the last three years," Adam said.

"Oh, and there's been no sign of him?"

"Have you heard us mention Kat Munro, the forensic accountant that I worked with on the CIP investigation?" Adam said.

"The girl with the false hand?" Eloise said.

"She's a little more than that," Adam said.

"Sorry, I didn't mean…" Eloise mumbled, exchanging a glance with Julian.

Adam inhaled. "I believe that she was one of the last people to see Jake before he disappeared. However, there are holes in her memory as she was involved in a car accident that night."

"That's awful. Did Kat see Jake before the accident, then?"

"She recalls seeing a man being questioned at South Hill Manor, which is near Jake's last known location. The owner of the house, William Huntly-Tait, has since confirmed that Jake was there but insists that he was alive when he left the property."

"And that's all tied up with the CIP case," Eloise said.

"Yeah," Adam said. "All of my enquiries into Jake's disappearance have drawn a blank. It is as though he's vanished into thin air. The one man who knows what happened is sitting in Holloway Prison awaiting trial and is not saying anything."

"Perhaps he's holding that piece of info to bargain with?" Julian suggested.

"It's possible," Adam said. "Eloise, can you find the letter from last week? I should have copied it."

"Sure, I filed it. I'll just go and get it."

"Can you send this to the lab on your way? I need fingerprints and any DNA from the seal."

"Okay." Eloise picked up the evidence bag and left the room.

"What's made you take notice of this one?" Julian asked.

"It suggests some knowledge of my past," Adam said.

"And it's definitely not Jake?"

"No," Adam said, scowling. "It's from someone who is messing with me, but if it leads me to the truth of what happened to Jake, then I'll play along, for now."

Eloise returned a short time later, a little red-faced and breathless from rushing.

"Here's the other note," she said, approaching Adam's desk.

Adam took the evidence bag from her and turned it so that the type on the anonymous note was visible.

'Mate, you need to find me. I can't hold on much longer.'

Chapter 6

Kat and Nate caught the District Line with Rosie to Plaistow. They walked for five minutes from the station along rubbish-strewn footpaths, past shuttered shops and an ugly seventies-build tower block. Halfway along a street lined with three-level red-brick terraced houses, Rosie turned and led them along a short path to a blue front door. There was a white van emblazoned with 'Newham Village Electrical' parked on the street outside. The tiny courtyard in front of the house was well maintained. It contained an outdoor table with two chairs, and red flowering bougainvillaea climbed over a trellis separating it from the weed-filled neighbouring frontage. Rosie slipped her key into the lock and opened the door.

A tired-looking man wearing slippers and a well-worn cardigan ambled into the hallway to greet them. "Oh, hello there, love. I thought it might have been Harry."

"No sign of him, then?" Rosie said. The man shook his bald head. "I've brought Kat and Nate to have a look at his computer," Rosie said, pulling off her raincoat and hanging it on a hook on the wall behind the door. "This is my husband, Terry."

Kat smiled her greeting, and Nate stepped forward and

shook Terry's hand. "Mr Compton," he said.

"Terry, please."

"Would you like a cuppa?" Rosie asked.

"No, we're good, thanks," Kat said. "Shall we take a look at Harry's computer?"

They followed Terry up two flights of steep carpeted stairs to an attic room.

"This is Harry's domain," he said, opening the door and leading them into a darkened bedroom. Rosie rushed to the window and drew the curtains across as Terry flicked on the light switch. There was a single bed in one corner, which looked to have had the covers hastily pulled up in an attempt to make it. The room was dominated by a large wooden desk with a computer, three screens and a printer. The walls were covered with posters advertising the latest science fiction movies, various computer games and e-sports events. A small bookshelf beneath the window was stacked with schoolbooks and loose pieces of lined paper covered in a messy handwritten scrawl. A thin laptop and a set of wireless headphones lay on the bed, and a long-lens camera sat atop a shelf on one wall among numerous gaming figurines. A pair of Vans lay abandoned at the end of the bed, along with a designer hoodie.

"He's got all the kit," Nate commented.

"Sawyer's Hill Grammar called earlier, wondering where he was today," Terry said. "I told them that we didn't know and unless he turns up tonight to expect a call from the police in the morning."

Rosie let out a sigh, and Terry put his arm around her. "I know, love, but if he doesn't get in touch soon, then something could have happened to him. I travelled his route to school today and called in at all his local friends' houses. Since the end of school yesterday, no one has seen him, and those who aren't at the school haven't seen him for weeks. He's moving with a different crowd, it seems – some of the boarders."

"Sawyer's Hill Grammar. That sounds fancy," Nate said.

"Harry won a scholarship to attend," Rosie said.

"Clever boy," Kat said, smiling at her.

Rosie beamed, unable to hide the pride in her expression. "He worked so hard to get in there."

"He's a lucky lad, naturally smart," Terry agreed.

"Mind if I take a look?" Nate asked, indicating the computer with a wave of his hand.

"Knock yourself out," Terry said. "I don't understand any of that stuff."

Nate sat down at the desk and tapped a key on the keyboard. All three screens whirred to life, and the keyboard began to flash with a pattern of bright coloured lights. The desktop box on the back corner of the desk had a clear side, and four colourful fans started to spin, sending a rainbow of lights across the desk. The centre screen had a game in standby mode, and the left-hand screen displayed a live stream of a popular online game called *Zombiegamez*. A browser window was open on the third screen. When Nate moved the mouse to activate the cursor, a password box popped up.

"I don't suppose you know his password?" Nate said. Rosie shook her head.

Terry handed Kat a piece of paper. "I don't know if Rosie mentioned this."

Kat looked at the printout of a bank statement in her hand. It had been screwed up, and the toner had smudged in places making part of it illegible. Kat held it up to the light. The account was in the name of Houdini Harry's Magic Tricks Ltd and had a closing balance of £104,392. There were deposits of between £500 and £5,000, two withdrawals of £1,000 each and several transfers to another account over the previous month.

"Is it real?" Terry asked.

Kat studied the header and footer on the printed page. The bank's logo and contact details appeared genuine.

"Do you have any more of these?" she asked, squinting at the page.

"No, that one was screwed up on the floor beside his rubbish bin. It looks like he'd printed it out."

"Rosie mentioned that Harry builds websites," Kat said. "Is this the company that he uses to bill his clients?"

"Yes, he builds websites, that's how we thought he bought all of this computer gear," Terry said. "But I didn't know that he'd set up a company. How would he even know how to do that?"

"Who are his clients?"

"Well, he built a booking site for our local pub's quiz night, a sales website for a neighbour who sells greeting cards at the market, that sort of thing," Rosie said.

"But only a handful of websites? There are twenty different deposits over as many days here during the last month," Kat said, referring to the page in her hand.

"He hasn't time to make more than two or three a month what with school and football," Terry said.

"Who's Bertie Bear?" Kat asked.

Rosie and Terry glanced at one another.

"Harry's old dog. He died last year," Rosie said. She gave Kat a strange look. "Why do you ask that?"

"That's the name of the account where a lot of these withdrawals are going to," Kat said.

"It's also his *Zombiegamez* username," Nate said. "Look." He pointed to an icon in the top corner of the centre screen. There was an avatar of a grizzly bear with the name Bertie Bear beneath.

"This isn't good, is it?" Terry said, sinking down onto the bed and running his hands through his thinning hair. "He's got more money in that account than we'll manage to save in our entire lives, and now it's as though he's disappeared off the face of the earth."

"We should call the police again now, love," Rosie said in a quiet voice. "Not tomorrow morning."

"You should," Nate agreed.

"We'll be back in a moment," Terry said. He followed Rosie from the room, and together they descended the stairs.

Kat joined Nate at the desk. "Anything?" she said.

"*Zombiegamez* is in standby mode. I can see that a few of his gaming mates are online. See the chat here." He pointed to a small window at the bottom of the screen where text was scrolling in a chat box. It was mainly trash talk.

"What's this?" Kat pointed at the third screen.

"That's where it gets interesting," Nate said. "That's The Onion Ring."

Kat looked blank.

"The Tor browser," Nate said.

Kat frowned. "The gateway to the Dark Web?"

Nate laughed. "Not quite how I'd have phrased it, but yeah, that one."

"Oh."

"Now, it looks like the kid is a bit of a computer geek."

"Takes one to know one, I guess," Kat said.

Nate grinned. "What I'm trying to say is that he has all the gear," he said, sweeping his gaze around the room. "So it wouldn't be unusual for him to try to get onto the Dark Web. Seventeen-year-old boys, curiosity and all that, but if you add Dark Web access to a bank account containing thousands of pounds, then I'd say he was up to something."

"Something illegal?"

"Not necessarily, it could be anything. But whatever it is, Rosie and Terry clearly don't know."

"And it could be why he's missing," Kat said.

The stairs creaked, and Terry returned. "We need to go and file a missing person report at our local police station."

"Okay, I think that's a good idea. You need to tell the police about the bank account and that Harry was accessing the Dark Web. They may want to look at his computers." Kat said.

"The Dark Web?"

Kat nodded.

"How do you know that?" Terry asked.

Nate pointed to the screen. "This screen is using an encrypted browser to access it."

Terry paled. "What would he want with the Dark Web?"

* * *

"They really had no idea what their kid was up to," Kat said as they headed back to the station. It was dusk, and the streets were busy with people returning home from work.

"Most parents don't," Nate said. "Technology has advanced so quickly, leaving many adults behind."

"Well, it looks like Harry has found a golden goose some-where. That's a lot of money for a teenager," Kat said.

"And that's just the account that he left lying around," Nate said. "A smart kid like that wouldn't just have all his funds in one account. I suspect the Bertie Bear account will have more."

"Yeah, you're right," Kat said. "I hope whatever he was involved in hasn't led to his disappearance."

"Hey, excuse me," an out of breath voice behind them called as they reached the entrance to the underground station.

They slowed and turned to see a teenage girl running along the well-lit street towards them. Her long sandy blonde hair was highlighted with pink streaks, and as she reached them, Kat saw that she wore heavy eye make-up. She was dressed in a short black skirt topped with a denim jacket.

"Hi, I'm Caitlyn. Rosie's daughter," she said. "You were just at our house, right?"

"Yes. I'm Kat, and this is Nate."

"I overheard you talking to Mum and Dad. You think something bad has happened to Harry, yeah?"

"I don't know," Kat said. "Your mum just wanted us to take a look at his computer to see if it gave any clues as to where he might be. Do you know anything?"

"Harry will kill me for telling you, but he was doing more than just making websites. He was selling Z-cash," she said.

"Z-cash?" Kat said, frowning.

"Zombie cash," Nate said. "It's the currency of *Zombiegamez*. It allows players to buy clothes, weapons, vehicles and magic potions to use in the game."

"Where would he get Z-cash to sell?" Kat asked

"You earn it through completing various tasks in the game

or by winning," Nate said.

"Harry must have won a lot," Kat said.

"He wasn't that good." Caitlyn shrugged. "He was getting it from somewhere, though, but he wouldn't tell me where," she said. "Anyway, I don't know if that's useful."

"It could be. Have you told your parents?"

A look of disdain crossed Caitlyn's face. "They don't know a cursor from a spreadsheet, let alone anything about online gaming, which is why they called you in, I suppose."

"Funny, your mum works with spreadsheets every day," Nate said.

"Really?" Caitlyn's surprise sounded genuine.

"They're off to the police station to report Harry missing, so you should tell them what you told us. It could help the police," Kat said. She slipped her hand into the side of her messenger bag and pulled out a business card. "Here, take this. You can call me if you think of anything else."

Caitlyn smiled, lighting up her features. "Okay, thanks. The little creep will probably already be sitting at home laughing at us all for being worried."

Chapter 7

Kat followed the maître d' across the restaurant to where Connor O'Malley was already seated. The lighting was subdued, and soft jazz tinkled from a piano in one corner. Each table was angled, so every diner had a view of the rooftops of the surrounding buildings and the lights along the river beyond. Connor rose as she approached the table. Kat had come straight from visiting Rosie's and still wore the tailored navy-blue trouser suit and high-heeled boots that she'd worn to work. Her dark auburn hair was bouncing around her shoulders as she strolled across the room. Kat had almost called to cancel, the thought of an evening batting away the man's flirtatious advances causing her stomach to clench with dread, but here she was.

"Kat," Connor smiled, standing to greet her. "I'm so pleased that you could make it."

"Hi, Connor, sorry I'm a little late; I had to help out a friend after work."

He leaned over and kissed her cheek, waiting until Kat sat down opposite him before retaking his seat.

"It's fine, I haven't long arrived myself."

She gave him the hint of a smile. "Thank you for inviting me," she said. "Although, I wasn't sure if this was a date or an interview?"

"I'm not thinking about work right now," Connor said. Kat raised an eyebrow. "But I am interested to know more about you."

"I'm pretty boring, really," Kat said.

Connor laughed. "You're not very good at this, are you? This is the point where you are supposed to regale me with stories highlighting your fabulousness."

Kat relaxed a little and allowed a smile to creep across her face. "I knew there was a reason that I hate going on dates."

"You're a forensic accountant with a very hi-tech looking prosthetic hand, who kickboxes in her spare time. I wouldn't call that boring. I would say there are several fascinating stories there," Connor said.

"So speaks the journalist."

"What can I say? It's in my blood. My father and my grandfather before him were newspapermen," Connor replied.

A waiter dressed in black arrived at their table, small tablet in hand. "Can I get you a drink?"

"I'd like a glass of red wine, please," Kat said, running her eyes down the wine list on the menu. "The Chianti looks good."

"Are you driving?" Connor asked. Kat shook her head. "Then let's make it a bottle."

"Certainly." The waiter turned on his heel.

"So, tell me about the kickboxing. Do you compete?"

Kat shook her head. "No, it's for fitness only. I started attending Marco's gym after the accident because he specialises in rehabilitation. I'm sure you already know that since you're writing about Tommy. Marco worked with me to get my strength up and anger out, and that included a kickboxing class, which I found I loved."

"Can you actually box with that hand?" Connor asked, glancing at her prosthesis.

"Not really, but it's good defensively."

"How did you lose it?"

Kat hesitated. "Has anyone ever told you that you're very direct?"

"Sorry, it's the journalist again," Connor said, giving her a sheepish grin. "You don't have to talk about it if you don't want to."

The waiter returned with the wine, and they were silent as he pulled the cork from the bottle and splashed a small measure of the ruby-coloured liquid into Connor's glass to taste. He took a sip and nodded his assent to the waiter who half-filled Kat's glass before adding to Connor's. He placed the bottle on the table and retreated.

Kat picked up her glass and took a gulp. "It was a car accident nearly three years ago. My boyfriend, at the time, Gabe, was driving, and my best friend died. I blamed him for a long time, but it turns out it wasn't entirely his fault." Connor opened his mouth to ask a question, but Kat held up her hand. "It's tied up in a case that's still going through the courts, so I shouldn't say any more, especially to a reporter," she said.

"Fair enough," he said. "I'm sorry about your friend."

"Thanks," Kat said. "Now, tell me about this story you're doing on Tommy."

"The article is part of a series on our armed forces. I'm particularly looking at how our injured servicemen and women integrate back into society after combat. Covering someone injured in the line of duty is only one angle. I'm also looking at the impact on families, future employment and mental health."

"Have you heard of The Valkyries?"

Connor took a sip of his wine. "Yes, but not much, I'm afraid."

"It's an organisation that I'm involved with, which specifically supports the rehabilitation of female members of the armed services who are injured. I can put you in touch with the head of the charity if that would be useful."

"That would be grand, thank you," Connor said as Kat retrieved her phone from the bag on the floor beside her chair. She scrolled through her contact list, selected Marjorie Peters' contact details, and forwarded them to Connor's number.

"There you go," she said, putting her phone down on the table.

"Thanks. I'm also researching a piece on how Eastern European syndicates are using online scams to fund their criminal activities," Connor said.

"Now that sounds interesting," Kat said. "How did you get onto that?

"My grandpa is in a retirement village in Dublin and has been taking seniors' computer classes. You know, they teach the oldies how to get online, send an email, browser searching, Internet banking and gaming."

"Gaming?"

Connor laughed at Kat's surprised expression. "You'd be surprised how many old folk like a good game of *Fortnite.*" Kat's features displayed her disbelief. "Okay, I'm kidding. But the class is taught how to play online scrabble and solitaire and the like."

Kat smirked.

"Anyway, the bank accounts of twenty of the residents were hacked, and their credit card details were stolen. Between them, eighty thousand euros was taken."

"Oh, no," Kat said. "How were they hacked?"

"Quite simple, really. One of the old dears shared a funny meme that someone had sent to her, and once it played, it installed a small virus on each device. The police lost the money trail fairly quickly. But before the cards were cancelled, money was spent all over the world."

"That's awful."

"When I started looking into it, I found out that fifty-six retirement villages in Ireland and the UK have fallen prey to similar schemes in recent months. Retirees have lost hundreds of thousands of pounds. I thought there was a story worth following, and it seems it's even more prevalent than I initially thought. Online crime is booming. There's been an exponential increase in crimes relating to online activities across all walks of life in the last five years. Interestingly, this has coincided with the growth of a new style of crime syndicate. They operate a bit like the gangs of the 1970s using extortion, theft and threats; the only difference is that 90% of the crime is carried out online," Connor said.

"Cybercrime," Kat said.

"Yeah, everything from identity theft, credit card fraud and blackmail is being conducted out of sight. People are being attacked and livelihoods destroyed by nameless and faceless hackers."

"We see it more and more. It's getting harder to track fund movements, especially where the Dark Web is involved," Kat said.

"Can I ask how you trace cryptocurrency transactions?"

"It depends on the coin and where it's transacted," Kat said. She picked up her wine glass and took a sip. "There's a lot of market data available on the more common currencies and organisations that analyse movements on the various blockchains. We have tools that allow us to dig into the more well-known cryptocurrencies. But with the more obscure currencies, there is a definite lack of transparency, making it attractive for criminals. Digital currencies are unregulated, unlike regular currencies, where the banking system controls everything."

"The lack of regulation can't last," Connor said.

"The growth of exchanges has legitimised digital currency trading in the last couple of years, which helps. The problems arise with the new crypto assets, which are emerging all the time. They often have ever-increasing levels of encryption and complexity, and very little in the way of anti-money-laundering compliance."

"Aye, it's nigh on impossible to know who's behind some of these things."

"Yeah, it's suspected that Satoshi Nakamoto, who is credited with founding the first cryptocurrency, Bitcoin, is just a pseudonym. No one knows for sure who's behind its development or the development of many of the newer crypto coins," Kat said.

"It's crazy, isn't it? Everyone is worried about the electronic trail that they leave, yet crypto transactions that occur between digital wallets are nothing more than a string of characters, a bit like a bank account number but more complex. Anonymity is guaranteed unless you know who owns a wallet."

"Yeah, if you know that, then you can track the transactions, but finding out that ownership is only possible if the owner tells you or lets that information slip in some way. There's no database of ownership, only a list of transactions associated with each digital wallet," Kat said.

"So we can know what transactions occur but not who is doing it."

Kat nodded. "The ability to move about the online world with little or no detection is certainly an attractive proposition for anyone committing financial crimes. The general public might be worried about their digital footprint. Yet, the criminals are becoming quite sophisticated at masking their identities. At least, that's what we see more and more of."

"I read recently that one South American country has adopted its own crypto as an official currency of the country. Although they appear to have fallen foul of international trade agreements by insisting on payment in crypto," Connor said.

"Even so, I think digital currencies are here to stay," Kat said. "It's interesting because the purists at one end of the spectrum espouse the virtues of a truly free market currency with no intermediary or regulation. But there's no doubt we'll see more regulation, which will go some way towards thwarting those who want to use them for more nefarious purposes."

"It's usually when the gangs decide to kill someone that they slip up. There have been five unexplained murders in the UK so far this year, all with links to one or other of the crime syndicates that I'm investigating," Connor said. "Deaths of otherwise upstanding citizens, whose side hustle has brought them into contact with the wrong people."

Kat shivered. "It's a part of life that most of us like to pretend doesn't exist, right?"

"Apparently, the National Crime Agency's biggest area

of growth in the last twelve months is cyber ransoms. As individuals have become more aware of phishing attacks, with fewer people falling victim, there's been an increase in malware attacks on organisations. I'm also working on a piece which digs into ransomware crimes, where businesses have been forced to pay to unlock their systems," Connor said.

"That's just plain old extortion, isn't it?"

"It is, but again, it's faceless," Connor said. "Some businesses that I've spoken to have simply paid the money over and not reported the crime."

"I thought the NCA and others were encouraging people to report these attacks and not pay up, to mitigate the wider impact."

"I'm not certain that's happening, at least not with some of the companies that I've talked to. They have taken their systems down, cleaned up their networks, installed better firewalls and security protocols, and hoped it wouldn't happen again. Businesses that have expanded quickly and whose IT function hasn't kept up with the growth have been hit. That sort of weakness makes them an easy target," Connor said.

"Makes sense, and I'm guessing the hackers are getting smarter too."

"Yeah, they are. The syndicates that I've been tracking employ some of the smartest computer techs around, and I'm afraid cybercrime is getting its tentacles further into everyday life in this country. Anyway, it's not really tantalising dinner conversation," he said, picking up his menu. "What are you having?"

* * *

"I really enjoyed tonight," Connor said as they closed the door of the restaurant. There had been a shower of rain while they'd been eating, and the pavement was damp.

"Me too," Kat said and was surprised to find that she meant it. She buttoned her coat up to combat the cool night air. They began walking along the narrow cobblestone street towards the underground station.

"We'll have to do this again," Connor said. "Are you free on Saturday for lunch?"

"I think so."

Connor grinned. "Great, I'll call…"

He stopped abruptly as two bulky men wearing dark clothes rounded the corner ahead and came to a stop in front of them, blocking their way forward. The smile slipped from Connor's face.

"Connor O'Malley?" said a heavy-set man with a shaved head and a fat, crooked nose.

"Who's asking?" Connor replied.

"This is your last warning," the man replied before his fist connected with Connor's face and sent him sprawling into the wall.

"Hey," Kat shouted, stepping between Connor and the man. He held up his hands. "I don't hit women, love."

"That's good to hear," she said, kicking out and catching him on the thigh. He grunted and staggered. The second man, younger and shorter, with a dark beard covering his jaw, reached for her, grabbing her arm. Kat raised her elbow at speed and heard a satisfying crunch as it connected with the soft tissue of the man's nose. He swore, and his hold on her dropped. She spun back around to the first man who had recovered his balance and had his hand raised, ready to slap her.

"I thought you didn't hit women, *love*," she said, bouncing on her toes and stepping to the side, back in front of Connor, who was on the ground, holding his jaw and groaning.

"I think I'll make an exception for you," he said.

Kat jabbed towards his face and landed another round kick to his leg.

"Hey, what's going on?" a voice shouted.

The man looked behind Kat in the direction of the voice. Kat could hear footsteps slapping against the wet road, but she kept her attention focussed on the two men in front of her. The man with the shaved head turned to Connor, who used the wall as support and climbed back to his feet.

"Consider this your final warning, O'Malley. Stop what you're doing. Next time we won't be so accommodating and you may not have your girlfriend to save you," he said before turning his attention to Kat and jabbing a fat finger in her direction. "And you, I never forget a face."

With that, the two men slipped back around the corner from which they'd come, and seconds later, Kat heard a vehicle pull away at speed.

"Connor." She rushed to his side and inspected his face. "We need to get some ice on that."

Their would-be rescuers reached them. "Are you okay?" a young woman in her early twenties asked, stopping to check on Connor.

"Thanks, you scared them off," Kat said.

Her friend kept running past them and looked around the corner for the assailants.

"Muggers?" the woman asked, looking askance at Kat. "You looked like you were fighting back."

"I was trying to," she said. "Thank goodness you guys came along. I'm not sure how much longer I could have kept that up, they were way bigger than me."

"Did they take anything?"

Kat shook her head and put out her hand to steady Connor as he wobbled and clutched the wall for support. "Come on, let's go back to the restaurant and wait there for a taxi."

"Thanks again," Connor mumbled to the couple as Kat hooked her arm through his and started to walk back to the restaurant.

"What was that about?" Kat asked, trying to control the shaking that had replaced the adrenaline surge.

"Just some thugs who clearly don't appreciate my literary talents," Connor said, taking a quick scan of the road behind them.

"Don't make light of this, we should call the police," Kat said, also looking over her shoulder with some trepidation.

"Nah, too late now," Connor said. "I have to say, you're proving to be a useful person to have around."

Chapter 8

The lights of several police cars, parked in front of the abandoned building in East London, flickered on and off. Once an electrical substation, the concrete structure stood at one end of a residential street. It was covered in colourful but pointless graffiti beneath its boarded-up windows. A baby-faced constable was trying to keep a growing crowd of onlookers behind the hastily erected crime scene tape.

Adam skirted around the edge of the group and showed his warrant card to a second police officer standing guard. The officer noted his details on the crime scene log and lifted the tape to allow Adam through.

One woman in the crowd, wrapped in a belted towelling dress gown, coffee cup in her hand, called out. "Oi, it's about time you lot came to sort out those druggies."

"This way, detective," a voice called, and Adam spotted one of the members of the squad's crime scene unit dressed in white coveralls, beckoning to him from one corner of the building. He climbed through a hole in the wire fencing to join her.

"Morning, Alice," he said, noticing the firm set of her jaw. From experience, he knew that it meant either a gruesome crime scene or the body of someone young had been discovered.

"Adam," Alice replied and handed him a matching forensic suit sealed in a plastic bag.

He pulled the coveralls on over his clothes, flicking the hood up to cover his hair. "Bit early," he said.

The sunrise was visible in the form of orange streaks gathering in the dark sky and his breath condensed in little white puffs as he spoke.

"Ain't that the truth," Alice agreed. "This way. You'll want these." She handed him thin blue gloves and disposable shoe covers.

"Thanks." Adam stooped, slipped the covers over the soles of his boots and pulled the gloves on before he followed Alice around the edge of the building.

They proceeded through a disused yard full of straggly weeds littered with all manner of rubbish, from empty takeaway packets to cigarette butts and items of discarded clothing. The area was illuminated by spotlights erected on temporary stands. Another crime scene technician was crouched down beside what, at first glance, appeared to be a crumpled heap of clothing. At the same time, a third stood a little further away, photographing the scene and the surroundings.

"What do we have?" Adam asked.

"Young white male, mid to late teens," Alice said.

"Overdose?"

Alice shook her head. "We'll know more once the forensic pathologist does his thing, but it looks like blunt force trauma. This was no accident."

"Dumped?"

Alice shook her head. "Unlikely, judging from the blood pooling."

Adam surveyed the scene for a moment before continuing towards the body, taking care to step on the plates already laid down by SOCO, the scenes of crime officers. It was a desolate spot, overlooked on one side by old warehouses backing onto a disused railway siding and hidden behind scraggly bushes and bent, broken wire fencing on either side of the substation. He raised his eyes to the adjacent buildings. Several of the warehouses had smashed windows and looked derelict from this angle. There appeared to be no security cameras mounted in the vicinity. Further on, a pair of residential tower blocks stood as silent sentinels overlooking the scene. Adam moved down the slight slope to where the body lay.

"Who discovered the body?"

"A guy out for his morning run."

Alice indicated with a flick of her head back in the direction they'd come. A man in his thirties, wearing a dark tracksuit, was talking to a uniformed officer behind the crime scene tape. The officer had positioned the runner with his back to the tracks and, more importantly, the body. However, the man peered over his shoulder every so often to check that he hadn't imagined his grisly discovery. The officer's questions drew his attention away from the body. Adam wondered whether the man would stick to more urban, well-lit routes in the future.

"ID on our vic?" Adam asked.

"No wallet or phone, but there was a student card in his back pocket," Alice said, handing a plastic evidence bag to Adam. The bag contained a small rectangular card with a photo. Adam looked from the image to the victim and back;

it appeared to be the same person. Marshall Tyler, a prefect at Sawyer's Hill Grammar School.

"That's the fancy school near here, right?" he asked. Alice nodded. "Time of death?"

"Again, we'll know more when we get him on the table, but less than twelve hours."

"So, sometime last night," Adam said. "I wonder what he was doing here."

Adam kept to the stepping plates as he followed her around the corpse. It was partially obscured among the weeds, although it appeared that no attempt had been made to hide the body. There were no tell-tale drag marks or trampled areas to suggest multiple attackers. The young man, clad in chinos and a black jacket, looked to have died where he had fallen.

They waited a moment for the crime scene officer to set a plastic number on the ground beside a half-smoked cigarette butt and continued once the photographer had captured the image. Adam crouched down while Alice lifted a bunch of tight curls, which had flopped across the victim's forehead, revealing pale, smooth skin, and unseeing blue eyes. Bruising on his cheek and dried blood caked beneath his nostrils suggested that he'd been beaten sometime before his death. The back of his head was misshapen, as though it were a boiled egg that someone had bashed with a spoon. The sandy curls were matted with congealed blood, and a large damp patch on the ground beneath his head was already crawling with insects.

Adam swore under his breath. He stood. "No phone, you said?"

"Robbery or drug deal gone wrong perhaps?" Alice said.

"Given the debris around here, I'd say this area is well used by the local junkies."

Adam shook his head. "I'm not sure. If this was a mugging, they wouldn't have left him with those nearly new Air Jordans." He pointed towards the victim's feet, clad in pristine white and grey trainers.

"And that's why you're the detective." She glanced up at the sky. "Where's TJ with that tent? I expect it will rain sooner rather than later."

"Thanks, Alice. I'll leave you to it. One of my team will be by later."

"One other thing, Adam, it looks like we might get something from beneath his fingernails." She lifted a cold, pale hand and indicated the torn and bloodied fingernails. "I know. I'll put a rush on it."

"Thanks." Adam left them to the unenviable task of evidence gathering and joined the officer interviewing the jogger. He paused to peel off the gloves and shoved them in a pocket before unzipping the coverall and stepping out of it. He rolled it up and added it to the crime scene team's gear bag.

"Morning, DS Jackson," the officer greeted him as he approached. "Mr Hamilton here has given his statement, and I've given him the number for Victim Support."

Adam reached out and shook Mr Hamilton's hand. "Thank you for calling this in. Here's my card in case you think of anything else. Constable de Santa will drop you home."

"Okay, thanks," Hamilton said. "Officer, he's so young, someone must be waiting at home for him. Do you know who he is?" His face held a look of anguish.

"Not at this stage," Adam said.

* * *

Adam grabbed a coffee back at the station before setting up a new incident board for the murder investigation between two wall-mounted screens at one end of the main CID incident room. He pushed the whiteboards for the two most recent murder inquiries that the team was currently working to one side and concentrated on the new case.

At the centre of the board, he added a photo of Marshall Tyler that he'd taken from the student ID card found on the body and printed out as soon as he'd arrived at the station. Marshall gave the camera what could only be described as a smouldering look through his mop of bleach-blond curls. Adam wrote his name and school address beside the photo and the location and approximate time of death.

'Newham sidings: 6pm Tues – 5am Wed.'

The rest of his small team arrived as he finished writing and grabbed their seats for the morning briefing. Adam stood to one side of the incident board, with his laptop on a table in front of him.

"Morning, all," he said. "In addition to the cases we're already working on, we have a new priority for today. The body of a young man matching the description of Marshall Tyler, a seventeen-year-old student at Sawyer's Hill Grammar, was found early this morning by a runner at a railway siding leading into West Ham. The cause of death appears to be blunt force trauma. Still, we'll know more once we get a preliminary report from the pathologist later today."

He tapped the laptop's keyboard and transferred four crime scene photos to display on one of the electronic screens hanging on the wall beside the board.

"Not a robbery then," Eloise said. "Since they left the trainers."

"My thoughts exactly," Adam agreed. "Although his phone, watch and wallet are missing. Eloise, can you get me his home address and the contact details for his parents. Tony, can you check the missing person reports filed in the last twenty-four hours?" he asked the middle-aged, plainclothes officer seated at a computer.

"Sarge," Detective Constable Tony Dupont acknowledged, rubbing a hand across his clipped greying beard.

"Julian, I want all CCTV footage from the approach roads to the crime scene and see if there are any cameras in the vicinity of the railway siding."

Julian straightened from leaning against a desk, moved across the room to a computer and sat down. He shed his jacket and started typing.

"We need to narrow down the time of death window. We currently have it as some time in the last twelve hours or so. Was he at school yesterday? Who last saw him?"

"On it, boss," Tony said, bringing up the missing person screen on the HOLMES database on his desktop computer. A moment later, he called. "Okay, four missing persons reported in East London in the last forty-eight hours that fit the profile, but nothing for a Marshall Tyler."

Adam rested his hand on the back of Tony's chair and leaned over to read the profiles. "You can remove the first two; they're too young," he said. "But those two are interesting, especially that most recent one. Look, he attends the same school as our vic."

Tony transferred the full missing person report onto the screen on the wall beside the incident board.

"Harry Compton, final year at Sawyer's Hill Grammar, reported missing by his parents Rosie and Terry Compton last night. They hadn't seen him for twenty-eight hours at that stage. No further updates since then," Tony said. "I wonder why it took them so long to report him missing?"

"Send their details to my phone, I'll pay them a visit," Adam said. "Who from Missing Persons has been assigned?"

"DS Cho."

"Good, let her know that we have a possible link and that I'll be in touch later in the day."

"Sarge, I have the CCTV for the roads between the school and the crime scene," Julian said, unbuttoning the cuffs of his shirt and rolling the sleeves up. "There's nothing for the actual road, but I'll start at 4 p.m. yesterday with what I've got."

"Good, let me know what you find."

"According to his social media, Marshall Tyler is a boarder at Sawyer's Hill Grammar," Eloise called across the room from her desk.

"In that case, call the school and see if they realise that he's missing," Adam instructed. "Tony, can you get back down to the crime scene and liaise with SOCO? I want to know what else they found in their wider search of the area."

Tony grabbed his jacket from the back of his chair. "On my way."

Eloise put the telephone down. "Marshall Tyler signed out after school on Monday to go and stay overnight with a school friend who is a day pupil, but he was absent from school yesterday. His parents live abroad. Geneva."

"Good work; I'll head over to the school now," Adam said.

"Hang on, Adam, you'll want to know this," Eloise said. "His parents are Conrad Tyler and Esmeralda Jefferies." Adam gave her a blank look. "Conrad Tyler is the British software developer who sold his business to one of the big tech companies several years back. Esme was a supermodel twenty years ago. They're wealthy and famous."

"That explains the pose on his ID photo," Julian called across the room.

"Thanks for the heads-up. It doesn't mean that they won't still be devastated," Adam said. "I probably should inform the DCI of his parentage before I go. Once the media get hold of this, it has the potential to be a circus."

Chapter 9

K at paused by the reception desk at the top of the stairs leading into the Forensic Accounting Associates office after lunch. Although it was cool out, she'd enjoyed a solitary walk along the river to clear her head.

"Any news? What did the police say?" she asked Rosie, seated behind the reception desk.

Rosie shook her head. She looked tired and drawn. "No sign of him."

"You should go home. You look exhausted," Kat said.

"I'm better having something to do," Rosie said. "Terry has stayed home again, so he'll let me know if… when Harry turns up."

"Okay, let me know when he does," Kat said, giving her an encouraging smile, before continuing on towards her desk.

"Actually, Kat," Rosie called. Kat turned and waited while Rosie caught up to her. "If I gave you permission, could you get access to Harry's bank account?"

"Not without a court order of some sort, unless either of you is a signatory. But are you sure that you want to do that? He might see it as a betrayal of trust," Kat said. "When he returns."

Rosie sighed. "Terry and I discussed it last night. Harry's a good boy, but there's no way he has earned all of that money from designing websites."

"Apparently, a lot of teenagers are making good money selling the game currency that they earn through online gaming."

"I don't think he has time to play online games all that much."

Kat shrugged.

Rosie's mobile rang. She pulled it from her pocket and peered at the screen. "It's Terry. I should take this."

Kat arrived at her desk at the same time as Nate and Shamira, who had just returned from a client visit.

"Hey, how did it go this morning?" she asked.

"Good, but more importantly," Shamira said, grinning at her, "how was the date?"

"It was alright, although it ended on a less than auspicious note," Kat said.

"Oh, yeah, tell me more," Shamira said.

Kat smiled at her enthusiasm. "Connor was attacked outside the restaurant."

"What?" Shamira screeched.

"And I suppose you fought off his attacker," Nate said, looking over. "Was he impressed?"

"Not exactly. Some bystanders intervened, and the men ran off," Kat said.

"Robbery?"

"No, they knew him, and this was the last warning, apparently."

"No way? What did Connor say? Was he hurt?" Shamira asked.

"He brushed it off, said it went with the job of being an investigative journalist," Kat said. "But, yes, he'll have a sore face today."

"He's not the right guy for you," Shamira said with a shake of her head. "You don't need any more drama in your life after everything that's happened."

"True, although I am seeing him again for lunch on Saturday."

Shamira's brow wrinkled. "Well, be careful."

"What?" Kat teased. "Aren't you the one who is always telling me that I need to get out more? Put what happened with Gabe and Adam behind me?"

Shamira rolled her eyes. "Stop using my words against me." She dropped the magazine she was carrying onto her desk as she set down her bag and removed her raincoat, hanging it on a wall hook behind her desk.

"You'll never guess who has a feature in the *Evening Standard* magazine?" she said.

"Who?"

"Deborah Sharp," Shamira said.

"As in our client, Deborah Sharp?"

"Yeah, there's a profile on her and the charity that she runs."

Nate leaned over and grabbed the magazine. He flicked through the pages until he came to the article, headed with a photograph of their client, a petite, dark-haired woman, leaning against a desk piled with various bits of computer equipment. "She certainly makes a glamorous frontwoman," he said.

"She does," Shamira agreed, snatching the magazine out of his hands. "Listen to this."

"Deborah Sharp is giving back to her community. On the

campaign trail fifteen years ago, the former Hackney girl-made-good met her husband, the Honourable Jeremy Sharp, when he was running for the Hackney Borough, and she was a youth volunteer. In the last year, her charity, Digital Kids, has provided computer equipment and wireless Internet access to over one thousand homes in the less privileged areas of London. 'Being born into a lower socio-economic household is an immediate disadvantage for a great many children. Often these homes cannot afford computers, or if they can, they don't have the means to access high-speed Internet,' Mrs Sharp said. 'And in today's digital world, that lack of access can compound the limitation of a child's future prospects.' And that's where Digital Kids steps in. Working with schools, they identify families in need. 'We have also set up computer labs at twenty local comprehensive schools. We run various training programmes and classes until the schools can manage themselves.' The success of a recent celebrity-studded fundraiser means that the charity will double its efforts in the coming year. If you'd like to contribute, details can be found on the charity's website."

"No mention of her impending divorce, then?" Kat said.

"No," Shamira said. "Perhaps the article was written a while ago and only just published now."

"Has Harry Compton turned up?" Nate asked. Kat shook her head. Nate looked thoughtful. "I wish we could have got into his computer. I'd love to know what he was up to."

"Yeah, there's definitely something strange going on. I've meant to look up the details of Harry's company at Companies House all morning," Kat said, typing into the browser on her computer. "You've reminded me."

The company details for Harry Houdini's Magic Tricks Ltd

filled the screen.

"He is the sole director and shareholder," Nate said, reading over Kat's shoulder. "What industry does it say the company is in?"

Kat clicked into another screen. "Other amusement and recreation activities," she read.

"That could mean anything," Shamira said, looking across from her desk.

Footsteps sounded behind Kat, and she saw Shamira's face light up.

"Hello there. Your receptionist said to come straight over."

Kat's heart sank as she registered who the voice belonged to.

"Hello, DS Jackson," Shamira said. Kat could hear the delight in her friend's voice.

"Adam, mate, how are ya?" Nate straightened from leaning on the back of Kat's chair and shook hands with Adam.

Kat closed her eyes for a moment and let out a calming breath before she spun her chair around to look at him. Adam was dressed in his usual attire of jeans, a black leather jacket and boots. His jaw was covered in dark stubble, and he looked tired and a little strained.

"What can we do for you?" Kat asked.

Adam registered her cool, even tone. "I'm working a homicide. A teenage boy found dead in East London this morning."

Shamira's hands flew to cover her mouth.

"Not Harry Compton?" Kat said in a whisper, her eyes wide.

Adam shook his head. "No, but the dead boy was a schoolmate of Harry's, whom I believe is your receptionist's son."

Kat looked over towards the reception desk, where Rosie was speaking into her headset. "We should talk in one of the meeting rooms," she said, standing, leading the way across the floor, and opening the door of an empty room with views along the Thames to Tower Bridge. Dark threatening rain clouds hung low over the city. Adam, Nate and Shamira followed, filing into the room and sitting down. Kat closed the door and took a seat at one end of the table, furthest away from Adam.

"Our victim is a boarder at Sawyer's Hill Grammar and told them he was staying at Harry's two nights ago. But I have just spoken to Harry's father, and that never happened. In fact, they reported Harry as being missing from that afternoon; he never came home from school."

"We know," Kat said. "It was Nate and I that encouraged them to report him missing."

"That's why I'm here," Adam said. "I'm curious; why did you two visit their house last night? His father mentioned that you looked at Harry's computer."

"Rosie wanted us to look into what Harry had been doing online," Nate said.

"His parents found a crumpled bank statement in his room for a business account with over one hundred thousand pounds in it," Kat said. "And they had no idea how he'd obtained that kind of money."

"They thought he'd been building websites, but you don't make that sort of cash building websites for local clubs and businesses," Nate added.

"We've just looked at who owns the company, and Harry does," Kat said.

"So, what had he been doing?"

"Hard to say, everything was heavily password-protected, but he did have a Tor browser open on one screen," Nate said.

"And a room full of computer equipment, designer clothes and other expensive toys," Kat added.

"Interesting," Adam said, rubbing the stubble on his jaw. "And now he is missing, and his classmate is dead."

"You don't think that Harry killed him, do you?" Shamira whispered.

"I'm not sure what to think at this stage," Adam said. "Harry, too, could be in danger for all we know."

"Poor Rosie," Shamira said.

"If I get his bank records and computer equipment delivered here, can I get you to look into it and report back to me?" Adam asked. "Our tech department has a two-week backlog. If what you're saying is correct, then the clues to his whereabouts, and perhaps my victim's death, could be on his computer, and I can't wait for two weeks. I assume your firm's overarching agreement with the Met is still in play?"

"Yeah," Kat said.

"In that case, I'll get you access to my victim's bank accounts too," he said, standing. "We need to know fairly quickly what these two were up to before Missing Persons makes the decision whether or not to issue a Child Rescue Alert."

"Harry's hardly a child," Nate said.

"He's under eighteen, so technically he is," Adam said. "But they need to show a reasonable belief that he is in imminent danger and have sufficient information for the public to help us locate him. We have neither."

They stood, and Shamira opened the meeting room door, holding it as the others passed through. Adam nodded towards the reception desk. "Needless to say, this is confidential," he said. "I'll talk to the Comptons again in due course, probably later today."

"Of course."

Adam began walking across the office towards the entrance before pausing and turning with a bemused expression on his face.

"What's this I hear about you being in an altercation in the West End last night, Kat?" he said.

She narrowed her eyes and approached him. "How?"

Adam waited.

"It was nothing; they ran off. Something to do with a story that Connor's investigating."

"Connor? You mean Tommy's reporter?"

"Yeah."

"I see," he said, studying her for a moment. "You should have access to those accounts by the end of the day."

Chapter 10

Adam drove through the gates and down the tree-lined avenue leading to Sawyer's Hill Grammar School, thinking about Kat. She was acting very cool with him, not that he could blame her, but he hated leaving things the way they had. He gripped the steering wheel until his knuckles turned white and took a deep breath. There was stuff to sort out before he could try to talk with her again about anything personal. Although a nagging voice in the back of his mind reminded him that Tommy had been correct, and she'd obviously been out with Connor O'Malley last night. Perhaps he was too late, and she'd already moved on. The thought pained him, and he shoved it to the back of his mind.

The manicured lawns surrounding the school's magnificent red-brick buildings were dotted with ancient oak trees and clusters of students walking in groups or kicking a ball around. All wore the school's uniform of dark grey trousers and a navy-blue blazer with a thin red pinstripe.

Adam pulled to a stop in the allocated visitor parking area and followed the signs to the headmaster's office. The school secretary showed him to a seat in a sunny waiting area beside a sizeable glass-fronted cabinet filled with various awards and trophies won by pupils over the years.

"Mr Beauchamp will see you now, detective," the secretary said, after a few minutes, ushering Adam through a doorway and closing the door behind him.

A short, round man wearing a navy double-breasted suit moved from behind a wooden desk to shake Adam's hand. He smoothed down his thinning hair with one hand and indicated to a pair of chairs in front of a window with the other.

"Please have a seat, detective. Were you offered tea?"

"No, I'm fine, thank you."

Adam handed him a card with his details. He sat down beside the window which overlooked the immaculate grass of the inner quadrangle of the school.

"So, what can I do for you? The officer who called mentioned a missing student."

"I'm afraid it's more than that, sir," Adam said. "A body was discovered this morning with Marshall Tyler's student ID in a pocket." The principal's face greyed. "Can I show you a photo?"

"Certainly."

Adam produced the photo of the ID card sealed in an evidence bag.

"Yes, that's Tyler's ID card."

"Why was he not reported missing?"

"Let me call his housemaster. I hope this is just a case of mistaken identity."

Adam watched a group of students walk around the path outside the window before cutting across the corner of the grass and running up the stairs into the building on the far side of the courtyard, while Beauchamp made a call requesting that Marshall's housemaster join them. This school was so different from the ones in the surrounding area and the one that Adam had attended. His co-ed secondary had been a comprehensive school, rough and rowdy, with the teachers spending more time controlling the class than teaching.

"Tell me a little about the housemaster," Adam said.

"Andrew Wilson has been with us around a year teaching economics and is popular with the students. He runs a finance club with a few of the boys, teaching them some of the more practical things that the curriculum doesn't allow time for," Beauchamp said. "The boys hear so much about investment markets in the media that it's great for them to have the chance to participate, even in a minimal, controlled way."

The door opened following a short, sharp knock and a thin man in academic robes entered. His straight, fair hair was cut in long layers and brushed his collar, and he wore a guarded expression.

"Ah, Wilson, this is DS Jackson; he's following up on Marshall Tyler's whereabouts."

Andrew Wilson acknowledged Adam before replying. "I believe he had a leave pass to stay overnight with a classmate, a day pupil, Harry Compton."

"Please tell me that he has returned and is on detention for tardiness?" Beauchamp said.

"No, sir, he's not returned, and it appears that Harry Compton has not been at school again today. I am waiting for his parents to call me back. I expect the boys are still at their house."

"They were friends?" Adam asked.

"As thick as thieves, one might say," Wilson replied. "Unusual, really, given that they were from completely different backgrounds."

"But, Wilson, didn't you just say that Tyler has been staying over at the Comptons' since Monday night?" Beauchamp asked.

"Not according to Harry Compton's parents. They filed a missing person report for their son last night. They haven't seen him in two days," Adam said.

"Oh, I see." Beauchamp peered at Wilson over his glasses, whose mouth dropped open.

"I understand Marshall's parents live overseas," Adam said. "I will need their contact details, and I'd like to see his room, if I may."

"Yes, of course, Susan will email their details to you," Beauchamp said, standing. "Wilson, can you show DS Jackson to Tyler's dorm?"

"Yes, yes, of course. This way, detective," Wilson said, opening the office door. Adam followed him out into the corridor.

"Thank you for your time, Mr Beauchamp. Please keep this to yourself until we contact his parents. I'll be in touch."

Adam followed Wilson along the wood-panelled corridor, where gloomy portraits of stern men in robes looked down on passers-by. Adam assumed from the authoritarian nature of the paintings that they were previous headmasters. Wilson led them out into the quadrangle behind the main building. Adam felt the prickle of observation on the back of his neck and checked behind him to see Beauchamp standing at the window of his office.

They skirted around the courtyard's edge and walked through an archway beneath the building on the opposite side. From there, they followed the path a short distance to the first of three smaller, matching red-brick blocks and climbed the steps to the entrance. Wilson took long strides and was silent the entire way, deep in thought. Several students were milling about in the hallway and stood to the side as they entered. Murmurs of 'sir' greeted Wilson, who led Adam up a carpeted staircase to the second floor and along a wide passageway past closed doors, each with several name plates attached.

"Here we are," Wilson said, arriving at a door at the end of the corridor. A bracket held a single name tag, which read 'Marshall Tyler, Prefect'. Wilson knocked before turning the knob. The door was locked. Wilson entered a code into the keypad set into the door, and a soft click sounded as it unlocked.

"The housemasters have an override code for instances such as this," he said.

Wilson tsked under his breath at the sight that greeted them: an unmade single bed, discarded clothes strewn across the floor and a messy desk. A sofa against one wall had a blanket bunched up on one end.

"The senior prefects have the privilege of being assigned single rooms, but young Tyler doesn't seem to appreciate the fact."

"Normal room for a teenage boy, I would have thought," Adam said, taking thin latex gloves from his pocket and pulling them on. "Now, has anyone else been in here since Marshall was last at school?"

"Not that I'm aware of," Wilson said.

Adam took several photos of the room on his mobile. He examined a framed picture on top of the bookshelf of Marshall Tyler with two people whom Adam assumed were his parents. The woman was stunning and looked vaguely familiar.

"Is there any chance that I could have a word with one or two of his friends? I'd like to see if they knew where he and Harry Compton were yesterday."

"I'll see who's around."

He left Adam studying the papers pinned to the noticeboard above the desk: a class timetable, an advertisement for an e-games tournament and a scrap of paper with a mobile phone number scribbled on it. Adam took another photo before pulling open the desk's top drawer, which contained pens, a pad of paper, and a calculator. The second drawer, however, was locked.

Wilson returned with a chubby teenage boy whose sandy fringe swept across his forehead. The front tail of his white school shirt was untucked. At Wilson's disapproving glance, he shoved it back into the waistband of his trousers.

"This is Samuel Rowley."

"I'm DS Jackson," Adam said. "I'm hoping that you can tell me where Marshall and Harry were yesterday?"

"I c-can't," Samuel said, adjusting his black-framed glasses.

"Can't or won't?" Wilson said.

"Marshall will kill me," Samuel whispered, as though Marshall was in the next room listening.

"Just answer the question, Samuel," Wilson said, sounding exasperated.

"You should ask Harry; didn't he stay the night at his?" Samuel said.

"That didn't happen," Adam said.

Samuel opened and closed his mouth. He fidgeted and peered up at Wilson from beneath his hair.

"Wilson, can you see if there is another of Marshall's friends around?" Adam asked.

Wilson hesitated, looking a little put out at being assigned the task of errand boy. He spun on his heel and left the room. Samuel's shoulders slumped.

"So, where were they going?" Adam asked.

Samuel looked over his shoulder to ensure they weren't going to be overheard. He lowered his voice. "To meet someone they've been doing business with."

"Business?"

"Yeah, he and Harry have some side hustle going. I don't know the details, but they're making some serious money. They're always splashing the cash."

Adam raised his eyebrows as he looked around the small room. "I don't see a computer."

"It'll be locked in the drawer there," Samuel said, nodding his head towards the desk. "Marshall didn't trust anyone."

"And you don't know where they were meeting this person?"

Samuel shook his head. "They didn't tell anyone the details."

Wilson returned alone. "The boys are back in class. Do you want me to take you?"

Adam shook his head. "That won't be necessary at this stage, but could you open this drawer for me?" He pulled a card from his pocket and handed it to Samuel. "If you think of anything else, give me a call."

"Off you go, Samuel," Wilson said and pulled a set of keys from his pocket.

"Okay, bye." Samuel darted for the door, looking relieved.

"Thanks for your help," Adam called to his retreating back.

Wilson sorted through his keys until he found one, which he fitted into the lock on the drawer. He pulled open the drawer. It was empty.

"No computer or laptop?" Adam asked.

Wilson looked around the room. "It doesn't appear so. He must have had it with him."

Adam pulled off the gloves and shoved them in the pocket of his jacket. "Why lock an empty drawer?" Adam asked, almost to himself. Wilson shrugged. "Well, thank you for your time. Can you seal off this room? There'll be someone by to process it later today. I'll see myself out."

Chapter 11

K at hurried through the ticket hall of the underground station on her way back to the office after a rather pointless meeting that could have been handled over the phone.

"Spare some change?"

Kat stopped walking and dug into her bag. She retrieved the banana and muesli bar she'd grabbed that morning when she left the flat and bent down to give them to the homeless man. She'd once been told by a social worker acquaintance that it was better to give food than money. She glanced at the man and did a double take. He sat beside a roll of blankets, a scruffy beard covering his cheeks and matted brown hair in desperate need of a trim hanging limply around his shoulders.

"Del?"

The man blinked and squinted at her. "Kat?"

"Del, what's happened to you?" she blurted without thinking.

Del's expression turned belligerent, and he rose to his feet. Kat took a step back and watched as Del's face crumpled and he hung his head. She reached out and laid a hand on his arm.

"Can I buy you a cup of coffee?"

He nodded and bent down to collect his belongings; the roll

of blankets and a bulging canvas bag.

There was a café next to the station. They had just sat down at an outside table at one end of the terrace when a waitress approached, wearing a pinched expression.

"Two flat whites, please, and would you like scrambled eggs on toast, Del?" Kat said, ignoring the waitress's glare and smiling at Del.

"Yes, please," he mumbled, keeping his eyes diverted.

The waitress harrumphed and stomped inside with their order.

"Sorry," Del said.

"Don't be, you've as much right to eat here as anyone," Kat said.

Del looked up at her, studying her face. "I heard about Felicity and you," he said, pointing to her hand. "I'm sorry. Felicity was a great girl."

"She was. I miss her so much."

"Can I look at your hand?"

Kat reached across the table and rested her prosthetic hand in his large dirty one. Del ran his thumb over the back of Kat's fingers and looked up at her.

"It looks so real," he said. "I always thought they just gave you a hook."

"I had a hook at the start," Kat said. "But I've been working with a group of scientists that my brother knows, who are building next-generation prosthetics. I've been assisting them for the last two years to help develop a properly functioning hand. We're not there yet, but this is pretty good. It sends electrical signals to my brain and back, which allows me to move it naturally and do a lot of everyday tasks."

"Amazing," Del said.

"What about you? Last I heard, you were running a market in Surrey," Kat said.

Del's head dropped again. "I got duped, Kat, mixed with the wrong people, and I lost everything. I owed so much money that I couldn't pay my rent, and, well, here we are. I think this is what they call rock bottom."

"Oh, Del, that's awful."

A different waitress returned with the coffee and a plate piled high with scrambled eggs and extra toast. "There you are, my love," she said, placing it in front of Del. "You enjoy that."

Kat gave the woman a grateful smile. "Thank you."

Kat sipped her coffee as Del demolished the food in front of him in a matter of minutes.

"When was the last time you had a hot meal?" she asked.

"There was a soup kitchen yesterday," he said.

"Why don't I take you to a homeless shelter that a friend of mine works at?" she said. "You can get a hot shower and a bed. They can get you registered for benefits and maybe even help you get a job."

"You need an address to get benefits," Del said. "And as you can see, the streets are my address…" He trailed off, waving his hand around.

"I think they provide the address for you."

"Look at me, Kat," Del said. "You were always lovely, but most people don't want anything to do with the likes of me, let alone give me a job."

"Could you go home to your mum?"

Del shook his head. "She died at the start of last year. That's when it all started going wrong. I was drinking too much, and it all got away on me."

"I'm so sorry, Del," she said. "I didn't know."

"I imagine you were dealing with your own stuff," he said.

Kat smiled at him. "Yeah, I was in a pretty dark place for quite a while."

"Look at you now, though, fancy clothes and nice hair; you obviously have a good job," Del said.

"It's all a work in progress, Del. Some days, I still feel like I'm operating on autopilot, just putting one foot in front of the other. I often feel like I'm being looked at and judged because of my hand. I sometimes think it would be easier just to stay home and avoid people." She stopped talking and looked down at the table. "I don't think I've ever really admitted that out loud."

Del reached across and enveloped her hands in his massive dirty ones. They sat in companionable silence for a moment.

"So, what are we going to do to get you back on your feet, Del?"

"I am not your responsibility, and besides I don't think there's a quick fix. There never is for the big problems."

"Del, you've got to have hope, things can only get better for you from here," Kat said.

"I just don't know if I have the energy to start again. You knew me, Kat, I had big dreams. Multimillionaire by twenty-one, retired to my mansion in Spain by thirty." He gave a wry laugh. "That dream sure as hell ain't happening."

"Then make new dreams." Del shrugged. "Let me take you to that shelter," Kat said.

"No, I'll find it," he said. "Where is it?"

Kat scribbled the address on the back of a serviette. She reached into her bag and pulled out her business card. "I come through this station most days, or you can call me if you need anything."

Del nodded and took the card. "Forensic accountant? Is that like those guys on TV that find all the bodies?"

Kat laughed. "No, we try to find the financial proceeds of crime."

Del stood. "Thank you for the food."

"You're very welcome," Kat said. "At the risk of insulting you, here." She thrust two £20 notes into his hand.

"Kat," he began to protest, but she turned her back and hurried inside to pay the bill.

"Don't bring homeless people here again," the original waitress snapped at her as Kat tapped her card against the payment reader.

"He's an old friend. I went to school with him," Kat said.

"I don't care if he's your brother; it chases the customers away."

Kat looked around the busy café. Her coffee with Del didn't seem to have bothered anyone inside or out on the terrace. "Well, you don't need to worry, I won't be back here, and neither will any of my colleagues from the corporate offices around here." She spun on her heel and left the waitress gaping open-mouthed at her.

There was no sign of Del outside the café or the station. Kat stood on the footpath, scanning the area.

"Hey, mate, who are you looking for?" Nate said, walking out of the station and joining her.

"An old school friend of mine, who I just bumped into," Kat said.

"Why the concerned look? Does he have teenage dirt on you? I need to meet this guy," Nate said, laughing.

"No, he's homeless. I just bought him lunch."

"Mate, that was nice of you."

"Not really; he was a good guy, Del. He's just fallen on hard times."

"Del? What's that short for?"

Kat smiled. "Del Boy, you know, after the character on the TV show *Only Fools and Horses*. I can't even remember his real name, Marc or Mike, something like that. Anyway, Del was a charming wheeler and dealer. He always had some money-making scheme going, right from when we were kids."

"Sounds like a character."

"He was," Kat said. "It's awful to think that his life has ended up like this. I encouraged him to go to the shelter that Amir works at. I hope he does."

"Surely he will, mate."

"He might be too proud. I think I'll call Amir to keep an eye out for him," Kat said.

"Good idea."

"It makes you realise how precarious life can be, doesn't it? Some bad luck or bad decisions, and it can all fall apart."

Chapter 12

Adam followed his boss DCI Joni Tanner into the incident room. The members of his team along with several uniformed officers seconded to the investigation, were gathered at one end of the room, some seated at desks, others standing and chatting. The wall-mounted screens were turned on, displaying the school ID photos of Marshall Tyler and Harry Compton. The incident whiteboard, covered with a handwritten timeline, lines linking scrawled notes and more photos, was positioned centrally beneath the screens.

DCI Tanner had been with London's Metropolitan Police for twenty years. She had a reputation for being tough to work for, but Adam enjoyed her straight-talking approach. The seated officers looked up and greeted her formally with calls of 'Ma'am'. She ran a hand through her short platinum blonde hair and gave a single nod of acknowledgement.

"Okay, team, DCI Tanner is joining us for this morning's review of the Marshall Tyler murder investigation," Adam said, striding to the front of the room and gathering the attention of those assembled. "We now know that Marshall Tyler died sometime between six p.m. and midnight on Tuesday. His friend and classmate Harry Compton has been missing since then too. Marshall's cause of death was blunt force trauma. From preliminary analysis, it appears he either fell and hit his head on a rock or was hit in the head by a rock. He also has some bruising to his face and some defensive wounds on his hands. His body hadn't been moved; he died where he fell, but his phone, wallet and watch are missing.

"Julian has reviewed the CCTV footage from the area. There is nothing on the road leading to the crime scene, but we have one individual matching the description of Marshall walking along Sawyer's Hill Road towards the location at 5:30 p.m. That's the last time he's seen alive. We've also discovered a significant sum of money in the name of a company owned by Harry Compton. I've asked Forensic Accounting Associates to analyse the bank accounts of both teenagers," Adam said.

"Do we have any clues as to the origin of the funds?" Tony asked.

Adam shook his head. "Still working on that; Harry was building websites, there's a suggestion the lads had a business operating on the side, and we know that Harry was accessing the Dark Web."

"Our priority is finding Harry Compton," DCI Tanner said, stepping forward to join Adam. "It's still unclear whether he too has fallen victim to whoever killed Marshall or whether he was involved in his death."

"We should expect a frenzy of media interest, now the name of the deceased has been released, which should help us to locate Harry," Adam said. "We need to monitor the tip line closely. Is everyone clear on what they are to focus on today?"

There were nods all round before the group dispersed.

"Marshall's parents are due here shortly," DCI Tanner said, looking at her watch. "Would you like to sit in on the meeting?"

Adam nodded. "Thank you, ma'am."

"Adam, there's a call for you from a Samuel Rowley," Eloise called across the incident room as DCI Tanner departed. "He said it's about Marshall Tyler."

Adam thought for a moment before recalling the name.

"Put him through," he said, striding to his desk in the corner.

He picked up his desk phone on the first ring. "Samuel, it's DS Jackson."

"Hello," Samuel said in a quiet, timid voice. "They've just told us that Marshall is dead." He sniffed. "That's why you were in his room the other day. You said to call you if I thought of anything."

"Yes," Adam said. "What did you want to tell me?"

"Marshall and Harry were working with Mr Wilson, our housemaster," Samuel said, his voice dropping to a whisper.

"A couple of evenings each week, they'd be doing something online. I overheard them talking about which company to use."

"They both belonged to Mr Wilson's finance club, didn't they? Perhaps they were rebalancing their portfolios or something?" Adam said.

"You know about the finance club?"

"Yes, Mr Beauchamp mentioned it."

"A lot of us are in the finance club," Samuel said. "No, what they did was different from what we usually do, and last week I heard Wilson threaten Marshall. He said that if the others found out what Marshall and Harry had been doing, there'd be hell to pay."

"And what did Marshall say?"

"At first, he laughed. I couldn't believe it, but he actually laughed in Wilson's face and said something like, 'well, we're not going to tell them, are you?'" Samuel said. "And then Wilson got mad and said, 'I hope you're not threatening me? This stops today'. Then he said something else that I couldn't hear, and when I peeked around the corner, Wilson was walking away, and Marshall looked genuinely scared."

"What day last week was this, Samuel?"

"Thursday, maybe?"

"Okay, thanks, Samuel," Adam said.

"Detective Jackson, the boys are saying that Marshall was murdered. Is that true? The police wouldn't be asking questions if nothing suspicious had happened, right?" Samuel blurted out.

"I can't comment on an ongoing investigation," Adam said.

"Oh, okay."

"Actually, Samuel, when did you last see Harry and Marshall?"

"On Tuesday afternoon," Samuel said. "I overheard them talking outside Marshall's room; that's how I knew they were going to meet someone."

"Do you know where Harry was on Monday night? His parents say he was missing from after school on Monday," Adam said.

"He stayed here," Samuel said. "He sometimes sleeps on the sofa in Marshall's room."

"That's really useful. Call me if you think of anything else," Adam said.

"Okay. Bye." Samuel ended the call.

"Remind me what housemaster Wilson's alibi is like for the night of Marshall's murder," Adam said. "It is airtight?"

"I think so," Julian said, scrolling through the case notes

on his screen. "He was present at dinner from 5:30 to 6:30, supervised homework from dinner until 9 p.m., and the housemistress spoke to him on three separate occasions between then and 10:30 p.m. There's not enough time to get to the crime scene and back."

Adam studied the photos on the screens at the end of the room for a moment, thinking. "Julian, where are the photos I took of Marshall's dorm room?"

"I've downloaded them into the folder, but I've posted the ones from Tony's more formal search on the incident screen," Julian said.

Adam joined him at his desk. "Humour me. I think there is something different between the two sets of images."

Julian scrolled through the photos downloaded from Adam's phone, on his desktop, with Adam looking over his shoulder.

"There, stop," Adam pointed. "That one there, of the noticeboard. Compare it to Tony's."

Julian enlarged the image, and the two photos appeared side by side on the screen on the wall. Adam straightened and walked towards it.

"The phone number," he said. "Someone removed it from between the time I was there in the morning and when you arrived in the afternoon, Tony." He reached for his mobile and dialled the number, putting the call on speaker for the team to hear.

"My money says it's a burner," Tony said.

An automated voice answered after one ring. "This number is no longer active."

Chapter 13

"I've just received Harry Compton's bank records," Kat said, as an email popped up on her screen during the afternoon.

"DS Jackson doesn't waste time, does he?" Shamira said. "How do they look?"

Kat clicked open the attachments and arranged the files across her two computer screens. "He certainly has a lot of money for a jobless teenage schoolboy. It looks like he's receiving regular deposits from several companies."

"Has he accessed the accounts since he went missing?" Shamira asked.

Kat scrolled to the most recent transaction in Harry's main current account. "No, the last entry was at a fast-food place on Tuesday afternoon. That's interesting since Rosie thinks he was missing from Monday after school. I suppose it might have just been someone using his card, a quick contactless tap, but if that's the case why not try and empty the account?"

"That's not good, Kat," Shamira said with a glance over her shoulder towards the reception desk, where Rosie sat. "I wonder where he was all day Tuesday?"

"I guess the police are looking into that."

Kat loaded the raw data into their in-house data analysis

tool and spent the next half hour sorting the other pieces of information from the police email. She consulted the Companies House website, ran several Internet searches, and then spent a further hour tracing payments and deposits through the various accounts. Finally, she summarised her findings using a pivot table.

"Nate," she said, looking over to the empty workstation where he was setting up Harry Compton's computer, which had just been delivered.

He looked up, pushing his hair out of his eyes. "What's up?"

"Take a look at this. Harry was operating three companies for the last six months," she said. She showed him the incorporation details downloaded from Companies House for Harry Houdini's Magic Tricks Ltd, Racing Tree Three Ltd and Warm Goo Products Ltd.

"Harry is the sole director of all three and joint shareholder with Marshall Tyler on the last two. I can't tell what business they were in."

"In the UK, you can be a company director from the age of sixteen, but you can't open a bank account without a guardian until you're eighteen, right?" Nate said.

"But you can buy a ready-made company with a bank account attached," Shamira said, overhearing the conversation.

"Ah, surely that has to be a loophole in the know-your-client banking process," Nate said.

"Yes, one that I believe has been closed," Kat said. "So someone has co-signed the bank account opening forms. We should request those and we'll need to get Adam to obtain bank statements for each of these companies."

Shamira nodded.

"Also, there are regular deposits into Harry's personal current account from one of the crypto exchanges, CryptoMania," Kat said, pointing to the statement on her screen. "Here, here and here in the last month, all for around £1,500."

"Interesting, what's the annotation?" Nate squinted at the screen.

"Bertie Bear," Kat replied

"Harry's dog," Nate said. "Could be the name of his crypto account."

Kat nodded. "So maybe he was trading crypto assets," she said. "That could explain the income."

"Let's see if we can get access to his account at CryptoMania," Nate said. "They're bending over backwards to help the authorities right now after the scandal with payments to that porn site last year."

"Good idea," Kat agreed. "Can you flick a request through to Adam for all of that?"

"Sure you don't want to do it?"

Kat shook her head. "Nate, do you think Harry could have been selling Z-cash and getting paid in cryptocurrency? Remember, his sister mentioned that she thought he was making his money by selling gaming currency. However, I've seen no evidence of that through his personal bank account."

Nate gave a slow nod, thinking. "We should also try to get access to Harry's *Zombiegamez* account to see what he's been doing. I'll add that to the request that I send to Adam."

"Okay." Kat turned her attention to her screen before looking back over at Nate. "Actually, Nate, what we really need is for Rosie to have another search in Harry's room, specifically for clues to his passwords. He's still missing, and his mate is dead; I don't think we can wait another day or two for Adam to obtain the necessary court orders."

"Have you received anything for Marshall Tyler yet?" Nate asked.

Kat shook her head. "The email from one of Adam's team said something about needing to speak to his parents first, but hopefully, we should have his records tomorrow."

"Hey, is that Rosie's daughter sitting with her?" Shamira said. "She's got a bit of an alternative look going."

Kat looked towards the reception desk, nestled into an alcove at the top of the stairs, where Rosie sat wearing a headset. Beside her, the pink streaks in Caitlyn's hair stood out like the candy stripes of a seaside umbrella.

"Yeah, that's her," Kat said. "I wonder what she's doing here? Perhaps there's news about Harry."

"We should take the opportunity to see what else she can tell us about Harry selling Z-cash," Nate said.

"The trouble is that she probably won't say anything in front of her mother," Kat said.

"Leave Rosie to me," Shamira said.

Nate and Kat crossed the floor to the reception desk. Rosie looked up as they approached. Caitlyn had her head down with her thumbs moving at pace across the screen of her phone. She was chewing gum and blew a pink bubble.

"Hi, this is my daughter Caitlyn," Rosie said. "Her dance class was held near here today, so she's waiting to go home with me."

"Hi, Caitlyn," Kat said, smiling at the girl.

Caitlyn glanced up from her phone, a flash of recognition crossing her face. "Oh, hi."

"I wondered if we could have a chat with Caitlyn about Harry?" Kat said.

"She doesn't know where he is," Rosie said, putting her hand on her daughter's shoulder.

"I know," Kat said. "It's just that she might be able to help us shed some light on his computer."

"Okay." Rosie sounded unconvinced. "I don't expect she'll be much help though, will you, love? Kat and Nate are trying to help us find Harry."

Kat smiled at the girl. Her eye make-up was heavy once again, and she wore a black top and a short coloured skirt over tight frayed black jeans.

"Caitlyn, I was wondering if you could tell us anything about Harry selling Z-cash," Kat said.

Caitlyn snuck a look across at her mother.

"Rosie, I've jammed the coffee machine again." Shamira came rushing over. "Can you help me to fix it?"

Rosie hesitated. "Ah, sure," she said, removing her headset and changing a setting on her screen to allow any calls to be diverted to the answering service.

Rosie looked at Caitlyn with uncertainty in her eyes. "Okay, love?"

Caitlyn nodded, and Rosie followed Shamira around the corner to the kitchen.

"I don't really know any more than I told you the other day," Caitlyn said as soon as her mother was out of earshot. "Just that he was selling a lot of it."

"To school friends?"

"To anybody that wanted it. All Harry had to do was advertise it in the forums, sell it at a slight discount, and people wanted it. Especially if it was cheaper than you could buy it in the game," she said.

"The game owners can't have liked that," Kat said.

Nate frowned. "Where did he get it from?"

"He… bought… it," Caitlyn said, emphasising each word as if Nate were a little slow.

"What with?" Nate said, matching her tone.

Caitlyn snapped her head up and glared at him. "I dunno, the money he made from selling it, I guess."

"But if he was selling it for less than it cost him to buy, then he couldn't be making any money," Kat said.

Realisation dawned on Caitlyn's face and her cheeks coloured. "Oh, yeah." She looked up at the ceiling and blew a bubble.

"How much can you win in one game?" Kat asked, turning to Nate.

"The top gamers can win up to one hundred Z-cash per game," Nate said.

"I might know Harry's cryptocurrency account details," Caitlyn blurted out.

Nate quirked an eyebrow. "How?"

"Harry sold some Z-cash to a guy I know, a week or two back. He gave me an address to give him to pay the funds into," she said.

"Do you still have it?"

"Yeah, I think so," Caitlyn said, picking her phone up from the desk. She scrolled through her messages until she came to one and turned her phone to show Nate. Kat leaned across and saw a peer-to-peer invoice with an alphanumeric sequence of numbers and a QR code on the screen.

"Can you forward that to me?" Nate asked.

"Sure," Caitlyn said. Nate reeled off his mobile number, and his phone buzzed seconds later as the message arrived.

"Thanks," he said.

"Dad said the police sent his computer here. The last I knew, his password was Zombieking##1," Caitlyn said, spelling it out without looking up from her phone.

Kat smiled at her. "Does Harry let you use his computer?"

She shrugged. "Only if he needs help with his homework." She grinned for the first time, and Kat saw a glimpse of the sweet girl beneath the sullen looks and the goth-like makeup. "Whatever you do, please don't tell him that I helped you when he turns up," Caitlyn said.

"We won't."

Nate returned to Harry's computer and spent the next few minutes logging in and searching the directories and browsing history before returning to Kat and Caitlyn.

"Anything?" Kat asked.

"Not really," he said. "The account number was just a single-use one. There's no crypto wallet saved on his computer that I can find, which makes me think he uses a hardware wallet to protect his keys. They're more secure and less open to hacking than software ones."

Rosie returned to the desk with Shamira hurrying behind her mouthing, "Sorry."

Nate turned to Rosie. "We think that perhaps Harry has been using a hardware wallet to save his crypto keys. You haven't seen one anywhere in Harry's room, have you? It looks a bit like a USB stick."

Rosie shrugged. "I can't say that I understood much of what you just said, but sometimes he has a USB drive stuck in his computer." She pointed to a port on her desktop box. "I just thought it was for his schoolwork."

"And his school bag wasn't at home, was it?"

Rosie shook her head.

"Did you know that he had a cryptocurrency account?" Nate

asked.

"Cryptocurrency, you mean like Bitcoin?" Rosie asked.

"Yeah."

Rosie looked confused. "No, how would he even know how to do that?"

"He probably learned about it at that fancy school, Mum," Caitlyn said.

"Can I ask a stupid question?" Rosie said.

"Of course."

"How exactly does cryptocurrency work?" Rosie said.

"Well, it's a digital currency," Kat said. "So, there's no cash, but you can buy and sell things with it without involving an intermediary, like a bank."

"So there are no records?" Rosie said.

"No, there are records. It's actually very clever and uses something called blockchain technology, which is basically just a giant ledger of transactions spread across thousands of computers worldwide."

"So, what has Harry been buying with cryptocurrency?"

"I'm not sure, his account is very secure with complex encryption algorithms, so without his access keys, we are in the dark," Nate said.

Rosie shook her head. "I'm afraid it's all a bit beyond me. Thanks for your help, though. When Harry turns up, he can answer some of these questions himself. There'll be an explanation for all of this, I'm sure. Harry's a good boy."

Kat and Nate exchanged a concerned glance.

"Well, I'll keep working on his computer and let you know if I find anything. We should have access to Harry's phone records in the morning, which may help," Nate said.

As Kat and Nate returned to their desks, Rosie sat down

again and put her headset back on.

"I don't think she realises how serious this is," Nate said. "Do you think she's even considered that Harry may have met the same fate as Marshall?"

"She probably can't even bring herself to go there," Kat said.

"Maybe." Nate shrugged. "If it was me, I'd be distraught."

"Unfortunately, we're no closer to helping find him," Kat said.

"I have to say, it looks like he had a lucrative little side hustle going," Nate said, dropping down into his chair and spinning around to face Kat.

Kat sighed. "I agree. Do you think he was getting money from somewhere to buy Z-cash and sell it at a discount?"

"He must be selling a lot of it if he's cleared £100,000 in the last year."

"Wouldn't the game manufacturers notice if one person was buying lots of gaming currency, though?" Kat asked. "Wouldn't that raise red flags?"

"Yeah, it would," Nate said. "But people sometimes have multiple accounts."

"Still, wouldn't the IP address that the game was being logged in from be reported somewhere? And wouldn't it flag if multiple accounts were logging in from a single IP address?"

Nate looked at her in surprise. "I'm impressed, Kat. Yes, everything is recorded somewhere; why do you think people are so worried about their digital footprint? But there are ways to disguise your IP address, especially if you have access to the Tor browser."

"Which we know Harry does."

"I don't think selling Z-cash could have generated that sort of income. Do you think Harry has been up to no good?" Nate said.

"I think perhaps he's been trading cryptocurrency," Kat said. "The value has gone up a lot over the last few months, so it's possible that he's timed it well and made a lot of money."

"That's true," Nate said.

"But the more important question is, where the hell is he?"

Chapter 14

Adam checked his watch as he exited St. Paul's underground station. Five minutes to get to the appointment at his lawyer's office on Holborn. He dodged around a group of tourists stopping in the middle of the footpath studying maps on their phones to get their bearings. He joined the throngs of commuters hurrying to their legal and financial offices in the modern buildings lining either side of the road.

The City always made him feel a little uneasy, as though he didn't quite fit. He looked down at his work boots, jeans and leather jacket and then around him at the smartly-dressed corporate workers. Yeah, he definitely didn't fit in around here; he felt like an untidy blot on a very uniform landscape.

His phone buzzed with notification of an incoming message. He pulled it from his pocket and read the text on the screen.

'Call me ASAP, Nancy'

Adam pocketed the phone without responding. This meeting with his friend and lawyer Noah Winbridge had come sooner than Adam expected. He didn't know whether that was good news or bad, but nonetheless, he needed to know. He wasn't sleeping well, and he knew that it was down to the situation with Nancy. He needed to talk to Noah before talking to his wife.

The office of Cannon McGarvey was situated in a Victorian five-storey building set back from the road, with a small fenced green area in front. Adam waited in reception for only a moment before the receptionist directed him to the second floor.

"Thanks for coming in, mate," Noah said, meeting him at the top of the stairs and shaking his hand. Noah's immaculate business suit was tailored to his large frame. Despite his somewhat intimidating size, his air of confidence was tempered with a ready smile. He led Adam to his office along a corridor hung with various pieces of three-dimensional art comprised of ceramics and wood. It was a bright space, with a wall of glass overlooking a courtyard formed by three other sandstone office buildings. A grand fountain sprayed a plume of water skywards in the centre of a grassed area.

Adam stopped to view a framed photograph of a group of young men and women in combat fatigues on the wall just inside the office. "God, we were young," he said.

Noah closed the door and came to stand beside him. "I know, can you believe that we'd just completed basic training? We were so green."

"I'm guessing that you have an answer for me," Adam said.

"Have a seat." Noah waved his hand to one of the two chairs in front of his solid oak desk. Adam sat down, sensing a change in Noah's demeanour.

Noah took a seat behind his desk and steepled his fingers for a moment before leaning back in his leather office chair.

"When I suggested this, I had no idea," he said. "I just wanted to make sure that you had all of the facts."

Adam swallowed, keeping his emotions in check.

Noah let the silence run for a moment as he looked over at his friend. "The paternity test results are back, and I'm sorry, Adam, the baby isn't yours."

Adam swore as Noah's words hit him like a physical blow. He jumped up and strode over to the window as a wave of fury passed through him. He stood with his back to Noah and stared unseeing through the glass, controlling each breath.

In, out, in, out.

Noah gave him a few minutes to compose himself before speaking again. "You don't need to do anything today."

"It was just one stupid night," Adam said, tugging his fingers through his hair. "I went back to collect some more of my things, and one thing led to another; I didn't even consider that she might be seeing someone else."

"I'm sorry, mate," Noah said.

Adam continued to stare through the window. "You know part of the reason we separated in the first place was my unwillingness to discuss my work with her. I didn't want to bring the awful things that I witnessed home. That house was a place of refuge for me, and I didn't want to sully it with violence and death and all the awful things that people can do to one another."

"That's understandable," Noah said.

"But Nancy just couldn't see it that way. She claimed since joining the police that I'd become distant, but it wasn't that, I just didn't want work and home to cross, especially after what it did to Mum."

"Your mother had a tough time being undercover," Noah said.

"I know that now, but she was difficult to live with when I was a kid. Still, policing is in the blood. Did I tell you Dad's about to retire after forty years?"

"How is the old boy?"

"Same as always."

Adam turned back to face Noah. He exhaled long and loud. "How could she do this to me? Pretend the baby was mine? I don't deserve that."

Noah shook his head. "You don't, but she may not have known."

"She was clearly seeing another man, so she must have known that it was a possibility," Adam said, giving a bitter snort.

"Perhaps, but she's not a nasty person."

"I know," Adam said, looking weary all of a sudden. "Draw up the divorce papers. I won't contest anything; she can have the house. I just want this over now, as quickly as you can."

Chapter 15

Kat joined the throngs of people milling about at the entrance to London Bridge Station and looked around for Connor but couldn't see him. She slipped through the crowds and waited at one side of the stone entrance near a homeless man selling *The Big Issue*, where she had a good view of the people coming and going. She reached into her bag for three one-pound coins to purchase a copy of the magazine and was rewarded with a toothless grin from the vendor. Her thoughts drifted to Del, and she made a mental note to follow up with Amir to see whether Del had made it to the shelter.

The weather had improved while Kat had been underground, and the sun was trying to break through the grey dome that seemed to enclose the city. Still, she shivered and buttoned up her soft camel-coloured overcoat and swapped the magazine for a hat from her bag and pulled it on. She was tired after spending the night tossing and turning. Seeing Adam again over the last few days had unsettled her more than she cared to admit, especially as she had tried not to think of him over the past few months.

"Kat." She shook her head to dislodge her thoughts and looked towards the voice. Connor was hurrying in her direction.

"Sorry I'm late; I hope you haven't been waiting long," he said, stopping in front of her and leaning over to kiss her cheek.

"No, I just got here. How's your jaw?" Kat said, taking in the faint bruising around his chin.

"It's fine," Connor said, waving his hand, dismissing her concerns. "You look cold. Let's grab a coffee to warm up."

"Great idea."

Kat followed him across the road when the traffic lights allowed. They strolled beneath the railway arches, stopping at an opening in the brickwork.

Connor ushered her through an archway and into a dimly lit room with a curving ceiling. A barista called out from behind a tall wooden counter as they entered.

"Connor, where've you been hiding?" His Irish accent sounded similar to Connor's.

Connor grinned at the wiry, bearded man who took his hand off the steaming nozzle for a moment to shake Connor's hand.

"Good to see ya, Paul," he said. "This is Kat."

"Pleasure," Paul said. "No further explanation needed, lad," he added with a wink.

Kat acknowledged the compliment with a wry smile.

"Ignore him. Paul and I were in school together," Connor explained. "He seems to think that means he can insinuate whatever he likes."

Paul laughed. "What'll you be havin'?"

"Cappuccino, please," Kat said.

"Make that two."

"I'll bring them over."

"This is a cute place," Kat said, looking around the tiny space. "I never knew it was here." Four small tables were attached to the bricks on the back wall, with two high stools at each. A long, narrow wooden bench ran along the wall opposite the counter and had room for as many as ten people to stand sipping their drinks. Several empty wine barrels stood on their ends in the centre of the room, acting as tabletops. The cosy café was busy with the buzz of chatter bouncing off the arch of the roof. A couple vacated one of the small tables at the rear, so Kat and Connor slipped onto the empty stools to await their drinks.

"I come here often," Connor said. "It's one of those hidden gems that you don't want to tell too many people about, or there'd be queues out the door, and you'd never get in."

"I can see that," Kat said. "Your secret is safe with me."

Connor smiled at her. "It's good to see you again."

"How's your week been?" Kat asked.

"Grand," Connor said. "My piece on the ransomware targeting of local businesses by crime syndicates has been given the go-ahead for next weekend's issue."

"Connor, that's great news."

"Yeah, I've finally got one firm, McHale Engineering, willing to go on record. The hack has basically destroyed their business. They think the virus got in through an employee's laptop one weekend. When he logged on to the company's network on the Monday, it installed itself on the main server. It locked each user out, one by one, and their IT professionals couldn't get back into the systems. Then the CEO received the ransom demand."

"Did they pay it?"

"Not initially. But after three weeks and finding out that

their backups had all failed, they capitulated and paid the ransom. But it was too late; they'd lost a major government contract to a competitor, along with the confidence of their other customers that they could deliver on time, and the business went under."

"That's terrible."

"Yeah, fifty employees and no redundancy, nothing. The ransom was five hundred thousand pounds and cleared out any cash reserves."

"Did they ever catch who was behind it?"

Connor shook his head. "No, although my research into similar scams at two other firms, Cartwright Construct and Temple Manufacturing, has given me a great lead. The businesses initially thought the criminals were Eastern European, based on the IP address of the ransom emails, but that was just a cover. The emails were bounced around several virtual networks. Still, I think I've uncovered evidence that suggests the scam was initiated locally," he said. "I'm investigating that for the follow-up story."

"I read recently that several hospitals across Europe have been targeted with what they called cyber-extortion attacks. You'd think that would have the potential to cause loss of life," Kat said.

"Yeah, it's the same concept, different target. The hackers basically get in and scramble the data by encrypting it in a certain way and demand a ransom to decode the system," Connor said. "Targeting the health system is despicable."

"Agreed," Kat said. "Anyway, I can't wait to read your piece. How's the article on Tommy going?"

"Good, it's not on Tommy per se; it's more on the seldom-discussed aftereffects of successive government interventions in conflicts abroad. Tommy is one of the physical casualties of the Afghan conflict, but many others suffer less obvious debilitating effects because of what they've experienced and don't always get the support they need once they're back home. The impact manifests itself in domestic violence, depression, homelessness and other mental health issues. I'm hoping to draw people's attention to this issue and highlight some organisations trying to help but who need more funding. I spoke to your Valkyries contact, by the way, who was most helpful."

"Good, I'm glad," Kat said. "Groups are trying to help, but I'm not sure the general public really understands the long-term effects. It's not only the soldiers but their wider family and friend networks. Grief can have a terrible long-term impact on people's lives."

"Well, I'm hoping that article will be published in a few weeks, so we'll see how it's received. I am trying hard not to come across as preaching," Connor said with a laugh. "I get a bit passionate about my various causes."

"Nothing wrong with that. It's probably what makes you such a good journalist," Kat said.

"Time will tell. It depends on what else is going on in the world when it's circulated. The editor tries to time these things for the biggest impact."

"Here you go," Paul said, arriving at the table balancing a tray with two coffees and two bite-sized pieces of chocolate brownie studded with walnuts. "See you at The Ship for a Guinness later?

Connor nodded. "For sure, and I might even persuade this one to join me."

"You'd be most welcome," Paul said, flashing a genuine

smile.

"Thanks," Kat said. "I might just do that."

The coffee was divine, as was the brownie.

"That's definitely warmed me up," Kat said.

"Sorry if I went on a bit earlier. I get so engrossed in my work sometimes that I forget that others may not be as interested," Connor said.

"Not at all, it's fascinating," Kat said. "My two brothers were in the British Army, so I get it."

"Were?"

"One still is."

"And the other?"

"One of the casualties."

"Oh, I'm sorry, Kat," Connor said, his eyes full of sympathy. "I didn't realise, or I wouldn't have…."

"All good, let's go and have a wander," Kat said, standing.

"Okay." Connor reached out to squeeze her arm in a show of condolence. "Do you come to Borough Market often?" he said.

"I haven't been here for a while," Kat said as they waved farewell to Paul and joined the crowds ambling along the lane.

They entered the green section of the market, housed under the massive arching Victorian iron and glass roof, pausing to stop at diverse stalls and try the various product samples on display. There was a colourful array of fruits, vegetables, meat, cheeses, and drinks. Kat was particularly taken by the enormous variety of mushrooms at one stall and purchased a small selection to take home. As they wound their way among the stands, a greengrocer at one booth, a Cornishman in his mid-thirties, sang out in his melodious accent, encouraging buyers to try his wares.

"Do you like chorizo?" Connor asked, pausing outside another vendor.

Kat nodded, and Connor fed her a slice of the spicy sausage from a tray of samples.

"Yum," she said.

They browsed in the small homewares shops and studied the vast array of fresh fish on display.

"I don't know about you, but all this food is making me hungry," Connor said.

"Shall we get some lunch?" Kat said, tucking the piece of cheese she'd just bought into her bag and dropping a glove in the process.

Connor stooped to pick it up as Kat noticed two men watching them from a side street at the edge of the market. Something about their demeanour appeared out of place. They were of similar age to many of the twenty-somethings shopping at the market, but they were alert and watchful, rather than dawdling and unrushed like those around them. She was about to draw them to Connor's attention when he straightened and grasped Kat's elbow.

"This way," he said, pushing her towards a gap between the stalls. They cut through, and Connor pulled her left along another row of stalls, then immediately right and behind the counter of a cider stand.

"What's going on?" Kat asked, shaking her arm free and staring at him.

"I just saw someone that I'd rather not engage with today," Connor said, pulling her backwards with him into a gap between two towers of stacked cider barrels.

Kat went to protest but noticed the sheen of sweat across

his brow and registered the look of anguish on his face.

"We'll just wait here for a moment," he said.

"Connor, who are you avoiding?" Kat said. "Is it the same men as the other night?"

"Could be."

"We can deal with them, especially in a crowded market," Kat said.

"No," Connor said. "Let's just wait here for a minute. Hopefully, they'll leave and then we can go for lunch."

Kat tilted her head. "Are you sure? Maybe we should call the police?"

Connor shook his head and checked over his shoulder. "Come on."

They slipped out from between the barrels, to the surprise of the man and woman working the stall.

"Get a room," the woman joked.

Kat blushed as she followed Connor under the arched market entrance and across the cobbled lane towards the doors of a renowned seafood restaurant. They went by people sitting at outdoor tables beneath heat lamps before Connor held the door open for her. Pounding footsteps sounded behind them as she passed through. She looked over her shoulder in alarm.

Connor snagged her arm and began hurrying through the busy restaurant. They weaved through the tables of diners as the door they'd entered through flew open and crashed against the wall. Kat looked behind to see two athletic men dressed in jeans and dark coats rushing after them. But there was something odd about their faces that caused her to do a double take. They both wore a clear plastic mask, distorting their features, so they appeared creepy and unrecognisable.

The men knocked into tables, upending wine glasses and sending cutlery to the ground with a loud clatter. Kat pulled over an empty chair blocking the floor behind them as they jogged among the tables. A woman screamed, and waiters started shouting at the men.

"Get out of the way," one of the men responded, vaulting over the chair.

Kat broke free from Connor's grasp and tracked her own route through the crowded room, meeting him at the doors leading out onto the laneway on the opposite side of the restaurant. They rushed through as a white SUV screeched to a halt in front of them. Before Kat could register what was happening, the men chasing them burst out of the restaurant. One pushed Kat roughly aside. She stumbled and fell, landing hard on her knees. Sharp pain lanced through her body, and she watched in horror as the second man lifted Connor up and pushed him into the back seat of the car. The other man leapt into the front seat, and the vehicle accelerated away.

Chapter 16

A restaurant waiter rushed to Kat's side and helped her to her feet. She recited the registration plate under her breath to memorise it.

"Call the police, my friend has just been kidnapped," she said.

The car braked halfway to the corner, narrowly avoiding a cyclist coming the other way. The cyclist wobbled and flew over the handlebars as his front tyre clipped the kerb. The driver overcorrected and sideswiped a blue van idling in the street before it collided head on with a two-door hatchback turning into the lane. The clash of metal resonated along the narrow road, and smoke rose from the bonnet of the oncoming car. The kidnappers' vehicle kept moving, pushing the smaller car out of the way as they reached the end of the road.

There was a squeal of tyres as the car sped around the corner, and the right rear passenger door flew open. Kat started running along the lane towards the car as Connor leapt from the back seat. A hand reached out and grabbed his ankle, arresting his progress. His shoulder and then his head hit the road. The car's momentum forced his would-be kidnapper to release his foot, and Connor's legs landed hard.

The car stopped and began reversing.

"No," Kat yelled. "They're going to run him over."

Several bystanders rushed to Connor's aid and pulled him up onto the footpath out of harm's way while a couple of others approached the car, shouting. The back door was pulled shut from inside, and the vehicle took off, with one man managing to thump his hand on the roof before it drove away at speed.

Kat reached Connor. She crouched down beside him and took his hand. He was pale, with blood dripping from a gash in his forehead. His left arm was at an odd angle, and he gave a soft moan.

"Connor, it's okay," she said. "Help is coming."

She sat with her feet in the gutter and rested his head on her lap. She unwound her scarf and pressed it against the wound on his head.

Connor drifted in and out of consciousness. "I didn't think they'd really do it," he murmured.

"Who, Connor?"

His eyelids fluttered closed.

A series of sirens sounded, coming closer. Kat watched as two police cars and an ambulance turned into the street, where a crowd of onlookers had gathered. Two uniformed police officers got out of their vehicle. They assessed the situation, moving the public back and setting up a perimeter around the damaged cars.

"Over here," a woman standing beside Kat called to the paramedics. One hurried over to Connor, while the other went to the aid of the cyclist and other motorists. More police cars, some unmarked, arrived along with a second ambulance. Three plainclothes police officers moved in their direction. A woman in a black trouser suit crouched in front of Kat and Connor, while the other two turned their backs and scanned the surrounding area.

"Can you tell me what happened?" she asked.

"Two men chased us through the market and forced Connor into a white SUV. He managed to escape when it collided with that other car. But he hit his head on the road."

"Sir, can you open your eyes?" the officer asked Connor. Connor's eyes flicked open, and a look of relief passed across his features. He looked up at Kat and gave a faint smile. "Sir, we need to let the paramedics take a look at you," she said.

Connor blinked.

A paramedic replaced the policewoman. "Hello, Connor, my name's Stevie. I'm going to check your head and arm, okay?"

Kat withdrew her hand from the scarf, and the paramedic lifted it. Blood spurted from the wound, and she reapplied the pressure. Connor sucked in a shallow breath.

"Just hang in there, Connor. We've got you," Stevie said in a soothing tone, swapping Kat's scarf for a gauze pad.

Connor's eyes drifted closed again.

A gurney was laid on the ground beside them, and two paramedics eased Connor from Kat's lap onto the stretcher, taking care to support his arm. They lifted the stretcher, allowing its legs to unfurl. Kat rose to her feet, stood aside and watched as an oxygen mask was placed over Connor's nose and mouth while he was wheeled to the waiting ambulance.

"Kat, what are you doing here?"

Kat turned to see Adam push past the uniformed officers, his warrant card in hand. His expression darkened as he took in the blood smeared across her cheek and coat and the blood-soaked scarf dangling from her fingers.

She followed his gaze. "The blood isn't mine," she said.

"Thank God," he said. "Are you sure you're okay? Is your hand alright? You didn't try your usual heroics, did you?" He reached for her prosthetic hand and examined it.

Kat shook her head and pulled her hand away. "It all happened so quickly. These men appeared out of nowhere and began chasing us. Connor was grabbed and shoved into a car, but he managed to jump out."

"Connor O'Malley?"

"Yeah."

Adam cleared his throat. "You were here with Connor?"

"Yeah, we were having a wander through the market before lunch," Kat said.

"Of course, markets and lunch, your weekend thing, right? Connor was lucky to get an invite."

Kat opened her mouth to say that Connor had invited her, but Adam had moved away to speak to the other police officers.

"When Ms Munro has given her statement, can you make sure she's driven home?"

Kat bit her lip. "Adam," she called. He turned back to her with a neutral expression. "I think Connor knew he was being targeted."

Adam raised an eyebrow. "What makes you think that?"

"Something he said."

"You'd better come with me," Adam said. "Who's the SIO?" he asked the nearest officer.

"Hang on," Kat said. "I need to check on Connor."

She looked over to where Connor's stretcher was being lined up with the open doors of the waiting ambulance. She ran to catch up with the gurney. Connor turned his head to one side and gave her a weak smile from beneath the mask.

"I'll come and see you later," she said.

"I'd like that," he replied, lifting the mask up from his mouth. "Rain check on lunch?"

Kat smiled. "Absolutely."

"Which hospital is he going to?" she asked a man in the dark green uniform of the ambulance service.

"Guy's."

"Thanks."

She watched as Stevie, holding a saline drip, leapt up into the ambulance. Connor's stretcher was pushed onto the flat back of the vehicle, its legs retracting as it slid forward. A second paramedic, clad in a bright yellow hi-vis vest, climbed aboard after him and pulled the doors closed. The ambulance's lights flashed, and the siren rang out once, clearing a path, and it eased away through the market and out into the traffic.

"This way, Kat," Adam said from behind her.

Kat followed Adam along the footpath to where several police cars were parked at the end of the lane. A senior officer was giving instructions to several people. He looked up as they approached.

"Jackson, what are you doing here?" he asked.

"My flat is nearby and came to see if I could help," he said. "I happen to know Kat Munro, who witnessed the attack. Her, er… companion is the man who was abducted."

"I'm Inspector Walker, Ms Munro." The thickset man looked down at Kat from over the top of his glasses. "You weren't injured too?"

"No," Kat replied. "It's not my blood." She looked down at her coat and shivered.

"Can you talk me through what you saw, and we'll get a formal statement from you later?"

"We were over there, walking out of the veggie market," Kat said, pointing, "when Connor started acting strangely. He said he spotted someone he didn't want to engage with today, so we hid out of sight for a few minutes before heading into the restaurant at the end of the lane. We'd just entered when these men burst in and started chasing us. We ran out the door onto this street, but they caught up with us. One pushed me over, and the other grabbed Connor and shoved him into a car which had just stopped in front of us."

"Are you okay to take me over to where this happened?" Walker asked.

"Yeah," Kat said. "And they were wearing these odd-looking plastic masks. They looked kind of creepy."

"Sounds like the type that screws with facial recognition software," Adam said.

"It does," Walker agreed.

Kat led Walker back along the street to the restaurant, and Adam followed. Some of the diners and kitchen staff were standing in a group outside. There was whispering as Kat approached. Other staff were visible through the window, righting tables and sweeping up broken glass and china.

"The car stopped here," she said.

"Did it pull up, or was it waiting?"

"It pulled up at speed." Kat turned towards Southwark Cathedral, towering over the far corner of the market. "It came from that direction."

"CCTV will give us more," Walker said.

"Kat thinks that Connor O'Malley may have known who his kidnappers were," Adam said.

Walker raised an eyebrow at her. "Is this true?"

"I'm not sure. It's just that Connor mumbled something like, 'I didn't think they'd really do it', while we were waiting for help to arrive," Kat said. "He's an investigative journalist, so he probably has a few enemies."

"We'll talk to him," Walker said.

"Will he have police protection at the hospital?" Adam asked.

"He will now," Walker said, turning away and talking to an aide who'd followed them. He spun back towards them. "Are you sure that you don't need medical attention?"

"I'm fine, thanks," Kat said.

"Jackson, can you see that Ms Munro gets home safely?"

Adam hesitated for a moment, "Sir."

"Ms Munro, we'll be in touch." Walker beckoned to his aide as he strode away.

Kat took a deep breath and looked down at the blood-stained scarf in her hand, and winced.

"Come on, let's find someone to drive us," Adam said.

"You're not driving me?"

"Sort of, but my car is parked streets away, and I think now the excitement is over that you're about to collapse, so I'll get someone to drop us there."

* * *

"You don't need to babysit me," Kat said twenty minutes later when she unlocked the door to her stylish Mayfair flat. "It wasn't me that they were after."

"I'm not," Adam said, following her through the door and securing it behind them.

"Coffee, then?" Kat dumped her bag on the kitchen counter, unbuttoned her coat, pulled it off, and dropped it on the kitchen floor. She shuddered and pushed it towards the washing machine with her foot.

"Why don't you get changed, and I'll make us some tea?" Adam suggested. He glanced down at her brown leather boots, which were stained with dark droplets across the toes.

"Good idea," she said and bolted along the passage to her bedroom. Closing the door, she toed off her boots and stripped off her clothes, dropping them into her laundry basket before grabbing leggings and a long jumper from a shelf in her wardrobe.

She sank down onto the edge of the bed and put her head in her hands, taking several deep breaths. She heard Adam banging about in the kitchen and forced herself up. She headed for the bathroom, where she washed her hands, taking care to clean all of the blood from her prosthesis. Kat dried her stump and slipped a clean sock over it before reattaching her hand. She raised her eyes and looked at herself in the mirror. She had a streak of blood across her cheek. A sob rose from deep inside, and she gripped the hand basin with her right hand as her vision blurred. She grabbed a washcloth and scrubbed her cheek clean.

There was a soft knock on the bathroom door. "Kat, tea's ready."

"Be there in a sec," Kat sniffed and pressed the heel of her right hand into each eye to stop the tears from falling, and with a final glance in the mirror, she returned to the living room. Adam was standing with his back to the French doors, studying the wall of stunning black and white photos taken by Kat's brother, Joseph, before his untimely death in Afghanistan. He looked up as she approached, and his expression softened when he registered the anguish on her face.

"Hey, it's okay," he said, reaching out and gathering her into his arms.

Kat took comfort in his embrace for a moment before pulling away. "I'm sorry."

"Don't be," he said. "You held up remarkably well, considering what happened today." He reached past her, tugging a tissue from a box on a side table. "Here, you've missed a spot." He dabbed the side of her neck with gentle strokes until the blood was gone. "There, that's better."

"Thank you," she said, peering up into his face. He looked a lot more rested than the last time she'd seen him. His hair was overdue a cut and curled around his collar. Sucking in a sharp breath, Adam stepped back at the same time Kat did.

He cleared his throat. "Have your tea."

She followed him to the sofa, where two steaming mugs were waiting on the coffee table. No sooner had Kat curled herself onto one end of the couch, than Zelda, Kat's smoky grey Persian cat, made her entrance through the cat door from the balcony. She leapt up onto her lap, turning circles, trying to get comfortable.

"Hey, Zelda," Adam said, sitting down on the opposite end of the sofa.

Zelda froze and looked over at him before giving a joyful meow and bounding off Kat's knee across to Adam's. She stood on his lap with her paws on his shoulder and rubbed her head under his chin.

"Traitor," muttered Kat.

Adam laughed and ran his hand down the cat's back, serving

only to increase the purring.

"Hey, there's something else that I should have told Walker," Kat said.

"Which is?"

"Remember the altercation that you somehow knew I got into one night last week?" Kat asked.

Adam nodded. "When I heard that a young woman with a prosthetic hand fended off would-be muggers, I figured there weren't too many people in London who fit that description." Kat gave a half-smile. "Why didn't you report it?" he asked. "It was a taxi driver who told one of the volunteer constables walking the West End beat, but you'd gone by the time he arrived at the scene."

"There didn't seem much point at the time; they ran away when some people came to our aid," Kat said.

"Connor's becoming a dangerous person to hang out with."

Kat noticed the slight clenching of Adam's jaw.

"Anyway, it wasn't a mugging; it was some thugs giving Connor a warning," she said.

Adam cocked his head to the side. "A warning about what?"

"I don't know, he wouldn't say, except that it goes with the territory of being an investigative journalist."

"And now someone has tried to kidnap him in a crowded market," Adam said, moving Zelda from his lap, standing and pulling out his phone. "Yes, you definitely should have told that to Walker."

Kat felt stung by the rebuke. "I was a little shaken and distracted, in case you hadn't noticed."

Adam relayed what Kat had told him to Walker's sergeant.

Kat leaned back on the sofa and closed her eyes. Adam ended the call, and the sofa cushions moved as he sat back down again. Before either of them could speak, Kat's phone, sitting on the coffee table, rang. She opened her eyes and leaned forward to glance at the caller ID. She groaned.

"I don't think I can deal with my mother right now," she said.

"This will have made the news, Kat," Adam said. "She may be worried."

"Can you talk to her? Tell her I'm resting, and I'll call her later." She gave him a pleading look. Adam sighed, scooped up the phone and walked over to the French doors.

"Hello, Mrs Munro, it's DS Adam Jackson."

"Yes, I'm with her now."

Kat watched as he gave a small smile.

"Yes, at her flat, she's resting, but I can get her to call you later."

"She's fine. A little shaken, but fine."

"No, I just brought her home."

"No, no, she doesn't need me to stay…"

Kat rolled her eyes.

"Of course, yes, you too. Bye."

When Adam finished speaking, he disconnected and tossed the phone to Kat.

"I'm not going to hear the end of that, am I?"

The corners of Adam's mouth twitched. "She was extraordinarily pleased to hear from me."

Kat groaned and shook her head.

Adam drained his mug and walked into the kitchen, placing the empty cup in the sink.

"I should probably get going," he said. "Do you need anything?"

Kat shook her head. "Thanks for the escort home."

"Thanks for the tea. I'll let myself out."

The door had only just closed behind him when her phone rang again. This time it was her friend and sister-in-law, Sara.

"Kat, are you okay? And what's this I hear about Adam being at yours?"

"Hello to you too," Kat said. "I see you've been talking to Mum."

Sara laughed. "Yeah, we saw you on the news, talking to the police. What happened at Borough Market today?"

"Someone tried to kidnap a friend of mine and injured a couple of people."

"Oh my God, Kat, you were with the guy – is he okay?"

"He's in the hospital. He hit his head when he fell from the car, and I think he might have broken his arm, but it could have been far worse."

"Was it the journo you had dinner with the other night?"

"Yeah."

"Are you sure you're okay? It's not that long ago you yourself had a gun to your head," Sara said.

"I'm not sure, if I'm honest," Kat said. "I feel a little unsettled now that I've stopped and sat still."

She gazed outside; the day was drawing in, and it was becoming gloomy inside. She reached out and switched on a side lamp, then jumped up, tucking the phone between her shoulder and ear and drew the curtains across the French doors, closing out the advancing night. A little voice in her mind reminded her that whoever was after Connor knew who she was. Or if they didn't, they soon would.

"Is Adam still there?"

"No, he's gone."

"How was that, seeing him again?" Sara asked.

"We've been working together over the last week, so it wasn't the first time that I've seen him since, y' know. But, yeah, it's weird. It's like there are things to say, yet there's nothing to say. It just is what it is."

"Aw, Kat, are you going to be okay on your own tonight? Georgie and I could be on the next train."

"Thanks, Sara, but I'll be fine. Zelda here is keeping me company. Although I'm a bit cross with her, she was all over Adam like a rash."

Sara laughed. "You know where I am if you need me or want to talk, okay?"

"Yeah, thanks. Give George a hug from me."

Kat put the phone down, sat back with her eyes closed, and tried to make sense of the day.

Chapter 17

Adam drove back to his flat, squeezing the Capri into an impossibly narrow space in the next street. After changing his clothes, he trudged along the riverside walk to Doggett's, the pub where he was due to meet Noah, Tommy, and two of their ex-army mates. They usually met every few weeks for a beer or a curry or a game of pool, and sometimes all three. The pub, named after the organiser of the original rowing race from London Bridge to Chelsea, offered some of the best views of the River Thames.

Tommy, Nev and Pete were already seated at a round table beside the window on the ground floor with half-empty pints of beer in front of them. The view across the river took in the famous Victorian façade of the former City of London School for Boys, now occupied by a US investment bank. Tommy's crutches were propped up against the wall behind his chair. He was deep in conversation with the man beside him whose dark shaved head shone in the decaying daylight. Opposite him, an overweight man with rosy cheeks broke into a lopsided grin as Adam entered the bar.

"Started early, I see," Adam said with a grin.

"Nah, you're just late," Tommy said as Adam headed to the bar.

Noah arrived a minute later, waving to the others before joining Adam and adding his order.

"How are you doing, mate?" he asked, leaning against the bar as they waited for their pints to settle.

"Fine."

"You know where I am if you need to talk some more," Noah said, resting a hand on Adam's shoulder.

"I wouldn't know where to begin," Adam said, nodding his thanks as the barman finished pouring their pints of Guinness, adding a shamrock motif into the foam.

They carried their drinks across to the table and joined the others.

"Cheers." Adam raised his glass and took a long gulp. "I needed that."

"Were you working today, Adam?" Nev asked. He puffed as he leaned forward to shake Noah's hand.

Adam shook his head. "Not really, although I got caught up in an incident at Borough Market. Anyway, I'd rather not talk about work. How are you doing, Tommy?"

"Today marks eight years since Jonno died," he said, rubbing at his eyes.

"Eight years," Adam echoed, shaking his head. "It doesn't seem that long, does it?"

"It does to me," Tommy said. "I miss him every day."

"To Jonno," Noah said, raising his glass.

The other men followed suit, and they were all silent for a few moments. Adam reflected on the incident that took the life of Tommy's brother and injured Adam, Jake and two others. The vehicle they were travelling in had been targeted by a handheld rocket launcher as they approached a village in the Helmand Province of Afghanistan. While in the hospital recovering from his injuries, Adam had decided to leave the army and join the police.

"Sure as hell glad not to still be on active duty in that place," Nev said.

"Yeah, I'm with you there," Noah said.

"What's the latest on Donny?" Pete asked, running a hand over his bald scalp.

Adam shook his head. "Nothing new, we're just waiting for the court date to come around."

"I still can't believe it," Pete said, shaking his head. "He was the most straight-up guy around."

"Yeah, well, apparently not," Noah said. "You don't mastermind an operation of that size if you're above board."

"I can't believe he got away with it for so long, and no one noticed anything," Nev said.

"Well, that's not entirely accurate," Tommy said. "Jake was onto him, wasn't he?"

Adam shrugged. "Not that he ever mentioned to me."

"And still nothing on Jake?" Nev said.

Adam shook his head.

"I wonder how long he was in military intelligence before we knew?" Tommy mused.

"Probably longer than we realise," Noah said.

"Adam, it can't be long now until Nancy's due," Nev said. "Are you ready to be a dad?"

Adam exchanged a glance with Noah.

"I'm going to say this once, then I don't want to discuss it, okay?" Adam said.

Interest registered in Tommy's eyes, while Nev and Pete gave slow nods.

"A paternity test has shown that the baby isn't mine, so once she's had it, we will be divorcing," Adam said.

"Mate," Pete said, shaking his head.

Nev was open-mouthed.

"Why, once she's had the baby?" Tommy said. "Why not now?"

"Because Nev's right, she's only a couple of weeks off, and she's under enough stress," Adam said, rubbing his forehead. "Listen, guys, I'm just trying to do the right thing here. It's not the baby's fault and a couple of weeks don't really matter to me."

"So, who's the father?" Tommy asked.

Adam put his hand up. "End of discussion."

"And time for the next round," Noah said.

"I'll get them," Adam said, jumping up. "Same again?"

There were nods all around.

"Where are you working now, Pete?" he heard Noah ask as he headed back over to the bar.

When Adam returned balancing a tray of drinks, the conversation had moved on.

"You won't catch me going up to the top of that thing," Nev said.

"Where's that?" Adam asked.

"The Shard or whatever it's called."

"The view is stunning from up there," Noah said. "There's a champagne bar on the seventy-second floor and let me tell you, sunset, champagne, a beautiful woman, it doesn't get much better than that."

The others laughed.

"You were always too smooth for your own good, Noah," Pete said. "No wonder you're still single."

"It's a choice," Noah said, reaching for a fresh pint from the tray.

"You keep telling yourself that."

"Give me the English countryside any day," Tommy said. "Green fields, a river, a starry sky and I'm a happy man."

"That sounds very patriotic. I'm sure there's a song in there somewhere," Nev said.

"I need a wee," Tommy said. "Pass my crutches, mate."

Pete leaned back and grabbed them from where they were leaning against the wall.

"There you go," he said as Tommy stood and gained his balance before moving off across the floor.

"I think I'll go too. He looks a bit unsteady," Nev said, rising and following Tommy.

"Good to tell them," Noah murmured to Adam. "Burden shared and all that."

"I know. What I don't know is how I'll ever trust another woman again."

Chapter 18

The hospital was a hive of activity. Kat noticed the discreet police presence as she crossed the vast entrance foyer towards the lifts at the rear. She wondered if they were there for Connor or whether police officers were stationed permanently at the hospital. They probably were, she figured.

Groups of people, some with a member seated in a wheelchair wearing a pale green hospital gown, congregated around tables at the hospital's ground floor café. The flower stall gift shop next to it was doing a steady trade. The atrium was bright and welcoming. An enormous glass art installation was suspended from the high ceiling, sending shards of coloured light across the floor.

Kat rode the industrial-sized lift to the fifth floor. A security guard asked for identification before directing her down the corridor to room 5B.

Connor was sitting propped up in bed with his laptop open on the over-bed table in front of him. His arm was in a sling, and an IV line snaked into the catheter port in the back of his hand. His hair was flattened on one side from sleeping, and he had a shadow of growth across his jaw, but his face lit up as Kat entered the room.

"Hello there," he said. "You're a sight for sore eyes."

Kat handed him one of the two cups of takeout coffee that she was carrying. "From my experience of hospitals, you'll be needing one of these."

"Oh, you truly are an angel," Connor said. "Come, sit."

Kat sat down on a chair beside the bed. The small room was painted pale green and had a single window looking into the car parking building on the opposite side of the street. "How are you feeling?"

"Honestly, I've been better," Connor said, touching his fingers to the bandage on his forehead. "Tell me, any word on the cyclist and the driver of the other car?"

"They're going to be fine, apparently."

"Good," Connor said.

"You were so lucky," Kat said.

"As were you, they could have grabbed you too," he said.

"Yeah, but it wasn't me they were after, was it?"

"Wrong place, wrong time, that's all. I'm going straight out to buy a lottery ticket when they let me go from here." He took a sip of coffee. "Ah, that's grand."

"But you said that you didn't think they would really do it after you fell from the car," Kat said, shaking her head.

"Did I?" Connor said. "I must have been delirious."

Kat gave him a look of disbelief. "Connor, you can't ignore this. If your life is in danger, then we need to get to the bottom of it."

"There's nothing that *we* need to get to the bottom of, Kat."

"But what about those guys who threatened you outside the restaurant last week? And now this?"

"It's just my line of work. I annoy people on occasion. There's nothing to worry about."

"Except when they grab you off the street. I think we both know that wasn't random. What were they planning to do? Beat you up? Kill you and dump your body?"

Connor leaned back against his pillows and smiled across at her. "Now you're being dramatic. I'm fine, really."

"What did the police say? I see you have some protection," she said, glancing at the door in the direction of the security guard.

"I'm not sure it's necessary," Connor said, looking confident.

"And you know that how?"

Connor waved his free hand. "I think a point has been made. As long as they believe that I will alter the angle of my investigation, it'll be fine."

"Is this about the ransomware or the armed services?"

"You do ask a lot of questions," he said, taking another sip of his coffee. "I don't know about you, but I'm starving. What they say about hospital food is true, as I'm sure you know."

Kat glared at him. "You're changing the subject."

"The subject is closed," Connor said. "Let's talk about something more pleasant."

"Connor..." she began.

Connor's shoulders slumped. "Kat, for God's sake, I don't want to involve you."

"I think it's too late for that."

"That's what I'm worried about," he said. "I would never forgive myself if you got caught in the crossfire."

"I can take care of myself," Kat said.

"Kat, they could have grabbed you yesterday."

"But they didn't. Now, you mentioned that you had uncovered a link to local organised crime with your investigation. Maybe you've rattled someone's cage?"

Connor gave a resigned sigh. "You're not going to drop this, are you?" Kat shook her head. "Do you remember me telling you about my grandfather and his seniors' Internet class being hacked and their credit card details being stolen?"

"Yeah."

"The same thing happened in several other retirement villages throughout the UK and Ireland. Varying amounts were stolen from each account before the cards were cancelled. I've been trying to trace the source of some of the hacks. Unfortunately, this has taken me down the rabbit hole of the Dark Web to several groups selling malicious software packages to the highest bidders."

"And you think it was one of these malware groups who tried to grab you yesterday?"

Connor shrugged. "Possibly."

"That makes no sense."

"Kat, yesterday's attack was amateurish at best. Organised crime is much more professional. If a crime syndicate had targeted me, I'd be dead rather than sitting here talking to you."

Kat absorbed that for a moment.

"What do the police say? Surely the retirement villages have called the police in," she said.

"Of course, but it's not clear that there's a link between them. The viruses unleashed are not all the same. The various police forces across England, Wales, Scotland, and Ireland don't appear to be working together on this. The individual retirement village thefts are small compared to the other cybercrimes they're dealing with. Still, together they're substantial, hundreds of thousands of pounds."

Kat leaned forward and looked up into his face. "Let me

help. I have skills that could be useful."

Connor looked hesitant. "I'm not sure that's a good idea."

"As you say, I'm already involved simply by being with you yesterday, so I might as well make myself useful," Kat said. "I think we should try to see if there are any similarities in what the credit cards were used for. One thing I'm good at is following a money trail."

Connor sighed. "I hope I don't regret this. My next step is to collate where and what the money was spent on and find the patterns, which I'm sure will be there somewhere. I've emailed the retirement villages that I spoke to originally to see if any of the residents would be willing to give me copies of their credit card statements. And I've already received some." He turned his screen around to show her an email containing several attachments.

Connor's phone began ringing with an incoming video call. He glanced down at the screen and grinned.

"Speaking of the old devil, do you mind if I take this call?"

"Go for it," Kat said, clicking on one of the attachments in the email.

"Grandpa."

"What have ya gone and done to yourself, lad?"

"Bit of a fall. I've dislocated my shoulder and bumped my head."

"Has it knocked any sense into ya?" His grandfather chuckled.

"That would be too much to ask," Connor said, laughing. "Hey, I'd like you to meet someone. Grandpa, this is my friend Kat." Connor turned the phone so that Kat could see the screen.

She put the laptop to one side and gave a small wave. "Hi,

Mr O'Malley, nice to meet you," she said.

"Hello there, Kat, and call me Paddy, everyone else does," he said.

"I was just telling Kat about your Internet class having their credit card details stolen," Connor said.

"Yes, dreadful business," Paddy said. "It's put a lot of the oldies off using the Internet now, which is a shame."

"Yeah, it really is," Kat said. "Do you mind telling me what happened?"

"Sure," Paddy said. "We have a weekly computer class which is taught by a lovely young woman called Sally. She's very patient with us. Some of them are a bit thick between you and me, and she has to explain things repeatedly, but we were getting there. The day it happened, we sent emails to each other to reinforce what she'd taught us the previous week. She was then going to teach us how to pay a bill using our Internet banking. Those who didn't want to use online banking were to play solitaire or Sudoku."

"Sounds like a good class," Kat said. "Very practical."

"Yes, it's grand. So we had just logged into our bank accounts when Muriel started laughing. She'd received a cartoon from one of her grandchildren. She asked if she could share it with everyone, and Sally explained how to forward it to more than one person. One by one, it arrived in our inboxes. Soon, everyone was chuckling until I went back to my Internet banking screen and saw the balance on my credit card was really high. When we checked, all these transactions had suddenly appeared that I hadn't initiated."

"That must have been a shock," Kat said.

"Yeah, it was, and then some of my friends started calling out to Sally because it was happening to them too."

"Within minutes, everyone's credit cards were maxed out," Connor said. "A virus was embedded in the meme sent to Muriel that wasn't from her grandson, by the way. Once she forwarded the email, the virus embedded itself on every machine and harvested the credit card details. They must have had some sort of automation set up to immediately spend up to the card limit across multiple fake retailers."

"That's just awful," Kat said.

"Anyway, young man," Paddy said. "I was just calling to check that you were okay, I will let you get back to your visitor, and I'll call you again tomorrow. Lovely seeing you, Kat."

"Bye." She waved before Connor ended the call.

"That's so despicable," Kat said. "Targeting the elderly like that."

"Now you can understand why I'm compelled to look into this."

Kat picked up the laptop again. "I can analyse these statements for you, see if there are any patterns."

"That would be amazing. My brain is still a little fuzzy from the concussion. Still, I feel that I'm this close," Connor said, holding his thumb and forefinger millimetres apart.

"And what makes you think that?"

Connor gestured to his arm. "Why else would they come after me?"

"So you really think it's the people doing this, not someone else that you've investigated?"

"Yeah, I do."

"I'll only help you if you also let the police know your suspicions," Kat said.

Connor grimaced. "Tell you what; I'll involve them if we

uncover anything concrete. Suppose it becomes a National Crime Agency investigation, then I can't break the story. We won't have to worry about the criminals coming after me because my editor will kill me. It's all a matter of timing and evidence."

Kat reached for the laptop and settled it on top of the sheets where they both could see the screen. She clicked open several of the attachments and reviewed them. "Could I send these to my work email? We've got systems that make short work of extracting data and putting it into a database to analyse."

"Yeah, sure," Connor said as a knock sounded on the door, and Inspector Walker and a junior officer entered.

"Ah, Mr O'Malley, good to see you awake," Walker said. "I'm hoping that you're up for some questions about yesterday's incident."

"I'll do my best, but it's all a bit hazy, I'm afraid," Connor said.

Kat forwarded the emails to her account before closing the laptop and placing it on the bedside table. "I'll leave you to it," she said. "I'll come back tomorrow, Connor."

"Okay, and thanks for the coffee."

"Ms Munro, I understand you gave your statement this morning?"

"I did," Kat said, standing and pulling her coat on.

"Thanks for that. I thought you'd like to know that the police have reviewed the CCTV footage from Borough Market yesterday and confirmed my suspicions," Walker said.

"What suspicions?" Connor asked.

"That this wasn't a random attack, but its execution was clumsy at best. Using the CCTV footage, we've been able to track the car that they bundled you into. It arrived at the same time you hopped out of a cab at the entrance to London Bridge Station," Walker said.

"Oh, that's where I was waiting for you," Kat said.

"It appears that they backed off when you disappeared into a hole-in-the-wall coffee shop," Walker said. "Instead, parking in the lane by the cathedral and waiting until you were spotted again."

"Has the car been found?"

"Yeah, burnt out in a field in Essex," Walker said. "It had been reported stolen yesterday morning. Any evidence was destroyed."

Chapter 19

Kat looked up as the managing partner of Forensic Accounting Associates, Charles Stephenson, crossed the floor from his office towards her desk. He was in his forties, a little overweight with short, thick hair and wire-rimmed glasses. He bounced on his toes as he walked, giving the impression of a younger, more athletic man.

"Hi, Charles," Kat said. "How was the conference?"

"Most interesting," Stephenson said, perching on the edge of Kat's desk. "The rate at which cybercrime is developing is staggering. I'm going to talk with some old colleagues from the National Crime Agency about some resource sharing. I think we, as a firm, need to upskill in a few areas to ensure we keep abreast of these issues."

"That would be great."

"I did learn several new things," Stephenson said. "Did you know that there's been an uptick in advance fee fraud? People are being convinced by criminals to pay an upfront fee for a non-existent product or service."

"They must be compelling salespeople to achieve that," Kat said. "What sorts of things are being sold?"

"Scams such as fees to release a fake inheritance or upfront loan fees for non-existent loans, and the most recent one they're calling 'work from home fraud'. For the chance to make easy money working from home, you pay an upfront fee for business leads and a website, which never eventuate."

"Unbelievable."

"Ransomware crimes are on the increase too. It seems that the most vulnerable part of many UK businesses is their supply chain, and that has been targeted lately, as a way into a firm's systems."

"A friend of mine told me that as individuals get smarter about avoiding phishing scams, cybercriminals are increasingly targeting businesses," Kat said.

"Yes, and something called double-extortion or data exfiltration is on the increase. Not only are networks encrypted, but threats to release certain data to the public are made, which intensifies the pressure to pay," Stephenson said.

"It's just extortion," Kat said.

"There's an unprecedented level of international co-operation on this since they are really borderless crimes, which can be enacted from anywhere in the world."

"Sounds like we definitely need to keep an eye on this," Kat said.

"Now, what are you doing, working on a Sunday?" he said.

"I've just popped in to look into something," she said.

"Which couldn't wait until tomorrow?" Stephenson raised an eyebrow. "And didn't I hear something about you being caught up in that incident at Borough Market yesterday?"

Kat gave him a guilty smile. "I was with Connor O'Malley, the investigative journalist who was injured yesterday."

"Ah, I've read some of Mr O'Malley's articles in the past," Stephenson said. "He's thorough and tenacious."

"Connor has been looking into a criminal enterprise that

has been stealing credit card details from the residents of retirement villages. I offered to help analyse the money trail."

"And has Mr O'Malley's media group engaged FAA?" Stephenson asked.

Kat shook her head. "No, but I'm doing this in my own time. I only need to use one of our systems to dump the data – is that okay?" She gave him a winning smile.

Stephenson shook his head. "Unless they engage us, I don't want you working on this. It has the potential to cross the line with our police work, and we don't do pro bono work, clear?"

"But…"

"No buts, Kat," Stephenson said. "The police contract is too valuable to us." Kat nodded, disappointed. "Now, I've had a message from Deborah Sharp's solicitors advising that we need to cancel our meeting tomorrow morning. It appears that the Honourable Jeremy Sharp is unavailable again."

"Surely he can't keep putting this off?" Kat said.

"Has your team found anything of interest?" Stephenson said.

"We can't account for all of his income, and one of his companies owns a flat in Pimlico that hasn't previously been disclosed," Kat said. "Also, we're still waiting on a final set of bank statements for an account that he 'forgot' to reveal in the initial discovery meeting." Kat drew air quotes to highlight the point. "Of course, that could account for the missing funds."

"Let me know once you've got that," Stephenson said.

"Okay."

"I understand you've done some more work for DS Jackson over the last few days?" Stephenson said.

"Yeah, I assume that's okay under our agreement with the Met," Kat said.

"Of course, but I'm a little confused as to what it has to do with Rosie's son?"

"We all are," Kat said. "Harry Compton has been missing for several days. A classmate, Marshall Tyler, a boarder from Sawyer's Hill Grammar, Harry's school, was murdered a few days ago. DS Jackson wants us to analyse both Harry and Marshall's bank accounts. It's possible the teenagers may have been selling gaming currency and receiving the proceeds in cryptocurrency."

"Were they trading cryptocurrency?"

"Also likely," Kat said. "We're still waiting on access to Marshall's accounts."

"Wait, Marshall Tyler, not the son of the software developer?"

Kat's eyes widened. "I hadn't made the connection."

Stephenson blew out a breath. "Everything by the book, okay? This one will hit the media." Kat shuffled in her seat and didn't meet his eyes. "What should I know?"

"Nate and I went out to Rosie's last Tuesday night and looked through Harry's bedroom and computer. He'd only just gone missing at that stage," Kat said, spying Nate crossing the floor towards her, whistling as though he hadn't a care in the world. He slowed, registering the look on Kat's face.

"G'day," he said, swinging his backpack off his shoulder and setting it down on the ground beside his desk.

Stephenson gave him a nod of greeting and turned back to Kat. "With or without DS Jackson?"

"Without," she said.

"From now on, everything needs to go through him,"

Stephenson said, standing. "The last thing we need is to be accused of tampering with evidence."

"Okay."

"And no favours for the journalist, I mean it." Stephenson wandered back across the floor to his office.

Kat tapped her fingers on the edge of the desk and turned to Nate. "You're working on a Sunday?"

"Nah, I forgot my phone charger, and I was passing," Nate said, watching Stephenson's retreating back. "What was that all about?"

"He doesn't want me to work on Connor's investigation," she said, as her computer chimed with a notification that the analysis was complete. She hesitated for a moment, considering whether or not to continue. Still, the process was finished, and it wasn't as though Stephenson was going to allow her to do any more, so she attached the resultant file to an email and sent it to her personal account before deleting the download from the system.

"Why's that?"

"Something to do with blurring the lines with our police work. It seems Stephenson is desperate not to lose the contract."

"How are you anyway, mate?" Nate asked, taking Stephenson's position leaning against Kat's desk and looking concerned. "It sounds like you had quite a day yesterday."

"Yeah, tell me about it," she said. "I've just been to see Connor, and he's going to be fine."

"Do they know who it was?" Nate said.

Kat shook her head. "It seems that there may be several possibilities. For a nice guy, Connor appears to have made more than his fair share of enemies."

* * *

It was 8:30 p.m. before Kat unlocked the front door of her second-floor flat. She'd gone straight from the office to the gym and taught her weekly Pilates class before working out herself.

Zelda greeted her with a sharp cry before stalking across the wooden floor into the kitchen. She stood beside her empty bowl, giving another indignant meow. Kat kicked off her shoes and hung her jacket in the entry hall before following the cat through the living room to the kitchen.

"Ooh, someone's hungry, or should that be hangry, you grumpy girl?" she said, reaching into the cupboard for a pouch of Zelda's favourite cat food and pouring it into the bowl. Zelda bumped her hand away with her furry head and started gobbling the food as though it could disappear any moment.

Kat changed into pyjama pants and a sweater before grabbing a premade salad out of the fridge and settling down at the desk in the small second bedroom that she used as a home office. She flicked through the post that had been sitting on the table inside the main door of her building. It was mostly junk, which she tossed into the bin beside her desk. One letter, the address handwritten, caught her attention, and she turned it over in her hands. No return address. She tore the flap open and withdrew a single sheet of paper with a single sentence typed in black ink.

'Has Adam told you his big secret yet?'

Kat screwed her nose up and jumped as Zelda leapt onto her lap, purring with satisfaction now her tummy was full.

"If Adam has a big secret, I'd be the last person he'd tell," she said, stroking the cat. "I wonder why someone would think

Adam's secrets had anything to do with me?"

She screwed up the paper and threw it in the direction of the rubbish bin, where it rebounded off the edge and landed on the floor. Zelda jumped after it and began batting it around the room. Kat watched the cat for a moment before scooping up the paper and smoothing it out.

"Sorry, Zeld, I probably need to show him this next time I see him." She slipped it into the side pocket of her bag.

Kat switched on her computer and downloaded the credit card statement analysis that she'd emailed home that afternoon before Stephenson had put an end to any further work.

Between forkfuls of dinner, she manipulated and sorted the data in various ways. Soon, a pattern of spending emerged at businesses that appeared to be located in Eastern Europe, Southeast Asia and Africa.

Opening a second browser window, Kat began the painstaking process of searching on the name of each business where the cards were used. If she found a reference to it, she drilled further. She then copied whatever information she could see into a new column in the spreadsheet.

After two hours she sat back, frustrated. Of the more than two hundred businesses, she'd been unable to find a reliable reference online for any of them. It was as though they didn't exist.

Kat grabbed her mobile and phoned Connor, but the call went straight to voicemail, and Connor's voice came on. "Leave a message at the annoying beep."

"Connor, call me when you get this. I've analysed the data from the four villages."

She searched up the number for the hospital.

"Ward 5B, please," she said when the operator answered.

"5B, putting you through."

Kat waited for a minute until a female voice came back on the line.

"Can I please be put through to Connor O'Malley's room?"

There was a pause. "I'm sorry, Mr O'Malley's discharged himself."

"Oh, okay, thanks."

Kat ended the call and retried Connor's mobile, but it went straight to his voicemail again. She disconnected without leaving a message and stifled a yawn. Kat saved her analysis and closed down her laptop.

She carried her dirty dishes back to the kitchen, adding them to the dishwasher. She drew the curtains across the French doors leading to the small balcony and switched off the lights before wandering along the passage to her bedroom with Zelda padding after her. She bundled her hair into a topknot, securing it with a hair clasp. She looked at her reflection in the mirror and allowed herself a moment of pride. A year ago, something as simple as putting her hair up seemed like an impossibility, and now she was able to do it without thinking.

Kat released the suction holding her hand in place and laid it on her bedside table. She unrolled the sock covering her stump and threw it in the direction of her laundry basket, where it bounced on the edge and fell in. She massaged the special lotion, designed for her by the team at New Century Orthotics, over her wrist, feeling for any points of soreness, before slipping a clean, soft sock over her stump.

A wave of exhaustion rolled over her. It had been a stressful couple of days, and right now, she just needed to sleep. She pulled back the covers and slipped into bed, just as her mobile rang.

"Kat, it's Del Boy. I hope I'm not calling too late."

"No, all good," Kat said, sitting up. "How are you?"

"I wanted to thank you for sending me in the direction of that shelter. They're good people."

"I'm so glad you went there," Kat said.

"They got me a job, Kat. I'm on trial, but I've just finished my first shift stacking shelves at a supermarket. It's not much, but it's something."

"Hey, that's great, Del. You have to start somewhere, right?"

"Exactly, the only way is up from here," he said. "Anyway, just want to say thanks."

"You're very welcome. Keep in touch. Goodnight."

Despite everything whirring around in her brain, the credit card fraud, Connor's attack and Del Boy's news, Kat fell asleep quickly and didn't hear her phone buzz again. It wasn't until the following morning that she listened to Connor's message.

"Kat, I've cracked it. I think I know who's behind all of this. You're not going to believe it. Call me in the morning. Actually, let's meet after work at The Ship & Anchor – it's around the corner from my flat. And bring your analysis, no matter how far you've got. It's all linked!"

Chapter 20

The sun was setting, casting its last long shadows while Adam walked back home. The flat, near London Bridge, belonged to a mate working in the United States who had sublet it to Adam on a somewhat temporary basis while he sorted out his living arrangements. Adam had lived there almost a year, and while the tiny one-bed flat didn't feel like home, it had become a refuge of sorts.

The walk from the office of CID at Bethnal Green station in East London took him along the Thames. Usually, it took around forty-five minutes, although it depended on the route he chose. It gave him valuable thinking time. Today's journey took him alongside the Tower of London and across Tower Bridge. He was striding along the riverfront walk when his phone rang.

"DS Jackson," he said.

"Detective Jackson, it's Jonathan Beauchamp, the headmaster at Sawyer's Hill Grammar."

"Good evening, Mr Beauchamp. What can I do for you?"

"Ah, it's a rather delicate matter, really. It's been brought to my attention that one of my housemasters may have some rather objectionable material on his computer."

"Oh?"

"We'd normally deal with this sort of thing in-house, you understand. But I'm told that the *Daily Mail* will be running the story tomorrow morning, so I need to be seen to do the right thing and involve the authorities," Beauchamp said.

"What sort of objectionable material?" Adam asked.

There was a pause. "Ah, pornography, but you see, it involves children."

"Okay, and you haven't tipped off the teacher involved?" Adam asked.

"No, but I really think I should speak with him first," Beauchamp began.

"Not yet," Adam said. "Can you give me his name?"

There was a momentary pause on the line. "Wilson, Andrew Wilson. You met him when you were here the other day."

"Let me contact the appropriate unit, and I will meet you at the school in an hour," Adam said. "Sit tight on this until then."

Beauchamp let out a heavy sigh. "I shall. See you in an hour. Come straight to my office."

* * *

Adam turned into the long driveway leading to Sawyer's Hill Grammar, following two unmarked cars. They parked beside a police car in the school's main carpark. The impressive red-brick structure glowed under the beam of floodlights. Soulful organ music drifted through the night air. The reflection of colourful light through stained glass windows streamed across the driveway at the far end of the building. Adam studied the shape of the gables, realising that both the light and music were coming from the school's famous chapel, built in the days when the school site was home to a monastery.

Adam greeted his fellow officers. "Martina, Daniel, sorry to bring you out so late," he said, shaking hands with a petite woman in her forties.

He turned to her companion, a rotund genial-looking man whose dark grey suit was pulling across his midriff.

"Adam, it's been a while," Daniel said, grasping one hand and slapping Adam's other arm in a warm gesture.

"Too long," Adam agreed, grinning at his old friend. "I hope they're looking after you over at the Child Protection Centre."

"Why did the headmaster call you?" Martina said, interrupting the reunion.

"I was here the other day on another matter, and I guess he had my card to hand," Adam said.

"Can I ask what that other matter was?"

"The suspicious death of a student off-site," Adam said. "In fact, I met the teacher accused of possessing the pornographic material. He's the housemaster of the deceased."

Martina frowned. "Interesting, and I suppose you'd like to tag along on the chance that there is any overlap with your case?"

Adam grinned. "You read my mind."

"Mmm…" Martina said, fluffing her short hair with one hand. "I'll allow it, but this is my investigation."

She beckoned to the two uniformed officers waiting beside their vehicle and turned towards the stone steps leading to the school's main entrance. Daniel raised his eyebrows at Adam, and they followed her up the wide staircase to the front entry. On the roof above the massive wooden doors, the Union Jack and a flag depicting the school's emblem fluttered at half-mast. The porch lights were on, and the headmaster stood in silhouette in the doorway.

"DI Martina Petrovski, DS Daniel Barker and I believe you know DS Adam Jackson," Martina said, stopping in front of him.

"Yes," Beauchamp said. The spider veins in his cheeks stood out beneath the harsh porch lights, and behind his glasses, he had dark circles beneath his eyes. "This way, please."

He ushered them along the wood-panelled corridor to his office.

"Wait here," Martina instructed the two uniforms when they reached the door.

Beauchamp led them into his office. A welcoming fire was crackling in the hearth, warming the room. He indicated that they could sit at the small circular meeting table in front of the window, where he had a laptop open.

"This is the email that I received tonight," he said, tapping the keyboard.

Martina sat down in front of the laptop and read the message aloud. "Mr Beauchamp, tomorrow morning the *Mail* will run a story about a suspected child pornography ring being run from a prestigious London boys' school – yours, unless I see evidence of Andrew Wilson's arrest tonight. The attachment will give you a taste of the material on Housemaster Wilson's computer. There's more, it's buried, but it's there if you look hard enough."

"It's not signed." She glanced up at Beauchamp. "Have you viewed the attachment?"

He nodded, looking ill. "It's sickening."

"And have you replied to the email?"

"No, DS Jackson said to sit tight until you got here."

Martina clicked on the attachment and a video opened on

the screen. In it, two young teenage boys sat naked on the edge of a bed. Each boy had a tourniquet around his upper arm. Their eyes were wide with terror. A man came into view with a syringe, grabbed the arm of the first boy and slid the needle into a vein in the crook of his elbow, while at the edge of the camera, a second man injected the other boy. The image was a little grainy, and the lighting in the room was poor. The video had been overlaid with a rock soundtrack giving it the tone of a music video. The two men moved out of the shot for a moment before returning. They wore face coverings, and their bare buttocks were in full view of the camera as they advanced on the two boys.

"I've seen enough. Daniel, forward the email and attachment to the unit, and we need an immediate trace of the IP address of the sender," Martina said.

"On it." Daniel turned the laptop towards him, closed down the video and began delving into the information contained in the email header. He pulled his own laptop from a bag, opened it, and started typing.

"Is Mr Wilson on site?" Martina said.

"I believe so," Beauchamp said.

"Let's get him over here and see what he has to say," Martina said. "Then we'll take a look at his computer."

"I assume you have a search warrant," Beauchamp said.

"Right here," Martina said, passing the papers to him.

Beauchamp ran his eye over them and looked up. "I will need to inform the school board."

"In due course. Let's talk to Mr Wilson first."

Beauchamp reached for his phone. "Yes, Wilson, would you mind coming across to my office now?"

Wilson's reply was unintelligible to those gathered in the

office, but the tone was one of surprise.

Adam stood with his back to the window while they waited.

After a couple of minutes of uncomfortable silence, Daniel spoke. "The person who sent the email has used a VPN to mask their location," he said. "In fact, they've used several. It's not worth our time going to the initial Internet service provider."

Martina let out a frustrated sigh. "That would have been too easy."

A knock on the door announced Wilson's arrival.

"Come," Beauchamp called, and the door opened.

Andrew Wilson hesitated in the doorway as his eyes roamed across those gathered in the room. He was dressed more casually than the last time Adam had seen him, in jeans and a sweater.

"Sir?" he addressed Beauchamp. "Is this about Tyler?"

"Take a seat," Beauchamp said. "This is DI Petrovski, DS Barker and DS Jackson you have already met."

Wilson looked wary as he joined them at the meeting table.

"Mr Beauchamp received an email tonight suggesting that you have child pornography on your computer," Martina said.

Wilson shot out of his chair, knocking it over. "What?" he said. "No way, that's ridiculous. Who emailed you? It must be one of the students playing a prank."

"It's a pretty nasty prank. The sender will out you in the press tomorrow."

The colour drained from Wilson's face, and he gripped the edge of the table. "It's not true. You can look on my computer."

"Lead the way," Martina said.

The uniformed officers joined them as Wilson hurried out of the main office, across the courtyard and down the driveway to the boarders' accommodation. Wilson's rooms were on the ground floor at the front of the building. They waited while he entered his code into the keypad beside the door. They entered a small cosy sitting room. An armchair sat on either side of the fireplace, which had burned to embers in the grate. *The Secret History* by Donna Tartt lay on a table beside one chair alongside a half-drunk mug of tea. Adam mused that the tale of murder in a New England college was an interesting choice for a housemaster.

"My computer is there," Wilson pointed to a heavy wooden desk in one corner containing a screen and keyboard. A desk lamp with a Tiffany-esque shade cast colourful light across the desk.

"Dan," Martina said, nodding towards the computer.

Daniel crossed the room, pulled the oversized leather office chair out from the desk, and seated himself. He tapped the keyboard, and the screen flashed to life with a password box.

"Password?" he asked, turning to Wilson who was standing looking uncertain in the centre of the room.

"Dionysis3435 with a capital D," he said.

"You'll have to spell that," Daniel said as Adam roamed further into the apartment.

A small kitchenette adjoined the sitting room and had a compact table beneath the only window with two chairs. The bench was clear apart from a toaster and kettle, and the dishwasher gave a quiet hum as it went about its work. Two doors opened off the kitchen. One room was a bathroom. Adam gave this a cursory inspection, opening and closing the medicine cabinet on the wall, which contained nothing of note. The second door led to Wilson's bedroom. The room was tidy with a neatly made double bed and a chest of drawers that held several photos in frames with groups of well-dressed people smiling for the camera. In one corner, a tall wooden wardrobe contained ironed shirts, pressed trousers, ties, and a set of academic robes.

"I have no idea how that got there," Wilson was protesting as Adam re-entered the sitting room. "You have to believe me. I'm being set up."

Adam glanced at the screen on Wilson's desk where Daniel was scrolling through some disturbing images of young children engaged in inappropriate acts with older men. Adam looked away. He didn't need those images in his head.

"What do we have here?" Daniel asked.

All eyes turned to the screen where a page was open, displaying code.

"What are you accessing on the Dark Web?"

Wilson hung his head.

"Andrew Wilson, I'm arresting you for possession of objectionable material," Martina began and read Wilson his rights.

Wilson dropped onto the closest armchair with his head in his hands. "No, this isn't right."

"We will need to take your computer as evidence, and we will conduct a search of your rooms," Martina said.

"You can't," Wilson said, looking up. His face was ghostly white.

"I think you'll find that we can," Martina said. "I presented Mr Beauchamp with a search warrant earlier."

"No, I don't mean that," Wilson said. He gave a flick of his hand. "Search away; I have nothing to hide. I'm being set up. I stupidly left the Tor browser open, and someone has hacked me."

"If that's the case, our techs will uncover that," Daniel said.

"Check the date and time stamps on those images. They must have all been uploaded in the last twenty-four hours. I run a virus check twice a week across the whole school network, and I did the last one the day before yesterday," Wilson said. "I would have discovered any unauthorised access then."

"But why the Dark Web, Wilson?" Beauchamp said, his voice ringing with displeasure.

"The finance club and I were dabbling with trading cryptocurrencies, some of the less common ones," Wilson said. "The Tor browser is the only way to access some of those platforms."

Adam looked over at him with interest.

"What?" Beauchamp exploded. "The board is not going to like this one bit."

"I think the board will be more concerned about the material on this computer," Martina reminded him.

"Marshall Tyler was in your finance club, wasn't he?" Adam said.

Wilson looked unsettled at the question. "Ah, yes, he was."

Martina beckoned with a flick of her fingers to the two uniformed officers standing by the door. They came forward as Wilson got to his feet.

"This way, sir." They led him back out into the corridor to the front entrance.

"Now, Mr Beauchamp, we're going to need access to the school network," Martina said.

"Why?"

"We need to see just how far these images have spread and who else had access to them."

"You'd better come back to my office, then," he said.

"Daniel, you wait here until the rest of the team arrives," Martina said. She turned to Adam. "Thank you for your help tonight."

Adam felt as if he was back at school himself, now being dismissed.

"Can you keep me in the loop?" he asked. "I have a strange feeling that this may overlap with my murder investigation."

"Of course."

"One thing, Martina," he said as she turned away.

"Don't you think it was a little strange that he put up no fight? I mean, why'd he give up his password so easily?"

Martina shrugged. "Who knows? People act strangely when under stress."

"Yeah, I suppose you are right."

Chapter 21

K at put her mobile down on the desk after the call rang once and cut off.

"That's strange," she muttered.

"What's strange?" Shamira asked, looking across at her.

"I can't get hold of Connor. I've been trying since last night," Kat said. "He discharged himself from the hospital and seems to have disappeared."

"Perhaps he's just holed up somewhere to recover and doesn't want to be disturbed," Shamira said. "Didn't you say the police were talking about protective custody?"

"Yeah, but he left me a message sometime during the night to call him first thing," Kat said.

"That is odd. Have you tried Connor's work?"

"That's a good idea," Kat said. She searched for the name and contact details of the media group that Connor worked for.

"Connor O'Malley, please," she said when the call was answered.

"One moment." There was a pause, and the phone rang again.

"Newsroom," a stressed male voice answered.

"Connor O'Malley, please," Kat repeated.

"Hang on."

Kat could hear voices in the background of the call. "Anyone seen Connor?"

"Isn't he still in the hospital?"

"Has anyone heard from him today?"

The man came back on the line. "Sorry," he said. "He's not here. Can someone else help?"

"No, but can I leave a message for him to call me?"

"Sure."

"It's Kat, Kat Munro."

"Okay, I'll let him know if I see him."

Kat put her phone down and sat back in her chair, her foot bouncing up and down as she thought.

"Something's not right," she said. "They haven't seen him at work either."

Shamira stopped typing and looked over at her. "What are you going to do?"

"He asked me to meet him at The Ship & Anchor down in the Docklands after work, so I guess I'll just have to wait until then," she said.

"Do you want me to come with you?" Shamira asked.

Kat shook her head. "No, it's probably nothing. I'm sure he's just left his phone somewhere and has his head down working."

But the excuse felt hollow, even as she said it.

"Mmm," Shamira said, her dark eyebrows drawing together. "Just be careful."

* * *

"Nate's going to join us shortly," Kat said, ushering Adam

into the corner meeting room at the Forensic Accounting Associates office with the view of Tower Bridge, during the afternoon. If she'd had her way, Nate would be giving the update on his own, or they could have simply emailed it to Adam, but he'd called and insisted that they meet in person.

"How's Connor?" Adam asked.

"Good, as far as I know, I haven't spoken to him today. He was fortunate," Kat said, sitting at one end of the frosted glass-topped table.

Adam took a seat along the far side with his back to the window and cocked his head. "As were you."

"It wasn't me they were after," Kat said, looking down at her hands.

"Not on Saturday, but they could be now that they know who you are."

"I don't think so."

Adam sat forward and drilled his gaze into hers. "What's Connor really involved in that's made him a target, Kat?"

"You'd need to ask him that. He's working on several stories that I'm aware of that have the potential to make a few people uncomfortable," Kat said.

"Such as?"

"He's been investigating the increase in the occurrence of ransomware crimes targeting medium-sized organisations in the UK. They lock a business out of all of their crucial systems, either operational or financial, and demand a ransom to unlock them."

"It's a growing problem," Adam said.

"Connor's been working with a couple of industrial firms who've been targeted."

"I hope that he's not encouraging them to pay the ransom."

"I don't think so, but you have to have sympathy for these companies. In some cases, the lockout has caused them to lose key contracts, and in others, it's brought the business down," Kat said.

"They should never pay," Adam said. "Haven't you heard the phrase, 'never negotiate with a terrorist'? That's all these guys are, cyber terrorists."

"Yes, I know," Kat said. "All I'm saying is that you must be tempted when you see your livelihood slipping away. Imagine logging into your computer and being presented with a screen informing you that your data has been encrypted. And then, you receive instructions on restoring the system by paying an amount in Bitcoin. You must be tempted to do anything to get your business up and running again."

Adam looked thoughtful. "Attempting to abduct someone at a busy market is a little extreme for an organisation who usually works online or in the shadows. He must be investigating more than that?"

"Like what?"

"I don't know, drug cartels or political terrorist groups. A targeted hit would be more their MO than some anonymous financial crime perpetrator."

"I really don't know. Both Connor and Inspector Walker seem to think they were amateurs, the whole snatch and grab thing was poorly executed."

"That may be, but it could have been you or some innocent bystander that they grabbed to use as leverage. I think you should keep your distance from Connor until this is resolved," Adam said.

"Excuse me?" Kat glared at him. "It sounded for a moment there like you were telling me who I can and can't spend time with?"

Adam tugged at his earlobe and closed his eyes for a moment. "No, Kat, that came out wrong. I'm concerned that you might get caught in the crossfire of whatever hornets' nest Connor O'Malley has stirred up. I don't want to see you get hurt."

"I can look after myself, you know that," Kat said through clenched teeth.

"Sorry I'm late," Nate said, bursting into the room. His gaze swung from Kat to Adam. "What did I miss?"

"We were discussing ransomware crimes. But Adam wants an update on where we've got to with Harry and Marshall's bank records," Kat said, dragging her gaze away from Adam and leaning back in her chair.

"Okay then," Nate said, clearing his throat. "First thing, it looks as though Marshall's mother co-signed the bank account opening forms for each of the three companies that the boys were operating. However, on closer inspection, it looks like a digital signature rather than an original."

"Forged, you mean," Adam said.

Nate nodded. "Harry appears to have multiple transactions into and out of cryptocurrency. And from what I see from the information that your team sent through yesterday, Marshall's set-up is similar. The issue is the source of funds, that is, unless they've made some savvy trades," Nate said. "The upshot is that I need to do some further digging."

"Okay, you're going to need to explain how you think these crypto transactions are working," Adam said. "Were the boys trading?"

"Yeah, they probably were, but it's also possible that the lads were involved in some scheme where they were selling gaming currency," Kat said.

Adam looked confused. "Gaming currency?"

"Harry's sister told us that she thought Harry was selling Z-cash at a discount via gaming chat rooms, forums and social media platforms. She thought he was being paid in cryptocurrency," Nate said.

"Z-cash?" Adam said.

"It's the currency of *Zombiegamez*, y' know, the wildly popular online game," Nate said.

"But wouldn't you have to sell an awful lot to make any profit?" Adam sat back and knitted his brows. "And wouldn't the game developers be wise to people doing that?"

"Yeah, that's where our theory comes a little unstuck. It wouldn't be so obvious if you have enough people doing it, but that means a bigger organisation, not just a couple of kids. Although, as Nate said, *Zombiegamez* is huge; they have around two point five million registered users worldwide, who regularly play," Kat said.

"But aren't these games free to download and play?"

"The basic version of the game is, but if you want to upgrade the way your avatar looks, its costume, abilities, weapons and potions, then you have to pay," Nate said. "You also pay to enter tournaments, play in more competitive leagues and unlock complex levels of the game. You can buy merchandise such as t-shirts, mouse mats, coffee mugs, phone cases – you name it, they've monetised it."

Adam shook his head. "I never realised. I thought the game developers made their money through advertising on the site."

"No, it's way more commercial than that," Nate said. "*Zombiegamez* actively markets its gift cards to parents on social media as the gift *du jour* for today's youth."

"I've never seen the attraction in gaming," Kat said. "I mean, I've got friends that are into it, but it's not for me. I always thought Gabe spent way too much time with a controller in his hand."

"I'm with you there," Adam said. "I overhear some of the young constables discussing their kills, rotations and loot. They might as well be speaking another language."

Nate shook his head at them. "Please don't tell me that you also think TikTok is the sound a clock makes."

"Ha, ha, very funny." Kat pulled a face at him.

"How about I play a *Zombiegamez* battle for you two geriatrics so that you have some idea what you're dealing with," Nate said.

Kat shrugged. "Sure."

Adam looked at his watch. "Alright, I have a few minutes before I need to get back for a meeting."

"Let me grab my laptop." Nate left the room and jogged over to his desk.

"Kat, about before, I didn't mean to suggest..." Adam began.

Kat waved her hand. "It's fine."

Adam ran a hand through his hair, his lips clamped together in a thin line.

Nate returned with his laptop and logged into his *Zombiegamez* account. "Sit either side of me," he said.

Kat and Adam moved their chairs.

On-screen, the humanoid figures tumbled from an aeroplane before one by one, parachutes opened above them, arresting their descent. One hundred bodies illuminated by the moon stood out against the inky night sky as they drifted downward towards an unknown landscape blanketed in darkness. As the Earth raced closer, the outlines of hills, trees and cliffs became apparent, then a village, houses, sheds, and farm animals.

"This is me," Nate said, pointing to a figure becoming more prominent in the centre of the screen. He swiped his mouse and the viewpoint changed to that of Nate's character. "Otherwise known as Surferdude222."

The ground rushed up, and Surferdude222 started moving his legs in a running position, ready for when his feet touched the earth. Static crackled in his earpiece, and his boots met resistance, then he was jogging for a moment before coming to a standstill.

"The graphics are amazing," Kat said. "He looks almost real."

Surferdude222 unbuckled his harness, releasing the parachute. With quick, efficient movements, he gathered it in and stowed it under a nearby bush. He straightened, tapping his night vision goggles to bring up a digital map and get his bearings. The village was southeast, over the hill in front of him, at the forest's edge.

"Beyond the forest, danger and possible death lies," Nate explained. "But if I'm to come out on top, I have no choice but to head in that direction."

Closing down the map, Surferdude222 checked that his knife was still tucked in its holster strapped to his leg, and started running on silent feet.

Frantic voices echoed through his earpiece, followed by gunshots and the sounds of fighting and death, as the zombies attacked the new arrivals. Surferdude222 altered his course towards a farmhouse.

"I need more weapons," Nate said.

Crouching behind a farm shed, he spied a box sitting in the tray of a digger in the farmyard. He crept forward and brought his knife down on the lid. With a flash of light, the wooden sides of the box fell away, revealing two Walter PPKs and a bottle of Z-kill powder. He holstered the weapons and pocketed the small bottle as the sounds of fighting came closer: the screams of the victims, the heavy rhythmic feet of the zombies and the spine-chilling sound of gnashing teeth.

Kat glanced at Adam and grimaced. Adam wore a bemused expression.

On the computer, Surferdude222 tapped his glasses again and checked his digital display.

"The enemy is cunning and vicious. Already the original one hundred parachutists are down to just forty-five combatants." Nate turned his head to look at Kat.

"Oh," Kat said.

Nate grinned. "No time to waste mourning my fallen comrades. It just means less competition and a greater reward for those who stay the course."

On-screen, he pulled out his assault rifle and began to run towards the battle.

Chapter 22

The Jubilee Line was crowded at six o'clock on a Monday night. Some were commuters rushing to get home. Others were office workers heading out to any number of pubs, bars and restaurants to celebrate the start of the week or whatever excuse had been fabricated that day. The days of being part of that scene seemed a distant memory to Kat. Before the accident, she and Felicity would often meet up to go out mid-week. She hadn't really done it since. It didn't seem right when Felicity could no longer join her. On the handful of occasions she had gone out, the sense of being carefree eluded her, as she felt as if people were looking at her hand and making judgements. Deep down, she knew that she needed to get over that, but it was easier said than done.

Kat caught the long escalator up from the platform to street level at Canary Wharf. She hurried through the concourse with its high arched roof to the exit and turned right, cutting through the busy shopping mall. She followed the boardwalk along the canal dotted with small boats until she reached the South Quay footbridge spanning the channel. Joining a stream of pedestrians, she crossed the waterway and made her way along the paved pedestrianised waterfront, turning right at the first corner. One block along on the opposite side, an attractive two-storey black and white brick building added a nostalgic touch of Olde England to the surrounding glass towers. Black lettering painted across the façade above the first-floor windows announced it as The Ship & Anchor.

When she entered the pub, Kat was surprised to find herself in a modern venue, with polished pale wood floors filled with round wooden tables. The buzz of voices filled the room, and she excused herself around groups of people as she made her way to the bar. But there was no sign of Connor. She drifted towards the back of the room and through an opening into the pub's restaurant, which held around twenty tables, set with white cloths, cutlery, and glassware. But Connor wasn't there either. Further on, the dining room opened onto a covered deck overlooking another waterway with yet more tables, all empty.

Kat retraced her steps, taking her time to check among the pub's patrons again before leaning against the bar and retrieving her phone from her bag. She shook her head, seeing that she had no messages. Where was he? She searched up his number and called again.

"What will you be having?" a young bearded barman asked as she put her phone down.

"Nothing yet. I'm supposed to be meeting a friend," she said. "Actually, you might know him since this is his local. Connor O'Malley?"

The barman grinned. "Yeah, I know Connor, but I haven't seen him for a few days and definitely not tonight."

"Oh," Kat said. "I'll try his flat."

Connor's flat was a modern low-rise red brick and glass structure two blocks from the pub. Kat recalled reading somewhere that the whole complex had won a sustainable architecture award.

She stood outside the main entrance and second-guessed herself. Perhaps Connor was just busy and didn't have time to see her, so he hadn't answered his phone, but then again, his colleagues thought it was unusual that he hadn't checked in; and it was he who suggested that they meet tonight, so he wouldn't have just changed his mind without telling her. The more she thought about it, the more she felt deep down that something wasn't right.

Connor's apartment was on the third floor. She located the intercom for his flat in a panel beside the glass entranceway and pressed the button several times. No answer, so she tried phoning again, but the call went unanswered.

She was debating what to do when the doors to the foyer swished open, and a young couple exited, dressed for an evening out, laughing. The man was wearing a smart dinner suit, and his partner wore a form-fitting neon blue dress and sky-high heels. Kat smiled at them and slipped through the doors before they closed again. She strode past a giant terracotta statue of Apollo in the centre of the lobby, to the lifts in the far corner. She walked inside and pressed the button for the third floor, but the doors remained ajar, and the elevator car didn't move. A light on the card reader at the bottom of the panel flashed. Kat cursed under her breath as she realised that, of course, for security reasons, you'd need a key card to access the appropriate floor.

She stepped back out of the lift and looked around the foyer with its soft lighting and scattered armchairs. She spied the entrance to the stairwell behind a shiny-leafed potted plant in the opposite corner. She rushed over and tried the door handle. Expecting this to be locked, she was surprised when the door sprang open. She hurried through and made her way up the wide carpeted stairs to the third floor. The fire door was propped open. She slipped through and prowled along a passageway painted pale blue, past framed watercolours of castle ruins set on picturesque lakes, to number 15, Connor's flat.

She knocked on the door before touching the doorbell button. She heard it chime inside, but no one came to the door. She pressed her ear against the wood to listen for any sound from inside and was surprised to hear the soft murmur of voices. It sounded like Connor had the television or radio on.

She hesitated, unsure what to do.

Down the hallway, the lift dinged, announcing its arrival. Kat looked up as a woman around her age strolled out carrying two heavy shopping bags. She moved in Kat's direction, stopping at the door to the flat next to Connor's.

"Hi there," Kat said, smiling at her. "I'm looking for Connor. You haven't seen him, have you?"

The woman tossed her shoulder-length blonde hair. "No, which is strange since he's always coming and going, and we often pass in the hall. He had quite a row with someone last night, though." She paused and looked warily at Kat. "It wasn't you, was it?"

Kat forced a laugh. "No, not me."

The woman unlocked her door and shrugged. "He usually tells me if he's going away, so I expect he'll be back later." She entered her apartment and closed the door.

Kat stood outside Connor's door and raised her hand to knock again but stopped, her unease growing by the second.

Someone had tried to abduct him, and now he appeared to be missing.

"Damn it," she muttered, making a decision and calling the first person she could think of who could help.

"Kat?" Adam answered on the first ring. He sounded surprised.

"Adam, I'm worried about Connor," she said.

There was a moment of silence before Adam replied. "He's a big boy. I'm sure he can look out for himself."

"No, listen, he was expecting me to contact him with details of some analysis that I was doing for him, but I haven't been able to reach him all day. He's still not answering his phone. He left me a message to meet him at a pub around the corner from his flat tonight, but he wasn't there."

"I'm listening."

"The thing is, he checked himself out of the hospital yesterday. He hasn't been to his office or spoken to anyone there since Friday." Kat swallowed the lump in her throat. "I'm outside his flat now, and I can hear the TV, but he's not answering the door. His neighbour just told me that he had an argument with someone last night. I'm worried that something has happened to him."

Adam sighed. "Where does he live?"

"Canary Wharf."

"Text me the address. I'll be there as soon as I can."

"Thanks, Adam."

Kat disconnected, messaged the address to Adam and caught the lift down to the foyer to wait in one of the comfy armchairs. She sat and watched the people wandering along the boardwalk lit by old-fashioned wrought iron street lights. The low thud of a bass guitar coupled with the rise and fall of voices from a bar close by flooded into the foyer each time the entry doors swished open. The longer she sat there, the more convinced she became that something had happened to Connor.

By the time Adam arrived half an hour later and knocked on the glass, Kat was pacing. She rushed to the doors and pressed the exit button and watched as they eased open for him.

"Thanks for coming," she said as he crossed the threshold. She looked up into his face, but his expression was guarded.

"Lead the way," he said.

They took the stairs to the third floor, but there was no answer at Connor's door once again.

"You can hear the TV or something, can't you?" Kat said.

Adam nodded. "Did you say that you spoke to his neighbour?"

"Yeah, the woman in number 14."

Adam strode along the corridor to her door and knocked. A few seconds later, the door opened on its security latch.

"Hello?"

Adam showed his warrant card.

"Hang on." The door closed for a moment, and the scrape of the security chain sliding off preceded the door opening fully.

"DS Adam Jackson, I'm looking for Connor O'Malley," Adam said.

"I'm Carrie Markov," she said, looking past Adam to Kat. "You were looking for him earlier."

"I was."

"Do you have the contact details for your building manager?" Adam asked.

"Connor's not in trouble, is he?" Carrie said.

"I'm not sure," Adam said. "He checked himself out of the hospital after the incident at Borough Market on Saturday."

Carrie's eyes widened. "That was Connor? That's why I haven't seen him since the weekend."

Adam nodded.

"Do you need to get into his flat?" she said. "Is that why you want the building manager?"

"Yeah."

"I have a key. Connor gets me to keep an eye on things and water his plants whenever he's away. I'll get it. It'll be quicker than trying to track down the building manager at night," she said.

"That would save a lot of time, thanks," Adam said.

Carrie left the door open and disappeared into her kitchen, returning with a keycard attached to a shamrock keyring. "Here you go." She handed it to Adam.

Carrie pocketed her own key and pulled her door shut before following Adam and Kat along the passage to Connor's flat. Adam knocked.

"Connor, it's Adam Jackson. Can you let me in?"

There was no answer, just the jingle from a commercial playing on the television or radio inside.

Adam held the key to the card reader, and the lock whirred as the door opened. Adam handed the card back to Carrie. "You two wait here," he said.

He entered the apartment, again announcing himself. Seconds later, he called out.

"Kat, in here."

Kat and Carrie exchanged an anxious glance and rushed through the entrance hall into Connor's lounge. Low voices murmured from the television screen on the wall as Adam leaned over Connor, sprawled unconscious on the floor between a wooden coffee table and a black leather sofa.

"Oh my God, is he..?" Kat said, a hand flying to cover her lips as if to hold in the words her mouth was forming.

"He's alive," Adam said. "Carrie, call an ambulance."

"Already on it," she said with her phone to her ear.

Adam rolled Connor into the recovery position, grabbed the sofa's throw, and draped it over him.

"His pulse is weak," he said.

Kat surveyed the room, open-mouthed. Empty beer bottles were lined up on the coffee table beside an unlabelled bottle of pills. A rolled-up £10 note lay across a line of white powder.

"What the…?" she began.

She knelt down beside Connor and ran her hand over his forehead, pushing his hair back. His skin was cool and clammy, his breath shallow. The injury from Borough Market was bandaged with mottled bruising spreading out from under it. His arm, still in a sling, was draped across his side. Kat felt tears prickling in her eyes.

Adam stood and looked at her as he pulled his phone from his pocket. "Looks like quite a party. Did you know he did drugs?"

"He doesn't," Kat and Carrie said in unison, as Adam called the situation in.

Adam ended his call and wandered through the flat, pulling on thin gloves from his pocket.

"What kind of investigative journalist doesn't have a laptop or computer of any kind?" he said, returning to crouch down beside Kat. He reached for the television remote and switched it off.

"He has a laptop with him most of the time," Kat said, looking around. "That looks like his office." She pointed to an area cleverly separated from the lounge by a stylish room divider. Adam wandered across the room and disappeared behind the screen.

"Well, it appears to be missing," he called. "The desk is empty, and he doesn't appear to have a briefcase or bag. Can you see his phone anywhere?"

Kat couldn't see it on the coffee table or sofa. She leaned forward and looked underneath the couch and spied a black notebook lying on its side against the leg of the couch. She reached out and picked it up. It appeared to be Connor's appointment diary and fell open on the current week. The two pages were covered in doodles; symbols and numbers. Her attention was drawn to an address circled in red.

"What's that?" Adam asked.

"I found it under the sofa. It looks like Connor's appointment diary," she said.

Adam held his hand out for it. Kat committed the address to memory before passing it to him and watched as he turned the pages.

Connor moaned, but his eyes remained closed.

Kat placed her hand on his arm. "Hang in there. The ambulance is on its way."

Kat looked up from where she was seated on the floor beside Connor. "Connor's message said he'd worked it all out," she said. "I wonder what he discovered that drove someone to do this?"

Chapter 23

When Adam turned his vintage Ford Capri into the Comptons' street, he was met by the flashing lights of two police cars. An ambulance was pulling away from the house, its lights off and siren silent. He eased into an empty parking spot and called Kat.

"Hello?"

"Kat, I thought you'd like to know that Harry Compton has turned up alive and unharmed," he said.

"That's fantastic news. When?"

"Just over an hour ago, while we were at the hospital with Connor. He simply walked in the front door of his parents' house unannounced. I'm on my way there now," he said.

"Have you had any more news on Connor?" Kat asked. "I just called, but I couldn't get the nurse to tell me anything."

"He's stable; we'll know more in the morning."

"I should have stayed at the hospital," Kat said.

"No, you need to sleep. You'll be more useful to him tomorrow if you're rested," Adam said. "Kat, you saved his life tonight. If we hadn't found him when we did, he'd be dead."

There was a moment of silence then they both spoke at once.

"Kat."

"Adam."

"You first," Kat said.

"I was just going to say, I thought knowing Harry was safe would help you sleep better," Adam said. "What were you going to say?"

"Thank you, I'm glad Harry's safe. Rosie must be overjoyed," Kat said. "I was going to say that Connor must have been onto something, for someone to go to those lengths to stop him. I think that I will…."

"Leave it to us, Kat," Adam said. "Whoever did this wasn't messing about."

"I know, but it can't hurt to go over the analysis that I was doing for him, again."

"Just be careful," Adam said.

"Of course."

"Mm, when have I heard that before?"

"Goodnight, Adam."

Adam stared at his phone for a long moment after Kat had disconnected. Ignoring the tightening in his chest, he climbed from the car and hurried along the street to the Comptons' house. He passed through the open gateway and along the short concrete path to the front door.

A uniformed officer checked his credentials at the door before letting him inside.

Rosie and Terry Compton were standing in the doorway of the sitting room to the immediate left of the front door, talking to a woman with short dark hair and glasses. They all turned as Adam entered the house.

"DS Jackson?" Rosie said.

"Good evening Rosie, Terry," he said before turning to the woman and shaking her hand. "Lee, it's good to see you."

"Hi, Adam, thanks for coming out so late," DS Lee Cho said.

"No problem, I'm interested to hear what Harry has to say."

"Come on through," Terry said, ushering them into the front room. A bright floral sofa with two matching armchairs dominated the small room. The room was tidy but had a cluttered, overcrowded feel. A sideboard and bookshelf framed either side of an ornamental fireplace and a rectangular coffee table stood in front of the sofa.

DS Cho sat down in the armchair nearest the fireplace and took a notebook from her pocket. Adam remained standing in the doorway.

"Harry arrived home at 9 p.m., and the paramedics have checked him over. He mentioned to the first officer to arrive that he's been hiding since witnessing his friend Marshall's murder," DS Cho said.

"Mum," a voice bellowed from above them. "Where's my computer, and who's been in my room while I was away?"

A young man with a messy mop of ginger hair, wearing a t-shirt and jeans, came to a stop halfway down the stairs. A scowl marred his features.

"The police and a couple of the forensic accountants from work," Rosie said. "The police have been analysing your computer to see if there were any clues as to where you were."

"What?" Harry exploded.

"You were missing, Harry. We were doing everything we could to try to find you," Terry said.

Harry looked down and saw Adam watching the exchange. He took a deep breath. "We'll talk about this later," he hissed to his mother before continuing down the stairs and brushing past his father. He threw himself down on the sofa. Rosie hurried after him and sat down at his side.

Terry raised his eyebrows at Adam and followed, sitting down on the opposite side of his son. Adam settled himself in the remaining armchair.

"Glad to have you home safely, Harry. I'm DS Cho, and this is DS Jackson. We'd like to get an initial statement from you tonight, and we'll come back in the morning to get further details. I'm sure you're exhausted," DS Cho said. "DS Jackson, do you want to start?"

"I'm investigating Marshall's murder, Harry," Adam said. "Are you able to take us through the events of last Tuesday night?"

Harry let out a sigh and looked down at his hands.

"Take your time," DS Cho said.

"Marshy wanted to pick up some weed before coming to spend the night here. On our way home, he got a call from a guy that he usually gets his gear from."

Rosie gave a sharp intake of breath but remained silent. Harry turned his head to look at her. "Sorry, Mum," he said, contrite. "All the lads do it."

Adam opened a notes app on his phone and made an entry to follow up on Marshall Tyler's toxicology report.

"But you weren't at school on Tuesday?" Cho said. "Where were you?"

"We were there, just not in class," Harry said. "We were working on a project all day."

"And Monday night?"

"I stayed over with Marshy – we worked late into the evening."

"You didn't think to call your parents?" DS Cho asked.

Harry turned to his mother. "I did, didn't I?"

Rosie shook her head.

"Back to Tuesday night, what happened after the phone call from Marshall's dealer?" Adam asked.

Rosie blanched at the word dealer.

"The guy said to meet him behind the old Sawyer's Hill substation at six o'clock, so we went to Maccas and hung out there for a while," Harry said.

"Which McDonald's?" Adam asked.

"Ah, the one near school," Harry said.

"In Plaistow?" Adam said.

Harry nodded. Adam made a note on his phone to request CCTV footage from the restaurant and surrounding streets.

"So at six, we went over to the substation and waited. We didn't think he was coming when a grey car with tinted windows pulled up, and this tough-looking guy got out. Marshy called out hello to him like he knew the dude. The guy said for us to follow him around behind the building to do the deal so that we wouldn't be seen."

Harry leaned forward, picked up a glass from the coffee table, and took a sip before setting it down again.

"The guy pulled a tin foil packet from the inside pocket of his jacket and handed it to Marshy, and Marshy gave him £50. We started walking back towards the street when these other guys appeared from around the side of the building."

"How many were there?" DS Cho asked.

"Three. All big guys," Harry said. "They taunted me for being in my school uniform. Marshy had changed out of his before we left school. They said that since we were rich grammar boys, the dope price had gone up and was now £500. Marshy laughed and said that we didn't have that kind of money, and they began pushing us around. Marshy opened his wallet and gave them the rest of his money, another £50,

I think, and they demanded my wallet. I handed it over, but Marshy didn't want to give his actual wallet, cos it was new. So one of the guys grabbed his arms and held him while the other pulled it from his pocket. When they let him go, he tried to grab it back, and there was a bit of a struggle. That's when the guy punched him really hard and knocked him out. He went straight over backwards."

Harry put his hands over his mouth and gave a sob. "His blood spurted over my shoes, and he just lay there with his eyes open, not moving. He looked dead. I started screaming that they'd murdered him. I leaned over to see if he was breathing when I heard one of them say that they couldn't risk me telling the police. They were arguing about what to do with me, so I just turned and ran."

Harry looked up; his eyes were red, and several tears spilt over and ran down his face. He swiped at them.

"Oh, Harry," Rosie said, pulling him into her arms and rocking him.

"I think that's enough for tonight," Terry said, standing up.

"Agreed," DS Cho said, also rising. "You've had quite an ordeal. We'll leave officers outside tonight and continue this in the morning. We're going to need you to spend some time with our Photofit team to get a good profile of these men."

"I have one other question before we go," Adam said. "Where have you been for the last few days?"

"In the caretaker's cottage at school. He's been away on holiday," Harry said, sniffing. "I risked turning on the TV tonight, and I saw you and Dad on the news, Mum, and I knew that I had to come home."

Chapter 24

"He's lying, and there are so many holes in his story that you could drive a truck through it," Adam said the following morning when Julian and Tony joined him at the whiteboard in the incident room. Both men had dark rings beneath their eyes, but they appeared sharp and alert. "However, he knows enough that he must have been there when Marshall was killed. The forensics lab has his clothes for testing. He claims he got blood on his trainers when Marshall's head hit the ground beside where he was standing, and his description of the crime scene was fairly accurate."

"Not so sure about that, boss," Tony said, studying the crime scene photos. "There were no voids in the blood splatter pattern to indicate anyone was standing close beside or behind him."

"Interesting," Adam said.

"So, where's he been all this time?" Julian said.

"He claims he's been hiding in the caretaker's cottage at the school," Adam said.

"You don't sound like you believe him?" Julian said.

"I'm not sure what I believe." Adam said. "Have you reviewed the notes from the uniforms' door-to-door enquiries near the crime scene?"

"Yeah, what are you after?"

"Was there any mention of a group of young men hanging around the substation the night of Marshall's death or a grey car with tinted windows?"

"Nope," Julian said.

"Unfortunately, Harry's mother let him shower while they called to let us know he was home, so any evidence on his body has gone. She'd also laundered his clothes and shoes before the first officers at the house thought to stop her, so I'm not sure what forensics will find. Anyway, I'm headed back there now. Julian, can you track down CCTV footage surrounding the Plaistow branch of McDonald's and surrounding area from 4 p.m. to 8 p.m. on Tuesday night?" Adam stood and grabbed his jacket from the back of his chair.

"Tony, can you get over to the caretaker's cottage at the school and see what the forensics team has found? I'll be over once I've sat in on the rest of Harry's interview with DS Cho."

"Okay, sarge, I'll see you there."

Adam made his way down to the garage beneath the building where he'd parked his car earlier. He pulled out and put a call through to Kat's mobile on his hands-free set.

She answered straight away. Adam could hear the rhythmic tapping of her heels as she walked.

"Adam, how are you this morning? What did Harry have to say?"

"I'm on my way back there now. We didn't get through his story fully last night."

"Okay," Kat said, sounding disappointed. "So we're no further ahead on where the money has come from?"

"Not yet, but I plan to ask about that this morning."

"Did he say where he'd been?"

"Ongoing investigation and all that, Kat," Adam reminded her.

"Yeah, but haven't I been read in since I'm doing the forensic accounting work on him?"

"True, but I'm just not sure he's telling the truth, so I won't muddy your version of events with misinformation."

"Not telling the truth? What makes you think that?"

"Just a hunch."

"Poor Rosie," Kat said.

"Have you heard how Connor is this morning?" Adam asked.

"He's critical but stable, is all they're saying. I thought I might head over to the hospital at lunchtime."

"Well, let me know if there's any change. Inspector Walker will be keen to speak to him."

"When you get a moment, there's something I'd like to show you," Kat said. "You know I said that Connor had me analyse some data for him? I may have found something."

Adam was quiet for a moment. "And you think this is to do with the attacks and this attempt on his life?"

"Maybe."

Adam swore under his breath. "Are you at work?"

"I'm almost there," Kat said.

"Change of plan. Stay at work today. Don't go to the hospital at lunchtime. I'll come and see you when I can, probably this avo, and we'll go and visit Connor together after work. Don't go anywhere alone, okay?"

"Now you're scaring me."

"I don't mean to, but I want you to be cautious. It seems that Connor is mixed up in something dangerous, and I don't want you or anyone else to get dragged down with him. We don't know if whoever attacked him knows that you're involved."

Adam parked his car in the street outside the Comptons' and rested his head on the steering wheel for a moment. How could he protect Kat when he didn't know who he should be protecting her from? A little voice at the back of his mind told him that it wasn't his place to protect her; she certainly hadn't asked him to. He shoved that thought aside before stepping out of the car and striding through the drizzle to the Comptons' front door.

A different police officer was on door duty. After checking Adam's warrant card, he opened the door and let him into the house. DS Cho was in the sitting room taking off her raincoat. Rosie came down the hallway from the kitchen carrying a tray containing cups of tea and a plate of biscuits.

"Good morning," she said. She looked like a different woman; the lines of worry from the past few days had faded, and she appeared a lot more relaxed.

They all filed into the front room, and Rosie fussed, ensuring that everyone had cups of tea. Harry lounged on the sofa between his parents, looking bored.

"Before DS Cho asks you her questions, I would like to see if you want to change your story at all?" Adam asked.

"Change my story?" Harry sat up straighter and glared at Adam.

"You see, in our door-to-door enquiries on the street leading to the substation where Marshall's body was discovered, there has been no mention of a group of youths in the area that night or a grey car with tinted windows, as you described."

Harry snuck a glance at his mother and let out a sigh. "Okay, I lied. I wasn't even there."

"Harry," Rosie said, her hand fluttering to her throat.

Terry said nothing, but the look of disappointment on his face spoke volumes.

"What?" Harry glared at him.

"Just tell the officers the truth, Harry," Terry said. He sounded and looked worn out.

"Marshall went on his own," he said. "I went back to school to work on a project for our finance club. Marshall was supposed to go, buy the weed and come back to school to get me, but he never showed. I tried calling him a couple of times, but he didn't answer. I could see on SnapMaps that he was moving through the West End, so I figured he'd forgotten about me and was out partying. I ended up falling asleep in his room. I waited until classes were about to start the next morning, but he still didn't show up. That was when the photos on social media started doing the rounds."

"Photos?" Adam said.

"Of Marshy. One of the kids saw the crime scene cordon on the way to school. He managed to take a photo of Marshy lying there with his head all bashed in. I didn't believe it at first, and I called him several times, but his phone was dead."

"So why lie to us?"

"Because I'm scared that the guy he bought the stuff off might come after me next, especially if he thinks I've told the cops. That's why I hid at the caretaker's cottage," Harry said.

"And the name of Marshall's dealer?" DS Cho asked.

Harry looked up, his eyes glinting with an expression that Adam couldn't read. "Tyrone Wetherby, he's a mate of Wilson's. Ask him. Tyrone supplies all the kids."

Chapter 25

Kat didn't hear from Adam again during the day and was dismayed to realise that the flat feeling was not just to do with being worried about Connor. She was disappointed that Adam hadn't called. Despite her attempts to be professional, working with him again had raised the spectre of the past. But he was most definitely off-limits, and while her head had accepted that, her heart didn't seem to want to. She just wished that her subconscious would get the memo and let her move on. Perhaps when this case was over, she would talk to Stephenson about assigning someone else to work with the police. They had plenty of other clients that she could focus on.

Stephenson stopped by their desks late in the afternoon.

"Kat, I hear that reporter friend of yours was found unconscious last night," he said.

"I found him."

Stephenson peered over the top of his glasses. "I don't think I need to reiterate that you're not to spend FAA time, or resources, on whatever it is that he's involved in. What we do is highly specialised and needs to be paid for as such. Working for free devalues our work."

"I understand," Kat said.

"So long as you do. If Mr O'Malley was investigating things that should be left to the police, then we need to report that."

When 6 p.m. rolled around, she logged off her computer and left the office with Nate and Shamira.

"What are you up to tonight?" Nate asked.

"Long bath and a good book for me," Shamira said, a wistful look crossing her face. "I have been out so much lately; I need a night in."

"Boring," Nate dismissed her with a flick of his hand. "What about you, Kat? Can I persuade you to come for a drink, or are you off to kick some poor defenceless punch bag?"

Kat smiled. "No, I'm going to go swing by the hospital and see how Connor is, and then I'm going home to look over my notes on the credit card fraud." She lowered her voice and checked over her shoulder to make sure Stephenson wasn't nearby.

"I hope he gets better soon," Shamira said. "I'm keen to meet this man who seems to attract danger like a magnet. You are beginning to have a type, my friend."

Kat laughed. "I don't know what you mean. Besides, Connor and I are just friends at this stage."

"Right," Shamira said.

"What about you, Nate? You obviously haven't got a hot date," Kat said.

"Sadly no, but I'm going to a pub quiz with some mates, which is always a laugh. Sure you guys don't want to come?"

"Not tonight, thanks," Kat said.

"Me neither, but I'll come next week," Shamira said.

Connor was still unconscious when Kat arrived at the hospital twenty minutes later. A uniformed police officer was sitting on a chair by the door of his single room.

"Hello," Kat said, approaching. "Can I go in and sit with Connor for a while?"

The young officer shook his head. "No visitors, sorry."

"Can I leave these?" Kat asked, holding up the bunch of flowers that she had just purchased in the gift shop.

"You'll have to ask one of the nurses," he said, pointing to the nurses' station at the end of the long corridor which separated the two sides of the ward.

"Okay," Kat said, glancing in at Connor through the window. He lay unmoving and pale beneath the sheets, looking like the shell of his usual gregarious self. He was hooked up to myriad machines that beeped and hummed. Kat gulped as the seriousness of his situation sank in. She tore her stare away and wandered further along the corridor to find a nurse to leave the bouquet with.

*** * ***

Kat got off the bus two stops earlier than her street and dropped into her favourite deli to pick up some groceries for her evening meal. She walked out minutes later carrying a bag loaded with fresh mozzarella, tomatoes, prosciutto, olives, and a handmade pizza base. After strolling the remaining distance to her flat, she was greeted enthusiastically by Zelda. She kicked off her shoes, put on some music and prepared dinner, picking basil and rocket from the plants she had growing in containers on her balcony.

Kat took the pizza into her tiny office and started her laptop. She opened the data analysis files and stared at the screen.

While she ate her dinner, her mind drifted to Connor and she wondered how someone had gained entry to his flat to stage the scene they'd discovered. She pictured the appointment book she'd found under the sofa, covered in doodles and patterns. What had Connor found?

Kat moved her empty plate to one corner of the desk, pulled the laptop closer to her, and began scrolling through the spreadsheet she'd assembled the previous evening. It contained the names of the various businesses where the retirement villagers' credit cards had been illegally used.

Over the next hour, a pattern began to emerge. No two payments were to the same account. When she started digging deeper into the payment details, it became apparent why she'd been unable to find any information on the companies the night before. They appeared to be fronts, names only. The underlying purchase was on a variety of digital currency websites. Kat started filtering and sorting the data on the names of the exchanges and the coins purchased. There was little to no data available on the Internet for most of them. Those that did appear legitimate didn't seem to have very rigorous rules around account opening and closing. This meant that anyone with an email address and a credit card could buy cryptocurrency, immediately sell it in smaller parcels, and then delete their account, in effect making the transaction untraceable.

Kat sat back, shaking her head from side to side as the implication of what she'd uncovered hit her. Over one hundred thousand pounds had been stolen from just four retirement villages. According to Connor, more than fifty had been targets, and they were just the ones he knew about. The thefts could be in the millions.

Kat sat back in her chair as she had a sudden insight. The scribbles in Connor's appointment book weren't just doodles;

they were the symbols for several lesser-known cryptocurrencies. Symbols that matched many of the digital currencies that she'd just uncovered. This wasn't just someone's credit card being used to purchase goods and services for a thief's personal use. This was theft, money laundering on a much larger, more organised scale. It appeared that Connor was wrong when he surmised that it wasn't organised crime.

She considered the possibilities. What was at the address that Connor had highlighted in his appointment diary? And why had he noted it down, then ringed it with red pen?

She racked her brain, trying to make the connection. She searched through the papers on her desk for the note she'd made of the address. She found the scrap of paper and studied it. There had to be a reason that he'd highlighted the address in Hackney. She closed her eyes, recalling the page. The address hadn't been written against a specific day or time, it had been scrawled diagonally across the top corner.

She searched up its location on her phone, switching to the street view to take a look. It was a two-storey end-of-terrace property. A sign hung on a bracket by the front gate, but Kat couldn't read it. She tried manipulating the angle of the image but to no avail. She checked her watch. It was 9 p.m.

She tapped the fingernails of her right hand on the desk, coming to a decision before scooping up her phone and calling Adam. It rang once and went to voicemail.

Kat ended the call without leaving a message and opened her ride-sharing app, entering the address from Connor's notes. The hourglass on the screen turned for several seconds before a message popped up on screen announcing that a car could be at her house in three minutes. She clicked confirm and jumped up, shoved her phone into her pocket and grabbed her coat, wallet and keys before rushing out of her flat.

The drive to Hackney along the A401 took just twelve minutes through the sparse evening traffic. The streets got more industrial and less gentrified the further they drove. Kat began to question what she was doing and pulled out her phone, and called Adam again. This time she left a voice message.

"Adam, it's Kat. I'm following up on an address that Connor had written in his notebook. It seems to be related to the data that I've analysed for him. I'm in a car on my way there now, just to see what it is. Call me when you get this, um… if you can."

Kat saw the driver glance at her in the rear-view mirror. "We're almost there," he said.

"Great, can you wait? I just want to see if they're home," she asked.

"You'll need to request the return trip in the app."

"Of course, sorry," Kat said, placing the request on her phone.

The car pulled to a stop beside an overgrown grass bank leading down to a darkened stretch of canal. On the corner opposite was the building she'd viewed earlier on her phone. The streetlights highlighted the yellow brickwork on the building, discoloured and darkened by years of exposure to London smog. The entire block looked tired and neglected. The end building had a single bay window beside the front door and straggly weeds poked from the paving stones in what would once have been the tiny front garden behind a low brick fence. The asphalt in the parking area at the side of the building was cracked and uneven. As Kat climbed from the car, she noticed no lights were on in any rooms or in the adjoining terrace.

"I'll only be a minute," she said to the driver.

She crossed the road and stopped to read the swinging shingle. The sign read 'Snapp Software.' The small wrought iron gate gave a loud creak as she pushed it open. A red light on a stationary camera above the front door blinked on and off. Kat veered off the path and skirted the weeds to peer in the front window. Her toe caught on a raised paving stone, and she stumbled, putting her right hand out and catching herself on the window frame.

From the light of a nearby streetlamp, she could make out a shabby looking front room with two desks with computers. Against the far wall, there were several stacks of boxes, but it was too dark to make out the writing on the sides. She retraced her steps, glancing across at the car. The driver signalled for her to hurry up. Kat held up one finger to indicate that she'd only be a minute. She hurried around the side of the building and through the carpark towards a gate that she assumed led to the property's back entrance. Her hand was on the gate latch when she heard a car approaching at speed and screeching to a stop. Kat looked over her shoulder to see the beam from the headlights of a vehicle pulling up in front of the building. The lights switched off, and deep male voices spoke as the car doors opened and slammed shut.

Kat looked around for somewhere to hide. The side street she'd turned onto had a long block of three-storey council flats, this time with their frontages right on the edge of the footpath. The balconies of the upper floors were crowded with all manner of junk, and the ground floor flats looked uninviting with torn curtains in the windows and graffiti on some of the front doors. The cars parked along the street appeared old and neglected. She rushed to the nearest car and ducked down behind it as the men's voices grew louder.

"It looked like his girlfriend, but she isn't here now," one said, in a deep voice with the hint of a Yorkshire accent.

"Let's check inside in case she broke in," the second man said.

In the crisp night air, she could hear their footsteps getting closer. She eased around to the street side of the car, her heart thumping in her chest. The squeal of tyres made her jump, and she looked across the intersection to see her taxi pull away at speed. The men's voices stopped, and Kat guessed that they too were looking towards the sudden noise. She eased herself up a little and peered through the car windows. Sure enough, one of the men, tall and with the physique of a body builder, was jogging back to the corner and looking in the direction of the departing car. Kat ducked back down again as he turned to re-join his colleague waiting beside the side gate leading to the rear of the building.

Kat felt in the pocket of her coat for her phone and was alarmed to find it empty. She tried the other pocket as panic began to rise from deep inside her chest. She patted her jeans. Where was her phone?

Kat crouched lower, her eyes scanning the houses opposite. It wouldn't do for someone to look outside and see her. They could alert the men to her presence, which wouldn't be good.

The side gate gave a loud squeak as the men opened it and passed through into the backyard. Moments later, light flooded the back of the house, spilling onto the footpath through the open gate.

Kat rose and crept back between the parked cars and

squatted down out of sight. She could hear the men moving about in the yard.

The security light in the backyard went off, and the voices faded as the two men entered the building.

Kat slipped out from her hiding place and ran to the corner. She half expected to see her taxi idling at the curb further down the street, but the road was empty in both directions. She cursed under her breath as she realised that she was on her own. She shuddered with unease and turned, walking away from the corner property, down the long road with the shabby blocks of flats on each side. After a moment, she looked over her shoulder and broke into a run.

In the distance, at the far end of the next block, she could see a building with lights on. She moved into the centre of the road and raced towards it. As she approached, she saw with some relief that it was a corner shop. The walls were covered in torn advertisements, and the windows had metal bars on them. A broken, flickering neon sign above the door announced that the shop was open. Kat pushed the door and entered.

A woman with limp, greasy hair scowled at her from behind the counter.

"Can I please use your phone?" Kat asked, out of breath from running.

"Does this look like a telephone booth?" the lady sneered.

"Please, my taxi has driven off with my phone in it," Kat said.

The woman looked unmoved until Kat pulled out her wallet and held out a £10 note.

"I can pay."

"Make it twenty, and you can have one minute."

Kat set two notes down on the counter and rested her prosthetic hand on them. The woman recoiled and looked up at Kat, a mix of fear and disgust on her face. "There." She pointed to a back room separated from the rest of the shop by a beaded curtain. "Be quick." Kat pushed the money towards the woman and rushed to the storeroom. The phone was attached to the wall just inside the curtain. She dialled the police non-emergency number and requested the Bethnal Green Station, where she asked to be put through to Adam's mobile.

"Just a moment," the operator said. "Who can I say is calling?"

"Kat Munro."

Adam came on the line seconds later. "Kat."

"Adam, did you get my message? I'm stuck in Hackney. Any chance that you could come and get me? I've learned something that might be useful to your case. I'm, ah, hang on." Kat put the phone down, stuck her head through the beaded curtain, and spoke to the woman seated behind the counter. "What's the address here?"

"The corner of Marlborough Road and Brown Street."

"Thanks," Kat said, picking up the handset again.

"I heard. Wait there. I'll be as quick as I can."

"Thanks," Kat said to the woman after hanging up and walking back into the shop. "Is it okay if I wait here?"

"No," the woman said. "I'm closing." She shooed Kat outside and pulled the door closed behind her. Kat heard the locks and deadbolts engage. The outside lights dimmed and turned off, leaving Kat out in the open and exposed on the corner.

Chapter 26

Adam's car squealed to a halt outside the shop, and he leapt from the driver's seat, his eyes scanning the street. There were no lights from inside the shop and the street was deserted. On the opposite corner a small park with a swing set and climbing frame was shadowed in darkness.

"Kat," he called. His voice carried on the still night air, his breath causing little clouds of condensation to form.

"Here." Kat rushed out from behind a tree at the edge of the children's playground and hurried across the road. Some of her hair had come out of its top knot and hung around her face. As she passed beneath the light of a streetlamp, he could see that the knees of her jeans were filthy, and she was shivering.

"Kat, thank God," he said, hurrying towards her. "Are you hurt? Let me look at you."

Kat put her hands up to show him, and he saw that the skin on both her right hand and her prosthesis was dirty. "I'm fine. Let's just get out of here." She gave a nervous glance over her shoulder before sliding into the passenger side of his car.

"Is it okay if we turn the heater up? I'm frozen," she said.

Adam closed the door after her and got into the driver's

seat. "I could ask what you're doing alone in the middle of Hackney at night, but from your earlier voice message, I can guess. Connor has you doing his dirty work."

"No, he's still unconscious."

Adam felt his anger rising. "What about my warning this morning, didn't you understand?" he said, starting the engine. "Connor has become involved with dangerous people. You need to leave this to the police."

"I'm beginning to regret calling you. I'll just walk, shall I?" Kat said.

"Hang on, why did you call from that shop? Where's your phone?"

"I must have dropped it in the back of the taxi," Kat said. "He drove off and left me."

"The taxi driver drove off and left you?" Adam repeated.

"Rideshare." Adam swore under his breath. "Adam, let's drive back past the building."

"What building, Kat?"

"Connor had circled an address in the notebook that had fallen under his sofa. I wanted to see what it was. I figured it might be related to my analysis."

"How did you know what was in Connor's appointment book?"

"I saw it when I handed it to you," Kat said.

"And you just happened to remember it?" Adam sounded as though he didn't believe her.

"I did, actually," Kat said.

"And what have you been analysing?" Adam ground the words out through gritted teeth.

"The illegal spend on a number of credit cards belonging to the residents of four retirement villages who'd had their bank accounts hacked," Kat said. "That's what I wanted to show you."

"And you were doing this for Connor's story?"

"I was going to show you today, but you never came by the office."

Adam's jaw clenched.

"And where did Connor get the credit card statements?" Adam asked, glancing across at Kat.

"From the retirement villages. Apparently, the various police forces haven't found much or linked the crimes, so the residents were happy to let Connor take a look."

"So what in your analysis suggested a link to this address?"

"Nothing specific, but what I did find was that not a single one of the businesses where the stolen credit cards were used, is legitimate. Behind the names, it appears the payments were made to offshore crypto exchanges, the sort that doesn't require much in the way of ID verification to execute a transaction. There were a variety of digital currencies purchased that I'd never even heard of. When I recalled that Connor had circled an address in red pen next to a whole lot of cryptocurrency symbols, I figured that it had to be related."

"Did you ever stop and think that you might have been going to the same place that Connor went to before he was drugged?" Adam's voice rose as his ironclad control slipped, and for the first time since picking her up, he sounded furious.

"I was just going for a look. I wasn't actually going to go inside," Kat said, looking sideways at him.

"Why didn't you wait for me?" Adam asked. "You have to be the most impetuous woman I have ever met." He took a deep breath.

"I called you, but you were busy, and I didn't intentionally nearly get caught," Kat said, glaring at him.

"What? This just gets better. You nearly got caught? I thought you were just going for a look." Adam didn't bother to try to disguise his annoyance any longer.

Kat looked down at her dirty clothes. "I thought I'd just have a look in the windows. It was an office of some sort. I must have triggered an alarm because these two guys pulled up out front when I was looking around the side of the building. There was nowhere to hide, so I crouched between the parked cars on the side street. But then they came around the corner and went into the yard through the side gate. I had to lay low until they went inside. Still, I got away, so no harm done except the bloody driver left without me, and I must have dropped my mobile on his back seat." Her words tumbled out before he could interrupt further.

Adam shook his head. "Kat, you realise that you could have compromised a police investigation. Those men could be there now destroying evidence."

Kat paled. "So you already had the place under surveillance?"

"No, but that's not the point. Interfering like this could put the whole investigation at risk. And, Kat, this could have turned out so very differently."

"I know, but it didn't."

Adam pulled out into the road. "So, what's the address?"

Kat grinned at him. "Down two blocks, on the corner on the right."

"Don't grin at me like you're forgiven," he snapped.

As Adam drove, Kat snuck another glance at him. His jaw, covered in several day's growth, was clenched, and he had one hand gripping the wheel and the other on the gear shift. She remembered that she hadn't had the chance to show him the note she'd received and wondered what exactly the secret was that he was hiding from her. But now wasn't exactly the time to ask.

Adam slowed the car when they reached the corner. The lights were off in the building, and the men's vehicle was gone.

"They've gone," Kat said. "The sign says Snapp Software. Have you come across them in the investigation?"

"No."

They drove the rest of the way in silence. Kat suddenly felt a wave of exhaustion as the adrenaline abated, and Adam kept his mouth shut in case he yelled at her again. When they stopped in front of Kat's building fifteen minutes later, he reached for his mobile.

"Let's see if we can get your phone back," he said, tapping the screen to call Kat's number.

"This is Detective Sergeant Jackson. A passenger of yours left the phone you just answered in your car tonight." Adam listened to the reply. "I suggest you drive to where you picked her up immediately and return it. I'll be waiting." He hung up.

Kat gaped at him wide-eyed. "You can be quite scary, you know."

"You don't know the half of it," he said. "Especially when I'm annoyed, and right now I'm so angry with you."

"I'm sorry, I didn't mean for it to turn out this way. I was just going for a look."

"Kat, I suspect Connor just went for a look too, and look what happened to him," Adam said.

"We don't know that."

"Actually, we do. The techs have traced his movements by triangulating GPS from the cell towers that picked up his phone. He was near that property, Kat, the day he was drugged."

Kat let out her breath with a whoosh. "I didn't know."

Adam looked across at her. "Wait for me next time."

Chapter 27

dam took a sip of coffee and set his cup down on a table adjacent to the whiteboard at the front of the incident room. Julian adjusted his shirt cuffs and studied the board as if he was hoping it would reveal the truth to him.

"We should get access to the data from Harry Compton and Marshall Tyler's CryptoMania accounts sometime today," Adam said.

"You mean cryptocurrency, sarge?" Julian asked. "How does that tie to Marshall Tyler's murder? That's quite a change in direction from a drug deal gone wrong."

"Right now, we have more questions than answers."

"What's this I hear about the journalist Connor O'Malley being attacked again?" Tony said, joining them. "Either that man has bad luck or he's made some nasty enemies."

"What happened?" Julian asked.

"I'm not entirely sure. Apparently he's been investigating, amongst other things, a wave of credit card fraud that targeted retirement villages over the past six months," Adam said. "The forensic accountants at FAA have discovered that the stolen funds were used to purchase a variety of cryptocurrencies through unregulated offshore exchanges. Unfortunately, I found Mr O'Malley last night unconscious from a suspected drug overdose."

"Self-inflicted or assisted?" Tony asked.

"The latter, I strongly suspect," Adam said. "The office of Snapp Software in Hackney is under surveillance from this morning. It's definitely a site of interest that Connor O'Malley was looking into, and near one of his last known locations," Adam said.

"Who or what is Snapp Software?" Eloise asked.

"I'll need you to look into that," Adam said.

"Okay, I'm on it," Eloise said.

The door opened and DS Cho entered.

"Good morning," she called, crossing the room to join them.

"DS Cho is the senior investigating officer on the Harry Compton missing person case," Adam said, introducing her to his team.

"Hoping to tie that one up today," she said.

"Harry's coming in this morning with his solicitor to be interviewed further. I don't believe he's telling us everything. I've invited Kat Munro from FAA to join us. They were digging through his records while he was missing and have discovered a few irregularities."

DS Cho bobbed her head. "And it would help if Harry didn't keep changing his story."

"Wouldn't it just," Adam agreed. "Now, Julian, anything further on the whereabouts of Tyrone Wetherby, the man accused of supplying drugs to Marshall Tyler?"

"No, still working on that, sarge," Julian replied. "He's a ghost. Also, I found footage of Tyler and Compton in Plaistow at 5:20 p.m. last Tuesday. They appear to be arguing before going off in different directions."

Adam pointed to a photo on the incident screen. "Andrew Wilson, housemaster at the Sawyer's Hill Grammar. I need background on him, Tony. He was arrested on Tuesday after the discovery of objectionable material on his computer. But he was released last night after his legal team were able to prove that someone else uploaded the images remotely."

"How were they able to prove that?" Eloise asked.

"Something to do with comparing his computer to a recent backup where there were no images. And when the forensic techs dug into the metadata of the images, they all had the same upload time stamp," Adam said. "I haven't seen the full report, but that's the gist of it."

"Wow," Eloise said. "Someone must hate him to do that. That's a hard stain to remove from a teaching career, even if proved innocent."

* * *

Harry Compton was slouched in a chair in Interview Room #2 between his father and his solicitor, Ali Singh, a dark-haired man with a high forehead and square black-framed glasses. DS Cho, Adam and Kat joined them, sitting on the opposite side of the table.

Kat studied Harry after she'd exchanged handshakes with his father and solicitor. She was curious whether the picture of Harry she'd built up through the analysis of his finances would be similar to the actual person. Harry stared back across the table at her, an almost defiant expression on his face. His eyes dropped to her left hand, and he glanced up at her with a puzzled expression.

Kat fought the urge to pull her hand onto her lap out of

sight and continued to hold the folder she'd brought with her.

"Thanks for coming in today to help us further with our inquiries into Marshall's death," Adam began, adopting a relaxed tone.

"Not sure there was much choice," Harry muttered. Terry Compton glowered at his son.

"You're not under arrest and can leave at any time," Adam added. Harry gave a slight nod. "Now, we're still investigating the circumstances of Marshall's death and trying to locate Tyrone Wetherby," Adam continued. "We're hoping that you can provide us with some further information on the special project you were doing for Mr Wilson."

Kat watched an expression resembling relief cross Harry's face. She studied him. Perhaps they weren't asking the right questions. Harry didn't answer straight away and appeared to be formulating his reply.

"Mr Wilson runs a finance club at school," he said. "A lot of us are members."

"And what do you do in this finance club?"

"We study the markets and buy shares," Harry said. "We each put in £100 at the start of the term. Then we meet once a week after school to review what's happening in the market. We make a collective decision whether to adjust our asset allocation or not."

"And the special project?"

Harry sighed as though reluctant to reveal the nature of the project. "Cryptocurrency trading. Marshy and I wanted to give it a go, but Mr Wilson thought it was too speculative for the finance club."

Kat glanced at Adam, who nodded. She opened the folder and slid a piece of paper across the table to Harry. "So you opened your own company to trade through?"

Harry looked at the Companies House extract and then back at Kat. "Where did you get this?"

"Companies House," Kat said. "It's publicly available information."

Harry sucked on his bottom lip for a moment. "Yes, that's my company."

"You must have been very successful traders," Kat said, smiling at him.

"Yeah," Harry said, resting his forearms on the table and interlacing his fingers.

Kat opened the folder again and took out several sheets of paper containing bank statements. "This is a lot of money for someone your age to have earned," she said, pushing the documents over to Harry. His solicitor reached for the pages, his face registering his surprise.

Harry glared at her. "Where did you get these?"

"After your friend was murdered and you were missing, we obtained your records to see if that could help us find you and those involved in Marshall's death," Adam said.

Harry's mouth twisted, but he didn't say anything.

"Where did your initial investment come from?" Kat asked.

"I had a bit of money saved from making websites," he said.

"And in a short time, you accumulated over £100,000?" Kat said.

"What can I say? We are good," Harry said, tipping his chair back on two legs. "And the market is hot right now."

Terry's hand shot out and applied pressure on the armrest, returning the chair to its four legs, eliciting a sneer from his son.

"Out of interest, which cryptocurrency have you been

trading?" Kat asked.

"A few different ones; Bitcoin, Ethereum, Tether, Ripple and others."

"Would we be able to look at those accounts?" Adam asked.

Harry turned to his solicitor. "Not without due cause. I'm not seeing that my client has done anything wrong here," Singh said.

Harry gave Kat a smug smile.

"What about taxes, Harry? Are your tax returns up to date, for you and for your company, or should I say companies?"

Harry's smile faltered.

"So far, we've uncovered three companies where you are a director and a shareholder. From what we can ascertain, neither you nor any of these companies has ever filed a tax return," Kat said. "You do realise that profits on cryptocurrency trading are taxable?"

"Looks like I'll need to refer that one to my accountant," Harry said.

"Are you aware of the term money mule?" Adam asked.

Harry scratched his ear. "No."

"It's when someone knowingly lets another person pass funds through their bank account for the sole purpose of money laundering. Your companies wouldn't be involved in anything like that?"

Terry's mouth dropped open, and he peered at his son.

"No," Harry said.

"Good." Adam let the silence run for half a minute.

"How much of your earnings has come from *Zombiegamez*?" Adam asked.

Harry tilted his head as he considered the question. "I don't make any money. I'm not that good," he said.

"Sorry, I didn't mean from playing. I meant from the sale of Z-cash or *Zombiegamez* tokens and gift cards," Adam said.

Harry shook his head and narrowed his eyes. "I don't know what you mean."

* * *

"He's still hiding something," Kat said after DS Cho escorted Harry, Terry and Singh from the small interview room. "I'm beginning to think those boys were up to more than cryptocurrency trading." She pushed her chair back and stood, picking her bag up from the floor and resting it on the table.

"Perhaps," Adam said, adjusting the blinds to allow more light into the room. "It will be interesting to see what he does next. I agree; he's not telling us everything, and I think there's someone he's more scared of than the police."

"Either that or he's a good actor."

"Did you check his phone records when he was missing?"

"Yeah," Adam said. "Nothing; he either didn't have it with him, or he didn't use it."

"That's surprising. How many teenagers do you know whose phones aren't almost surgically attached to their wrists?" Kat asked. "Nate found nothing in Harry's emails about his trading activities and I would expect there to be deal confirmations from the more well-known exchanges. You don't think he has another device that you haven't found?"

"That's exactly what I'm thinking," Adam said. "And another email address that we haven't connected to him. We haven't found Marshall Tyler's laptop either. And there hasn't been any location data for his phone since the night he died. Hang on, I'll just update the team."

Adam left the room, and Kat watched through the window as he spoke to Tony, who jumped up and left the office. Adam returned as Kat slid the papers scattered across the table back into a folder and pushed it into her bag. She hesitated before speaking. "Ah, Adam, I need to show you something." Kat unzipped a pocket on the outside of her bag and pulled out an envelope, holding it out to him. "I received this in the post a couple of days ago."

Adam looked wary before taking it from her hand. He lifted the flap and pulled out a single crumpled sheet of paper, reading its contents.

'Has Adam told you his big secret yet?'

Adam closed his eyes for a moment. "Someone is playing with me, Kat, and it looks like you've been caught up in it too."

"What do you mean?"

Adam ran his free hand through his hair. "Can I keep this?"

"Sure." Kat narrowed her eyes. "What's going on?"

"Do you have time for a coffee before going back to your office?"

"Yes."

"Sarge," Julian said, leaning around the door frame. "There's something you need to see."

"I'll be there in a sec," Adam said. He turned to Kat. "I'll meet you in the café on the corner in fifteen minutes," he said.

"Okay." Kat lifted the strap of her bag over her head and across her body. "I'll find my own way out," she said.

Adam followed Julian back to his desk, where Eloise was waiting.

"Sarge, Snapp Software is a defunct software developer. I spoke to one of the two founders. After it collapsed last year, they sublet the property to another firm."

"And the other firm is?"

"That's the thing; it's a cash arrangement, paid up front, until the lease runs out next year. Snapp Software doesn't actually know who the tenant is," Eloise said.

"Great, another dead end." Adam ran a hand over the back of his neck and stretched his head from side to side. "What have you got, Julian?"

"I've just spoken to the CEO of Late Night Entertainment, who owns *Zombiegamez*. They're reluctant to share user data, citing commercial sensitivity."

"We'll see what a court order says about that," Adam said.

"We may not need to. He did tell me that they've noticed an unusual uptick in the purchasing of Z-gift cards in recent months. They've run their own internal investigation and concluded that there is nothing untoward going on, and it's just a reflection of the success of their marketing efforts."

"You mean, so long as they're getting paid in full for the gift cards, they don't care where the money is coming from, so no need to dig any further?"

"Something like that," Julian said. "They did send me the time and date access records for both Harry and Marshall's accounts over the past three months, and they don't appear to be heavy gamers."

"Interesting."

"Also, I was tidying up a few loose ends and ran the Comptons' address through our system to see if there were any hits. There are records of two visits to that address five years ago," Julian said.

"Were the Comptons living there then?"

Julian nodded. "It appears a caution was issued for some

kind of computer hacking."

"Now that's interesting," Adam said. "Which family member?"

"It was referred to juvenile division at the time but doesn't appear to have been followed up," Julian said.

"So young Harry has been at this for a while," Adam said.

"So it seems," Julian said. "And I would wager that the caution only served to improve his skills so that he wouldn't be detected again."

* * *

Kat was seated at a table near the entrance of the café when Adam pushed the door open a short while later. Two cups of coffee sat untouched on the table in front of her. The interior of the building was in stark contrast to the historic exterior. Modern décor and artwork abounded, and the entire room was light, airy, and welcoming.

"I ordered you a latte. I hope that's okay," she said, pushing one of the cups towards him.

"Thanks," he said, sitting down opposite her at the small dark table.

The café was quiet, just a handful of customers, but the staff bustled about preparing for the midday rush. Adam watched as a waiter wrote the day's lunch special in chalk on a blackboard behind the counter.

"So, according to my anonymous correspondent, you have a big secret to tell me?" Kat said.

Adam sighed and looked off into the distance. "It's complicated, Kat."

She frowned. "Is everything okay?"

"Everything's fine. Now, is this the only note you've received?"

Kat studied him for a moment. "Why do you do that, Adam?"

He raised an eyebrow. "Pretend that everything is okay when clearly it isn't?"

"People in glass houses, Kat."

It was Kat's turn to sigh. "We're not talking about me. We're talking about the fact that you look stressed and tired."

"Gee, thanks." Adam picked up his cup and took a sip.

"What I meant was you look like you haven't slept in days. I know you're busy with this case, but you should be getting all the sleep you can now because when the baby comes…"

"It's not my baby," Adam interrupted in a soft voice.

"What?" Kat opened and closed her mouth as the implications of his statement sank in.

"That's my big secret."

Neither spoke. They stared across the table at one another, the silence stretching between them full of unspoken and unanswered questions.

"I don't understand," Kat said.

"You and me both," he said.

"Adam, I'm so sorry." Kat reached out, touching his arm.

Adam shook his head and pulled his arm away, forcing her to withdraw her hand.

"I don't want your pity, but since someone has chosen to involve you, I needed to tell you," he said.

"Okaaay," Kat said, unsure where he was heading. "Have you talked to anyone about this?"

Adam hung his head. "It's a long and tortuous story that I'm not ready to share with anyone."

"Maybe, but you need to get it out; believe me, I know the

consequences of bottling stuff up. It doesn't have to be me, but you should discuss it with someone."

"My lawyer, who's also a mate, knows," he said. "Actually, it was him that suggested the paternity test."

"Adam, I'm really sorry. Why did she say it was yours?"

"She said that she really hoped that it was." A muscle in Adam's jaw twitched.

Kat shook her head. "Adam," she began.

"This was a mistake. I should go," he said, pushing his chair back from the table. "I'll call you if there's any update on Harry."

"Adam, stop," Kat said, reaching out and touching his arm. Adam hesitated.

"But why would someone involve me? I mean, hardly anyone knew about us."

"That's a good question, I don't know," he said.

"It could be someone who read or heard about the CIP case in the news," Kat said, her brow furrowing as she considered this. "Or…"

"Sorry, Kat, I can't do this," Adam said, rising from his chair. "Do what?"

"You and me," he said, waving his hand back and forwards between them. "This."

Kat sat back, his words hitting her hard. "But there is no 'you and me'," she said.

"Good, let's keep it that way."

Chapter 28

Kat was still smarting from her conversation with Adam when she got back to her office. She sat down at her workstation and called the hospital to get an update on Connor.

"How is he?" Shamira asked, overhearing the conversation. She pushed her chair back from her desk and turned to face Kat.

"No change."

"You really like him, don't you?"

"He's a nice guy, easy to be around," Kat said.

"But?"

"No buts, I just haven't known him for long."

"Haven't known him long, or he doesn't excite you like a certain detective?" Shamira said.

"Excite?" Kat gave her an incredulous look. "I don't think that's the right word. Maybe annoy, or irritate would be better."

"Well, you two certainly have chemistry."

"No, we don't."

"Whatever you say," Shamira grinned. "But I've seen you and Adam together, and there is definitely something there."

Kat shook her head. "He's just made it clear that there isn't, so please let it go."

Shamira's smile disappeared. "I'm sorry, Kat."

"Are you crazy, or what?" Nate said, hanging up his desk phone and turning to her.

"You sound just like Adam," Kat snapped, rolling her eyes. "What have I done now?"

"That was Adam. He just told me that he had to pick you up from Hackney in the middle of the night because you were chasing down one of Connor's leads. Please tell me he was exaggerating."

"He wasn't," she said. "I just went to an address for a look, and some guys turned up, and my taxi drove off with my phone, leaving me stranded."

"Oh my God, Kat," Shamira said. "That sounds dangerous."

"It wasn't meant to be, and if the driver hadn't left, it wouldn't have been. I won't be using that rideshare company again."

"What did Adam say?"

"You don't want to know, but suffice to say, he was fairly annoyed with me. I think the words impetuous and that I don't listen were mentioned," Kat said with a shudder.

"Sounds fair," Nate said.

Kat shrugged. "Anyway, I did sit in on an interesting interview with Harry Compton this morning."

"What did he have to say?" Nate said.

"Apparently, his story keeps changing. He implicated Wilson in knowingly allowing drugs to be sold to the students, but Wilson claims to have no knowledge of the person that Harry named.

"Wilson also runs a popular finance club with some of the kids at the school. Adam had a call from another student who says that Marshall and Harry were doing a special project with Wilson, one that seemed to be making them a lot more money than the share club's dabbling. Harry says they were cryptocurrency trading, but the other student claims he overheard Wilson threatening Marshall. Something about if the others find out."

"So whatever they were doing with Wilson could be the source of Harry's unexplained wealth," Shamira said.

"Precisely," Kat said. "And I'm not sure it's entirely legal, otherwise he wouldn't be hiding something."

"I find it hard to believe that someone like Marshall Tyler would need to resort to theft. He must be loaded," Shamira said.

"His parents are, for sure," Nate said. "Sometimes, people like him just break the law for the thrills."

Kat thought for a moment. "Shamira, can you cross-reference the analysis that I've done for Connor on the credit card theft with what we have from Harry and Marshall's bank records? See if there are any matches in amounts or timing. I don't think Stephenson will have a problem with that."

Shamira spun her chair around to face her computer and began typing. "Do you think they're related?"

"No, maybe, I'm not sure."

"I'm going to take another look at Harry's computer," Nate said.

"One of Adam's team has just sent through the credit card statements from a further ten retirement villages, so I'm going to run those through the data analytics software and see if the same patterns emerge as with the four that I've already analysed," Kat said.

* * *

Nate pushed his chair back. "I can't get anywhere," he said, running his hands through his hair in frustration. "He has crazy levels of encryption on here. It's going to take days to break it."

"I might have found something," Kat said. The excitement in her voice made Nate jump out of his chair.

"What?"

"Look at this. Across the ten new retirement villages, more than £50,000 has been spent purchasing *Zombiegamez* gift cards," Kat said.

"Not crypto?" Shamira said.

"We're going to need to get the sales transaction data from *Zombiegamez*," Nate said, "so we can see the email addresses for the transactions and how the gift cards are being used."

"Can you call Adam?" Kat said. "See if he can get us access to their records."

* * *

Kat hurried through the foyer of the hospital and caught the lift to Connor's floor. There were three others in the elevator with her, two chattering elderly women carrying bunches of flowers wrapped in plastic from the flower seller at the entrance to the tube station, and a short man wearing a shirt and tie with a hospital lanyard around his neck. They all got out on the floor before Kat. She took the opportunity of being alone to check her hair in the mirrored side panel. When the lift arrived, and the doors opened, she stepped out onto a quiet floor. The whirr and beep of medical equipment seemed oddly loud as she turned left and then right towards Connor's room halfway along the ward.

The chair where the police officer had sat the previous day was empty, and there were no staff rushing about the ward. Kat came alongside Connor's room and looked in the window. A male nurse in pale blue scrubs was attending to Connor. Kat kept walking to the end of the corridor to wait at the nurses' station to get an update on Connor's condition.

The heels of Kat's shoes echoed in the strangely silent ward. She looked over her shoulder, wondering where everyone was. From her considerable experience of hospitals, she knew them to usually be hives of activity. She glanced through the window of the next room, where a patient slept surrounded by machines and poles holding medicine bags. As she reached the nursing station, a machine in one of the rooms gave off a series of loud beeps, followed seconds later by the shriek of an alarm.

She took another step and gasped as she saw the police officer sprawled on the floor behind the desk and a nurse slumped in a chair. They both had their eyes closed. Kat reached out and patted the back of nurse's hand. It was warm and she murmured at Kat's touch. She leaned over the policeman. He too was unconscious, but his chest was rising and falling with a steady rhythm.

Kat heard steps behind her and stood as the male nurse hurried out of Connor's room and dashed towards the lifts. Kat caught his side profile as he left the room.

"You," she shouted, rushing towards the man. He hesitated and turned back towards her, his mouth twisting into a cruel smirk. The machines keeping Connor alive screamed with urgency as she came alongside his room. She made the mistake of taking her eyes off the man for the briefest second to look at Connor, and the world went black.

The voices sounded distant.

"She's coming round."

"Quick, bring the cart."

Kat forced her eyes open and tried to scoot backwards as a male nurse reached for her.

"It's okay, you're safe," he said.

Kat looked at him, more clearly this time and relaxed. He wasn't her attacker. His name tag introduced him as Pierre.

"Let's help you up, love," a woman said.

Kat allowed the nurse and the woman to help her stand.

"Connor?" she said.

"They're working on him now," the woman said.

"The man, he was dressed as a nurse," Kat said. "I have to stop him."

"Let's look at your head first," Pierre said. "You took quite a knock into the door frame."

Kat looked past him to the entrance to Connor's room. A smear of blood slashed across the door surround at head height. She reached her hand around to the back of her head, but the nurse grabbed her fingers. "Don't touch, I need to clean the cut."

"Where was everyone?"

"We were called to an emergency on the next ward, which turned out to be false."

"A way to get most of you out of here, so he could…" Kat couldn't finish the sentence.

She looked over to where several doctors and nurses were working on Connor's prone form. The machines attached to him had been silenced, but Kat noticed that the screen showed three neon green flat lines. She gasped as electronic paddles were applied to Connor's chest and, with a shout of 'clear', an attempt was made to restart his heart.

"Oh no," she whispered. Silent tears began tracking down her cheeks.

Pierre placed a gentle hand on her back and guided her away from the room down the ward to the nurses' station. The nurse and the police officer were sitting up, looking dazed, while doctors attended to them.

"Are they going to be okay?" Kat asked.

"Yeah, looks like they were hit with a strong sedative, not fatal," Pierre said. "Now, if you can sit here, I'll tidy up that cut on your head."

Kat winced as he sprayed the back of her head with a cool sterile cleanser.

"Is Connor going to be okay?" she asked in a whisper, barely able to voice the thoughts racing through her brain.

"He's got the best doctors working on him."

"We meet again, Ms Munro."

Kat looked up as Inspector Walker and several uniformed officers swarmed into the ward.

Chapter 29

"We didn't expect to see you today," Nate said when Kat strolled across the open plan floor of the FAA office. She dropped her bag on her desk and draped her jacket over the chair.

"One day stuck at home with my thoughts was enough, so I decided to come in," Kat said.

"Ooh, you're here," Shamira said, arriving at their workstations carrying two cups. "Here, take this; I'll make myself another one." She handed Kat a cup of coffee. "Are you okay? How's your head?"

"It's a bit tender, but I was just telling Nate that I'm better here than at home," Kat said.

"You're not concussed?"

"No, I was lucky. Hey, I wondered if you guys would mind going over what Connor was working on with me? He seemed to think he'd discovered a link before this all happened to him. And I may have worked out what part of that was."

"Of course," Shamira said. "Let me grab another coffee. Meeting room three?"

"Stephenson should be okay with this now that Connor's investigation has been linked with the police case," Kat said.

"Regardless, he's out at a meeting," Nate said.

Kat gathered her notes and followed Nate into the meeting room.

"Is Connor going to be okay after the attack?" he asked.

"I'm not sure," Kat said. "They've moved him to an 'undisclosed location', so I don't know. The doctors were all very concerned about how long he was technically dead."

"That's awful."

"I know," Kat said. "He was just doing his job and trying to expose injustice. I feel like I owe it to him and his grandfather to try to finish this."

"So long as no one realises that's what you're doing," Shamira said, joining them and closing the door behind her.

Kat shrugged and approached the smartboard on the wall at one end of the room and picked up a pen.

"Let's go over everything we know. Connor was working on several investigations at once. The impact of military interventions abroad, credit card theft and ransomware crimes. But, I think it's his interest in exposing cybercrime that seems to have attracted the wrong kind of attention."

She wrote 'Investigations' as a heading with bullet points beneath for 'malware', 'identity theft' and 'army'.

"Connor had spoken with several firms in the UK that had been hacked and locked out of their systems."

"And then issued a ransom note to unlock their data," Nate said.

"It's more widespread than most people know," she said. "Many firms just quietly pay the ransom."

"Can I play devil's advocate and question whether the government or armed forces might want to silence him if he was exposing a problem in the care of those with long-term physical and mental injuries?" Nate said.

"Fair point and I asked him something similar after the incident at Borough Market, but he indicated that it was the cyber angle. I also don't think he was exposing anything about the rehabilitation of veterans that people don't already know. There are plenty of organisations focussing on that, such as the Valkyries and Invictus," Kat said.

"Agreed," Nate said.

"What about the credit card thefts?" Shamira said.

Kat drew a line through the word 'army' on the board. "So the reason he was looking at the retirement village credit card thefts was that his grandfather had been a victim. Lovely old guy. We spoke on a video call the other day."

"And from what you've said, the theft used a form of malware," Nate said.

"That's a good point. I have been thinking of the two as separate," Kat said. "Connor felt that whoever was behind the first attacks on him were amateurs, but this latest attempt on his life seems more like a hit. If I hadn't arrived when I did, he would be dead."

"A hit is not something an amateur usually organises," Nate said.

"Exactly, except that the man posing as the nurse was one of the street thugs who attacked Connor and me outside the restaurant," Kat said. "And that warning didn't seem all that professional."

"Interesting," Shamira said, taking a sip of her coffee. "So, what have you found that you think might link all of this?"

"This is where it gets a little hard to track," Kat said. "We know that the stolen credit cards were either used to buy Z-cash or to purchase a variety of cryptocurrencies at obscure exchanges around the world."

"Kat, we got some info from *Zombiegamez* yesterday," Nate said. "The email addresses that purchased many of the gift cards weren't the same as the ones that redeemed them in around seventy percent of the purchases over the last six months."

"So they were being on-sold?" Kat said.

"Looks that way."

"Just when we thought we'd seen every kind of money laundering there was," Shamira said.

"That's really interesting because it's a link to what Harry's sister suggested he was doing," Kat said.

"What does Harry say?" Nate said.

"He denied selling Z-cash when Adam asked him at the interview the other day," Kat said, twirling the whiteboard marker in her hand. "And there's no evidence that he was doing anything like that."

"True."

"Connor is big into finding patterns, so last night, I turned my focus to the malware angle. I looked at the UK firms that have been the victim of a ransomware attack in the last few months to see if they had anything in common."

"How many are there?" Nate said.

"Thirty-five who reported it. I've found news articles on some of them. Connor mentioned the names of another three companies to me and I assume there are additional ones he found who didn't report an attack," Kat said.

"How much money are we talking about here?" Shamira asked.

"Connor told me that one of the firms that he'd had discussions with paid five hundred thousand pounds, so multiply that out."

Shamira gave a low whistle. "That's more than twenty million pounds. People have been killed for less."

"So what do the businesses have in common?" Nate asked.

"This is where it gets a little strange. Remember I showed you that article on Jeremy Sharp and his work helping UK businesses?"

"Yeah," Shamira said. "It had a funny acronym."

"FSBI; Future Sustainable Business Initiative," Kat said. "Anyway, I knew when Connor told me the names of the firms he'd spoken to, that they seemed familiar somehow, so I ran an Internet search on them as a group last night and that article popped up. They were among those mentioned in the report and I worked out that each firm was visited by a representative of FSBI in the weeks before they were attacked."

"That's a coincidence, surely," Shamira said.

"That's not all. I extended my search to include the thirty-five firms who'd reported a malware breach to the authorities and twenty have either a mention of FSBI on their websites and social media accounts or have photos in a local newspaper with a FSBI rep."

"Do you think someone saw the media reports of the visits and used that to build a list of targets?" Nate said.

"Maybe, but I think it's worth us digging deeper into the finances of the Honourable Jeremy Sharp."

"I knew he was a dirt-bag," Shamira said.

Chapter 30

Terry drove home from an emergency call out to a household that'd had a power cut due to an overloaded circuit board. One lane of his street was blocked by a police car with its lights flashing on and off.

"I still can't believe that you made me come with you. That was so boring," Harry said.

"Son, I don't think you're in a position to argue at this point."

"Hey, isn't that the cop who was at our door this morning?" Harry said, pointing through the windscreen to a police officer talking to a distraught older woman beside a silver four-door car stopped at an odd angle across the street. Its bonnet was crumpled, and the front bumper was hanging off. The driver's door of a blue car parked at the curb was crushed inwards.

Terry slowed his van to a crawl and wound the window down. "What's happened?" he asked a second police officer, who was sweeping up broken glass from beside the woman's vehicle.

"It appears that the driver swerved to avoid a pedestrian but lost control and crashed into a parked car," the officer said.

"Oh no, is the pedestrian okay?" Terry asked.

The officer shrugged. "He was gone by the time we arrived

on the scene, so one would assume so."

"We just live further down the road. Are we good to continue?" Terry asked.

The officer nodded and waved them on.

Terry drove along the block and pulled into an empty parking space opposite their house.

"Come on, lad, I think we need to have a talk about the responsibilities of running your own business," Terry said, turning off the engine and unclipping his seatbelt. "And if you're buying and selling things, even Internet things, then you're running a business." Harry rolled his eyes. "I'm serious; that accountant from your mother's work was right. You have to do your accounts and pay your taxes. It's rule number one of business, I'm afraid."

They crossed the road together and walked up to the door.

"You're right, it was our cop up the road," Terry said. "He's not here at any rate. He must have heard the crash and gone to help." He stuck his key into the lock, but the door swung open before he had a chance to turn it.

He looked at Harry, bewildered.

"Rosie? Are you home?" Terry called, stepping through the door.

Harry followed his father inside, and the two froze. To the left, in the lounge, the sofa had been slashed open and armchairs overturned. The drawers of the hall table were upended on the carpet, their contents splayed across the hallway.

Harry bolted up the stairs to his room and seconds later gave a cry of dismay. He thumped back down to where his father stood, rooted to the spot.

"Dad," he said, his voice rising. "The whole house has been

ransacked."

Terry turned his head and looked up to where his son stood on the bottom tread. "What were they after, Harry?" he asked in a low, controlled voice.

"I, ah, dunno."

"I think you do, and you need to start telling the truth," Terry said. "What if your mother or sister had been at home when this happened?" He pushed the front door closed, but it sprang open again. "The bloody lock is busted."

"Why wasn't that policeman guarding the door?" Harry said.

"I doubt he could have stopped this." Terry gave him a withering look as he reached into his pocket for his mobile. "Do you have the card that DS Jackson gave you?"

Harry pulled it from the back pocket of his jeans and listened as his father relayed the details of the break-in.

"Come on, Harry," Terry said after he'd finished the call. "We're not to tidy anything. Let's have a cuppa while we wait for the police to arrive, and you can tell me why this is all happening. Truthfully, this time."

"What do you mean?" Harry said.

"I mean, why you've gone behind our backs. Why didn't you tell us that you were trading Bitcoin and whatever else it is that the police seem to think you and Marshall were up to?"

"Because I know you wouldn't have let me," Harry said, following his father into the kitchen, where the evidence of someone searching was apparent. Cupboard doors hung ajar, papers were scattered across the floor, and utensil drawers were open.

"You don't know that," Terry said, filling the kettle and

lighting the stove.

"You wouldn't have," Harry said, dropping onto a chair at the small round dining table. "You never let me do anything that you don't understand."

"We just want to protect you," Terry said with a tired sigh.

"But the world has changed," Harry said. "You don't have to wait until you have a degree or get a job in the City to earn serious money. Anyone with an Internet connection and a few smarts can do it these days."

"I hope you weren't doing anything illegal."

Harry held his father's stare and said nothing.

"I'm serious, Harry," Terry said. "What was DS Jackson meaning about being a money mule? And why do you need three companies to trade cryptocurrency?"

"It's complicated, Dad," Harry said. "But we were making loads of cash."

"Why this sudden obsession with making money?" Terry asked.

Harry looked at him as though he'd grown two heads. "You try going to a school where you're the poorest kid," he said. "There are guys at Sawyer's who have everything. The newest tech, the latest fashions, winter skiing holidays, summers on their family's Caribbean island, and what do I have? Clothing from the Tesco sale, a second-hand outdated laptop, trainers from some bloke down the market, and a reconditioned phone from a company no one has ever heard of."

The kettle whistled as Terry dropped a teabag into each mug.

"Oh, Harry, those things don't matter," Terry said, pouring boiling water into the cups.

"Maybe not to you, but they do to me," he said. "How did

you think I was going to fit in with the kids at that school?"

"You fit in because you're so smart," Terry said in a whisper.

"Being smart is not everything," Harry said. "You need to project the proper image too. And a poor scholarship kid definitely isn't the right image to get ahead in this world."

"We worked so hard to give you every opportunity," Terry said, opening the refrigerator and grabbing the milk. "And you're what, ashamed of us or where you came from?"

Harry hung his head for a moment, and when he raised it, his eyes glistened with tears. "You don't understand. I knew you wouldn't."

Terry placed a mug of tea on the table beside Harry and rested his hand on the boy's shoulder, but Harry twisted out of his reach, standing and wiping a hand across his eyes.

"Without money, you are nothing. Money gives you power," he said.

"But you are on your way to making more money than either your mother or I could dream of. That school is your path to a top university and a job in the City," Terry said.

"That might be your dream," Harry said. "But that future is years off, and I need money now. The other kids have everything, and I have nothing. Do you remember that awful big, heavy laptop that you sent me to Sawyer's with? The kids all laughed at me on my first day, and for weeks after, they called me a 'gutter-punk'. How do you think it felt every time they all pulled out their sleek, slim devices with superfast Internet, and I had that chunky brick of a thing that was so unbelievably slow? The class would be half-finished by the time the bloody thing loaded whatever we were supposed to be working on."

"Why didn't you say something?"

"I did," Harry said. "You just called me ungrateful because you had to work that night security guard job for six months to afford everything I needed for school."

Terry sank down onto a chair at the table and put his head in his hands.

"You have no idea how much I hate being poor," Harry said.

A loud knock at the front door interrupted them. Terry looked defeated as he rose to his feet and shuffled out to see who was there.

"Oh, hello, you're back," he said to the young policeman standing there inspecting the broken lock.

"What's happened?"

"While you were off attending to that car accident, someone broke in and ransacked our house," Terry explained, without rancour.

The officer put his hand to his radio.

"I've already called it in. Someone is on the way," Terry said. "Would you like to come in for a cuppa while you wait?"

"No, thank you, sir. I think I'd better wait here."

Terry closed the door and returned to the kitchen.

"Where were we?" Terry said.

"I was telling you how much I hated being the poor scholarship kid. I'm finally at the stage where the kids have stopped making snarky comments about my background, and some even look up to me. And why do you think that is?" Terry didn't answer. "Money; I have enough now that I fit in. I've been accepted. Why can't you understand that?"

Terry studied his son for a long moment. "Tell me this, lad," he said. "This burglary, what were they after?"

Harry shrugged. "Dunno."

"Why don't I believe that?"

"Look, whatever," Harry said, shoving his chair back and jumping to his feet. He pushed past his father and opened the back door. "I've had enough of your questions." He slammed the door behind him and strode down the narrow bins alley at the side of the house out to the street.

Harry crossed the road and started walking to the underground station, trying to control the rage he felt at his father. Partway along the street, he noticed a man and woman climb from a parked car and cross the road towards him. He felt a jolt of alarm in his chest as he registered the intent on their faces. They were coming for him, and they didn't look friendly. He turned, jogging back the way he'd come, before cutting down a walkway between two houses, where he broke into a sprint.

Glancing over his shoulder, he ran a back route to the station, favoured by the locals, and clambered down the steps to the westbound platform. A disjointed computerised voice announced that the train was ready to depart, and the doors began to close. Harry leapt aboard and stood holding on to a pole as they swished shut and the train started to pull out. Harry watched as the couple following him came into view at the bottom of the stairs and glared at the departing train. Harry felt a jolt of recognition. He'd seen the man somewhere before.

Harry looked around the half-empty carriage, selected a seat well away from anyone, and pulled out his phone. His heavy breathing subsided, and his heart rate returned to normal as he scrolled through the hundreds of images saved on his phone with trembling hands. After a minute, he paused and flicked back through the previous four photos. In them, standing next to a car in the lane outside the school grounds, two men were shaking hands with Wilson. Harry recalled Wilson introducing the men to a group of students as '*Zombiegamez* representatives'. Harry and Marshall had suspected it was rubbish. The two boys had followed them when they left, and these photos were the result. Harry zoomed in on the image.

"Holy crap," he murmured. Clearly visible in the photo was the man who'd just chased him to the station.

Chapter 31

Kat looked at her watch and logged out of her computer. "Hey, thanks, guys, for helping today."

"I feel like we're just missing that last piece of the puzzle," Nate said, rolling his chair back from his desk as Kat added her phone and laptop to her bag. "I haven't been able to find anything else on Jeremy Sharp or FSBI."

"Have you told Adam your theory?" Shamira said.

Kat shook her head. "As I told you the other day, things are not great between us right now, so no."

"Maybe we should?"

Kat shrugged. "It's just a theory and we haven't been able to back it up with any evidence, so I wouldn't want to go tarnishing the man's reputation. He's an MP after all.

Anyway, I'm leaving early since I've got Sara and George arriving tonight, and I need to get organised."

"It will be good to have them around, to take your mind off Connor," Shamira said.

"George is always a bundle of energy, so it should be fun."

Shamira reached across her desk for Kat's hand. "You know I'm here if you need to talk. Don't go internalising everything that's happened, Kat."

"I know," Kat said before bolting from the uncomfortable

conversation. She pulled her jacket on as she hurried across the office and raced down the stairs. She crossed the foyer, waving to the security guard seated behind a glass counter, and pushed through the revolving door to the street outside.

"Kat?"

Kat jumped at the mention of her name and turned to see Harry Compton leaning against the wall outside the building.

"Harry? If you're looking for your mum, she's already left."

Harry pushed himself off the wall. "No, it's you I'm after. I didn't know who else to talk to, and I thought maybe you could help."

Kat weighed up her need to get home with the responsibility she felt to help Rosie's son, no matter how untrustworthy he was proving to be.

"Do you want to come back into my office?" Kat said, relenting.

"Okay." Harry followed Kat back into the building and up to the first floor. She led him into a small meeting room at the top of the stairs and closed the door. She indicated where he could sit with a wave of her hand.

"So, what can I do for you?" she asked, sitting across from him.

Harry was silent for a moment as he looked through the window at the river. "When Dad and I got home today, someone had broken into our house. They'd been through everything. The whole place was trashed. Then when I left the house, I was followed to the station, but I managed to get away and get on a train just as the doors closed."

"Oh no, have you told the police? Kat said.

"About the break-in? Yes. But not about being followed. I came straight here. I know what they want, and I think you can help me," Harry said.

"We should call…" Kat began. "Hang on, what were they looking for?"

Harry grinned. "See, I knew you were smart. Everyone else gets hung up on the mess, but you just cut to the chase."

"Don't try to flatter me," Kat said, glaring at him. "What were they looking for?"

"A USB stick," Harry said. "It contains all the information on the scam that Marshy and I discovered Wilson was running from the school."

Kat's eyes widened.

"We were trying to gather enough evidence on Wilson before taking it to the police. Somehow he must have found out what we were up to, and now Marshy is dead. I'm worried I could be next."

Kat felt a flash of sympathy for the teenager sitting across from her before remembering Adam's concerns that Harry kept changing his story to suit the situation. She sat back and considered whether she believed or trusted him.

"Do you have proof that Wilson was behind Marshall's death?" she asked.

Harry shook his head. "Nah, but it's a bit convenient, right?"

"So Marshall wasn't out buying weed the night he died?"

"I'm not sure, but you don't get killed over a bit of weed," Harry said.

"If you're mixing in those kinds of circles, who knows what can happen?" Kat said. "Tell me, what exactly was it that you think Wilson was doing?"

"Wilson told us that he was mates with the creators of *Zombiegamez*, you know, the online game," he said.

"Yeah, I know the game," Kat said.

"Anyway, Wilson told us that we were conducting testing for *Zombiegamez*. We were rewarded with gift cards, wild card entries to e-game tournaments and *Zombiegamez* merch," he said.

"You and Marshall?"

"No, there were others, some of the finance club," Harry said.

"But what were you really doing?"

"We think that he had us buying *Zombiegamez* tokens and gift cards using stolen credit cards and single-use email addresses," he said. "We thought we were stress-testing the system with pretend data. You have to believe me."

Kat leaned her right elbow on the table and rested her chin in her hand, running through in her head the conclusion that she and the team had come to. What Harry was saying tied in with what they'd uncovered.

"And this USB drive of yours has evidence of all of this?"

"Yeah, photos, screenshots, and a video of Wilson talking to these two guys that he said worked for the creators of *Zombiegamez*. I'm sure it was one of them that followed me to the station today. They must somehow know about it. Maybe Marshy told them before…" Harry paused and drew in a deep breath. A sheen of sweat spread across his forehead, and his earlier bravado had disappeared. "We can't prove any of this without that USB stick. Can you help me to get it back?"

"Where is it?"

"It's hidden at school, and I can't go back there to get it, and I can't call one of my mates to get it, in case they're monitoring my phone."

"Why didn't you tell this to DS Jackson when you were at the station earlier?"

"Because they'd go rushing in, and Wilson would have time to talk his way out of it again," Harry said.

"Again?"

"You know, with the porn thing?"

"How did you know about that?"

Harry blushed. "All the kids know. Can I use your phone to call my mate Sammy? I'll tell him where it's hidden, and he can retrieve it," Harry said.

"No, why don't you tell me and I'll go and retrieve it?" Kat said, glancing at her watch. "You don't want to involve any more of your friends in this, especially if Wilson is as dangerous as you claim."

"You'll need someone to let you in," Harry said. "The school is like a fortress."

"Perhaps Sammy can do that much; meet me at the entrance and sign me in," Kat said.

Harry sat forward and held his hand out for Kat's phone. "Let me call him and see if we can do this."

"Put it on speaker," Kat said.

"Hello?"

"Sammy, it's Harry," he said.

"Harry? Wait a sec."

They heard a door close.

"Okay, that's better. Are you alright? We heard about Marshall," Sammy said. "What the hell happened?"

"Sammy, I'm here with a lady called Kat, who works with the police. She's coming to the school to pick something up for me. Can you sign her in and show her to the library?" Harry said, ignoring Sammy's questions.

"Hi, Sammy," Kat said.

"Um... hi," Sammy said. "It would have to be by 6:30 p.m.

We all have to be in the common room for a movie marathon after that."

Harry rolled his eyes and shook his head.

Kat looked at her watch again. "I can make that if I leave now."

"Okay, I'll wait for you at the front gate," Sammy said.

Harry punched the end button and pushed the phone back across the table to Kat.

"I hope I'm not going to regret this," Kat said. "Do you want to wait here?"

Harry shook his head.

"Where are you going?"

"Home," he said. "It's the last place they'll think to look for me. Can you swing by and drop the USB to me?"

Kat gave a slow nod and stood. "I'll just leave my laptop here," she said, walking out onto the office floor and across to her desk.

Turning to watch Harry standing with his back to her, looking out at the view of Tower Bridge, she called Adam at the station. Tony answered his phone.

"He's in a meeting with the DCI and Marshall Tyler's parents," he said.

"Can I leave a message with you for him?"

"Of course."

"Tell him to come to my flat around 7:30 p.m. I should have gathered the evidence which explains why Marshall Tyler was killed."

Chapter 32

"The library's in here," Sammy said, leading Kat to the end of a dark wood-panelled corridor. He opened a pair of heavy wooden doors and ushered Kat into a book-lined room with high ceilings and a balconied mezzanine running the entire circumference of the massive room.

"Wow," Kat murmured. "This is amazing."

Dotted around the room were polished wooden tables with ornate desk lamps. Kat could imagine them occupied by students with books and laptops open. But of course, it being a Friday night, the library was empty and silent.

"Come on, this way," Sammy said, dragging Kat's gaze from the room. She hurried after him, past book-laden shelves and down four steps to another area of the library. "Harry said to find *The Odyssey* in the Classics section, which starts here and goes the whole way along to there." Sammy pointed to the far end of the room, where leadlight windows opened onto a grassed courtyard.

"What actually happened to Marshall? And why hasn't Harry been back to school?" Sammy asked as they crossed the room.

"I can't answer that," Kat said.

"Is Harry in trouble?" he asked.

"I'm not sure," Kat said. "But whatever we find here could help him and help the police work out who killed Marshall."

"I hope so," Sammy said.

"Look for Homer," Kat said, coming to a stop in front of the Classics section. "I assume this is alphabetised."

They strolled along the row, running their eyes up and down the shelves until they found several volumes by Homer.

"Here," Sammy said, pulling out a paperback copy.

"No, it'll be a hardcover if he's hidden the memory stick in the spine," Kat said, reaching past him for a book bound in navy blue. She pulled it from the shelf and turned it around so Sammy could see it. The cover image was of an ancient sailing boat.

Kat carried the book over to a small side table and laid it down. As she opened it to the centre, she felt a bulge in the spine. She tipped the book on its end and gave it a tap on the table. Samuel's eyes widened, and he looked around as the sound echoed through the quiet library. Kat wriggled her fingers into a gap in the binding and grazed the edge of something which she couldn't quite reach. She lifted the book up and gave it a good shake. A bright blue USB drive slipped out and bounced on the edge of the desk before coming to rest on the floor. Kat dropped the book on the table and stooped to pick it up.

"Quick, someone is coming," Sammy said, grabbing the book and shoving it back into its space on the shelf.

Kat went to slip the USB stick into the pocket of her jeans but instead tucked it into her bra.

"And who do we have here? Shouldn't you be at movie night, Samuel?"

Kat turned around as Andrew Wilson strode into view, followed by a bulky man with military-style cropped hair.

"I, ah," Sammy spluttered.

"I'm Kat, Sammy's aunt," Kat said. "Sammy was just showing me your wonderful library. But, yes, goodness, look at the time, I must be going. Sammy, I've held you up long enough." She linked arms with the shaking boy and started back towards the stairs.

"Not so fast," Wilson said, stopping in front of them. "If you'd be so kind as to come this way." He held his hand out, indicating a door cut into the wood panelling that Kat hadn't noticed.

She hesitated before stepping in front of Sammy. "I don't think so," she said.

"You realise that I'm not asking." Wilson's tone turned cold. His companion stood further away with his meaty hands clasped in front of him like a bouncer at a nightclub, blocking their only point of exit.

"Run when you can," she whispered to a frightened Sammy.

Wilson reached for Kat's arm as she aimed a jab at his face. The unexpected blow grazed his jaw, and he stumbled. The other man started towards them. Kat followed through with a solid push kick, which sent Wilson staggering backwards into his accomplice. The two men lost their balance for a moment.

"Go," she shouted, gripping Sammy's hand.

Together they ran through the library with the two men chasing them. They reached the main door leading back into the corridor as it flew open, and they found their way barred by a third man. His lined face broke into a sneering grin as firm hands gripped each of their arms from behind.

Chapter 33

Sara opened the door of Kat's flat to Adam's knock.

"Oh, hello," she said. "I thought you might have been Kat."

"What do you mean?" Adam said, surprised to see Kat's sister-in-law. "She asked me to meet her here."

"She's not home yet. We got here around 5 p.m., and she wasn't here," Sara said. "I tried her mobile about half an hour ago, but it's switched off."

"That's odd," Adam said.

"Do you want to come in and wait?" Sara asked. Her long honey blonde hair was pinned in a messy bun and she looked effortlessly elegant in a white shirt and dark trousers.

"Yeah, if that's okay," he said.

"Sure, I'm trying to get George to bed, but he wants to wait up to see her."

Adam followed Sara through to Kat's living room. A little boy dressed in stripy pyjamas was reclining on the sofa watching a cartoon on an iPad. Zelda lay snuggled up beside him, purring loudly.

"Hello," he said, looking Adam up and down.

"Hello, George," Adam said.

"I've seen you before. What's your name?"

"I'm Adam. I'm one of your Auntie Kat's friends."

Zelda looked up and gave a loud meow before rolling over and burrowing deeper into the little boy's side. Satisfied with Adam's reply, George turned his attention back to the show.

"Can I get you a tea or coffee?" Sara asked.

"Tea would be great, thanks," Adam said, taking out his phone and calling Kat. The phone was switched off. He scrolled through his contact list and made another call. After several rings, it was answered.

"Stephenson."

"It's Adam Jackson, Charles. Sorry to bother you so late, but I'm looking for Kat. Is she still at the office?"

"Good evening, Adam. No, she left early. I think she mentioned that her sister-in-law was staying."

"Okay, thanks, Charles. You don't have Nate and Shamira's numbers handy, do you?"

"Sure, I'll text them through."

Adam ended the call.

"Here you go." Sara placed the mug on the bench in front of Adam. "Milk?"

He nodded and shed his jacket, laying it over the arm of the sofa. "Kat's boss says that she left early because you were staying."

Sara frowned. "Well, where is she then?"

"That's an excellent question," Adam said.

"It's really unlike her not to call if she's been held up," Sara said.

"Maybe she went to see Connor on the way home," Adam said, glancing at her.

Sara smiled at him. "She wasn't planning to because he's been moved somewhere secret. You like her, don't you?"

Adam was thrown by the directness of her question. "Yeah, she's a smart woman."

"It's more than that. I've seen you two together, remember? If you don't mind me saying, you seem like kindred spirits."

Adam was silent for a moment.

"We've both suffered trauma and lost people close to us. I think when you've been through that sort of stuff, you recognise it in others."

"Mmm."

"Plus, she's so resilient. Nothing fazes her." Adam realised that he was rambling and clamped his mouth shut.

"Have you told her this?" Adam shook his head. "What's stopping you? You're both single."

Adam ran his hand through his hair. "Did she tell you about Nancy and me?"

Sara nodded. "I'm sorry." Adam didn't reply. "So, what happens with you and Kat now?" Sara pressed.

"She's seeing Connor," he said.

"I'm not sure a couple of dates constitute 'seeing' someone," Sara said as Adam's phone beeped.

Adam pulled it from his pocket and checked the message.

"Excuse me while I call Nate," he said, tapping the screen, grateful for an excuse to escape the awkward conversation.

There was crowd noise in the background when Nate answered.

"Nate, it's Adam Jackson. I'm looking for Kat."

"Hang on, I'll go outside."

Adam listened as Nate excused himself, and a door opened, then closed, and the rise and fall of voices subsided.

"Sorry about that," Nate said a moment later. "Kat's not with me. She left work early because she had something to do before Sara and George arrived."

"Did she say where she was going?"

"Not to me," Nate said. "Is everything okay?"

"I'm not sure. I'm at her place with Sara, but she hasn't been home, and she's not answering her phone."

"What can I do?" Nate asked.

"Nothing at this stage, but let me know immediately if you hear from her."

"Will do and same."

A thud in the lounge made them both jump. Sara rushed past Adam and found that George had fallen asleep, and the iPad had slipped from his hands onto the floor. She scooped him up in her arms and carried him to Kat's bedroom.

Adam's next call was to the station.

"It's DS Adam Jackson. I need an immediate location on a phone," he said, reciting Kat's mobile number. "Yes, I'll hold."

"Plaistow?" he said. "Okay, thanks."

He was frowning at his phone when it rang again.

"DS Jackson."

"Adam, it's Shamira. Nate just called me. Kat was going to see a kid called Sammy at Sawyer's Hill Grammar on her way home. Harry came to the office to talk to her as she was leaving. He asked her to meet Sammy and collect some evidence about Wilson from the school."

"Thanks, Shamira, that's really useful. I'll get over there now."

Adam's next call was to the police officer stationed at the road entrance leading to Sawyer's Hill Grammar.

"It's DS Jackson. Is Wilson still at the school?"

"I believe so, sir."

"Has anyone else arrived?"

"There were some paparazzi hanging about in the lane earlier," the officer said. "I guess the death of a celebrity's kid brings those guys out. But the security guard on the gate moved them on."

"And no one else?"

"There's been a pizza delivery, and a woman arrived a couple of hours ago."

"Dark reddish hair, medium height?"

"Yeah."

"Has she left?" Adam asked.

"No, the headmaster was the only one to leave tonight, apart from the pizza delivery guy."

Adam shoved his phone back in his pocket and cursed as Sara returned to the living room.

She registered the look of thunder on his face. "What's up?"

"Your sister-in-law," he began, with barely concealed fury. He grabbed his jacket and let out a controlled breath before speaking again. "I know where she went. Why does she think that she's bulletproof?"

Chapter 34

Sammy broke down in tears. He shuddered as gulping sobs racked his body.

"I'm sorry," he sniffed. "I'm so scared."

"Yeah, me too," Kat agreed, shuffling her chair closer to the frightened boy and nudging him with her shoulder. Their hands were secured to the armrests with cable ties and their ankles tied to the chair legs. The only illumination in the room came from a single light bulb hanging in the centre. The room was used to store surplus and broken desks and chairs stacked haphazardly throughout the space.

"We'll get through this. There will be people already out looking for us."

But in reality, she wasn't so sure, especially after the way she'd left things with Adam. What if he hadn't got the message that she'd left with Tony? Or worse still, received it and ignored it? She should have texted him to say where she was going rather than trying to prove something to him by coming up with the trump card to solve the case.

"Harry said the people that Mr Wilson works for would kill me if I told the police anything. But DS Jackson seemed to know everything already," Sammy said.

"Well, maybe not everything, but he'd probably worked out

enough that you just filled in the gaps," Kat said.

"I hope they do kill me," Sammy said. "Because if they don't, my grandmother will. She'll be so disappointed in me."

"I think you'll find that she'll just be glad when you're safe," Kat said.

"You haven't met my grandmother," Sammy said, shuddering again and letting out a slightly hysterical laugh.

"Well, we can't always please everyone," Kat said.

"That's easy for you to say, you're an adult."

"You haven't met my mother," Kat said. "All she wants is for me to settle down, get married and have children. She's always trying to set me up on dates with these awful, boring men."

"Why can't you get your own dates? Is it because of your hand? You're hot, I would think lots of men would want to go out with you," Sammy said. "I mean, ah…" He trailed off, and Kat could feel his embarrassment.

"Thank you, Sammy," she said. "That's very kind of you to say. No, the problem is me. I don't want to settle down, and my mother can't understand that. But she loves me, and I'm sure, even if your grandmother can't understand how you got involved with Wilson's scheme, it won't stop her loving you."

"I guess you're right," Sammy said.

They sat in companionable silence for a few moments as Kat racked her brain trying to remember a personal safety video she'd once watched on YouTube. A girl was able to free herself from cable ties using her belt and shoelaces.

"What happened to your hand?" Sammy asked. "Were you born without it?"

"No, I lost it in a car accident," Kat said.

"Oh, I'm sorry."

"Thanks. Sammy, can I ask you some questions about what you were doing for Wilson?"

"Um… okay."

"So you were buying *Zombiegamez* gift cards, is that right?" Kat asked.

"Yeah, he asked me one day if I wanted to help him with a project. He said I would get extra privileges," Sammy said. "And at this school, you want all of the extra privileges you can get."

"Where did you get the money to buy the gift cards?"

"He gave me a sheet of paper each time with, like, twenty sets of credit card details on it."

"Didn't you think that was unusual, and they might have been stolen?"

"I asked him whose they were, and he said they weren't real and that we were testing the system," Sammy said. "He showed me how to log in using a series of VPNs, which I now realise was disguising our movements. We bought the gift cards in varying amounts, sometimes £500 and sometimes £1,000."

"How long have you been doing this?" Kat said.

"About two months, after school a couple of times a week," Sammy said. "I thought that I was the only one until one day I overheard a couple of the other boys talking. He had a little team of us, all sworn to secrecy. That's when I realised it wasn't really testing. I asked him about it and found myself on detention for a week with all privileges revoked."

"Why didn't you tell one of your other teachers?"

"We didn't think anyone would believe us. Wilson had promised to give some of the boys better grades, but he got angry and threatened us with expulsion when we questioned him. He told a couple of the lads that he'd announce on social media that they were gay when they hadn't even told their parents. He even threatened to take his belt to us. We were scared of him."

Sammy relaxed as he talked, leaning against Kat's side. Kat continued wiggling in her seat, trying to move to the right-hand side of the chair so that she could reach her belt buckle with the fingers of her right hand.

"So you haven't talked to anyone about this?"

"Only the other boys in the finance club that were doing the same project."

"Where did Wilson get the credit card details from?"

Kat felt Sammy's head shake. "I don't know."

"What about Harry and Marshall?" Kat asked.

"They were doing something else, but I know they hated Wilson. I overheard them talking about 'aping into a coin that's flippening', whatever that meant. Still, to his face, they were really matey with him," Sammy said.

"Are you good friends with them?"

"What, Marshall and Harry?" Sammy snorted. 'No, I'm a year younger and certainly not cool enough to be their friend. They only put up with me because Wilson needed lackeys to do the computer work."

"I've met Harry, but what was Marshall like?"

"He was a bully," Sammy said. "A charming one, though. Everyone thought he was amazing. He made you feel special until you got on the wrong side of him. Then he could be quite nasty."

"Who do you think killed him?"

"Wilson, I guess."

"I believe Wilson has an alibi for that night, so it can't have been him. Not Harry?"

"No, Harry was here. I saw him come back into the dorm around 6 p.m., it was just after we'd eaten. He let himself into Marshall's room, grabbed his laptop and left."

"Did you speak to him?" Kat worked her right hand to the back of the chair's arm and turned her body towards it. Her fingertips pulled the loop of her belt free from the buckle and worked the prong from its hole. She felt the belt loosen around her waist and eased it from the belt loops of her jeans using her right hand.

"Yeah, he said he was getting Marshall's laptop for him and not to tell anyone that I'd seen him. He left by the back entrance, heading towards the gate. What are you doing?"

"I'm trying to see if I can use my belt to snap these cable ties. I saw someone do it online once."

"I don't have a belt," Sammy said, sounding disappointed.

"It's okay; I might need you to help me since my prosthesis is at an odd angle, and I can't seem to make it work properly. Anyway, I wonder what Wilson had on Marshall and Harry to make them keep working for him?" Kat mused.

"I've always wondered if it was around the other way," Sammy said.

"You mean what did Marshall and Harry have on Wilson?" Kat said.

"Yeah, I mean those of us in the finance club thought we were special getting the opportunity to earn *Zombiegamez* merch. But Harry and Marshall seemed to get a lot more than the rest of us. They had a lot of new stuff lately; the best laptops, the latest tech, games, clothes, mopeds, you name it. I mean, Marshall's parents are wealthy, but Harry's aren't. He's a gutter-punk," Sammy said, a blush rising on his cheeks. "I mean, a scholarship kid. And I believe Marshall's father had him on a very strict allowance because they were self-made; he thought Marshall should be too. So, Harry and Marshall had to be getting their money from somewhere."

"I think you're right," Kat said.

"You do?" Sammy sounded surprised.

"Harry told DS Jackson that he made his money trading Bitcoin and other cryptocurrencies."

"It's possible, although on the days when Wilson was actually teaching us about finance, he warned us against cryptocurrency trading," Sammy said. "He said it was too speculative."

"So were Harry and Marshall buying the game cards too?"

"I think so, but they did other things. Harry could hack into anything. He got into the school's network once and increased all of our grades. One time, he got into the private email account of a politician and found some dirty photos. Wilson hit the roof and banned him from doing it."

"Maybe someone found out what they were up to, and that's what got Marshall killed," Kat said.

"And now that we've worked it out, they're planning to kill us too."

"Not if I can help it," she said.

Kat slid her hands forward on the arms of the chair and fed the buckle through the small gap between her ankle and the chair leg. Holding the other end of the belt, she leaned forward, sliding her hands to the edge of the chair arms, grabbed the buckle and tugged it towards her. She threaded the end through the clasp with the fingers of her right hand. Doubling over, she grabbed the end of the belt with her teeth and sat up, pulling it tight.

"Okay, Sammy, this is where I need your help," she said, her voice muffled around the belt. "I'm going to pass you the end of the belt, and when I say, lean forward and tug it sideways as hard as you can. Ready?"

"Alright." Sammy slid his hands to the end of the chair arm, twisted his wrist as far as it would go, and opened up his fingers. Kat leaned across, angling her head towards the arm of the chair. Sammy's fingers closed around the belt, and Kat released it from her teeth.

"Okay, now tug it sideways."

Sammy yanked on the belt, and Kat felt the cable tie cut into her ankle.

"Stop, try again. Short and sharp tugs," she said.

Sammy pulled again and again until the cable tie snapped.

"Yah," he said, delighted. "What now?"

"I need to get my shoelace and try the same thing with the wrist ties."

The only sound for the next few minutes was Kat's heavy breathing as she worked to get free. Kat pulled her right leg up and rested her heel on the edge of the chair, and unlaced her shoe using the fingers of her right hand. She pulled the laces from the eyelets, leaving the last two in place, and double knotted the lace to the top eyelet to secure it. She fed the lace through the tiny gap between her wrist and the chair's arm. Leaning forward, she double knotted the lace around the laces of her left shoe, using the fingers of her right hand.

Kat held her right arm tucked between her thigh and the inside of the chair arm. She lifted her feet off the ground, working them backwards and forwards in a sawing motion. To her astonishment, after thirty seconds, the cable tie snapped, and her hand was free. "It worked," she exclaimed before turning her attention to her left arm. She pushed up her sleeve and rolled down the sock covering her forearm. Taking care, she released the suction, holding her prosthesis in place, and her arm came free, leaving the hand attached to the chair. Kat eased it out of the cable tie and reattached it, flexing her fingers to re-engage the sensors. She looked up to find Sammy staring at her.

"That was pretty cool," he said. "Sorry, can I say that?"

She smiled at him. "You can. Now let's get you free," she said, looking around the room and spied a splintered broken chair leg lying nearby to use to saw through Sammy's bonds.

Five minutes later, they were standing looking at the locked cellar door in frustration.

"Maybe we can hit him over the head with a chair when he returns," Sammy suggested.

"I think that only works in the movies," Kat said, turning to examine the room. "We'd be better to try one of those high windows." She pointed to the far side of the room. At regular intervals, there were long narrow windows along the wall just below the ceiling.

"Let's climb on those old desks and see if any of the window latches are loose."

Sammy's face fell. "Even if they are, I don't think I'd fit through." He looked down at his round middle.

"If your head fits through, then the rest of you will," Kat said, dragging a chair over to the wall and using it to climb onto a desk beneath the windows. She reached up and gave the first window a push, but it wouldn't budge. At the opposite end of the room, Sammy did the same. After a minute of trying each window in turn, he called out. "The latch on this one is broken."

Kat jumped down and raced to his side. "Can you pass the chair up onto the desk for me so that I can reach?" she asked.

Sammy jumped down and passed it up to her, holding it steady as she climbed up. The latch was broken, but the window was stuck. It was hinged along the top and looked as though it would open outwards. Kat pulled the sleeve of her jacket down over her right hand and hit the bottom right-hand edge of the window surround with the edge of her fist. It moved a little. Encouraged, she repeated the action on the opposite corner of the window, releasing it further. When she pushed against the first corner again, the wood gave a squeal, and the window sprang ajar. Kat pushed it fully open and peered through. The window was at ground level, opening onto a grassed area. It was dark outside, and the air was cool. Kat twisted her head to the side, looking up to the floors of the building above. There were no lights on in any of the windows, but she could still see quite a way across the lawn courtesy of the school's security lights.

"Can you give me a boost?" she asked Sammy.

"Ah, sure," he said, climbing up on the desk beside her chair.

Kat pulled herself up and through the window using her forearms. Sammy put his hands behind her knees and gave her a push. Using her shoulder to wedge the window open, she curled her legs up and rolled out onto the grass. She sat up and looked around, half expecting an unwelcome welcome party, but there was no one about. She pulled the window open and reached in for Sammy. He too pulled himself up and managed to squeeze through the small window with a bit of manoeuvring. Seconds later, he lay on the grass on his back, panting. Kat jammed the window closed again and looked around, trying to get her bearings. They were outside one section of the school complex next to an abundant rose garden.

"What's the safest and quickest way out of here?" she asked, as the crash of a door opening and hitting the wall sounded in the room they'd just left.

"I don't know," Sammy said, leaping to his feet. "There are cameras everywhere around the buildings and on the main driveway."

"We need to keep moving," Kat said, crawling away from the window.

Behind them, they could hear voices in the cellar.

"There are plenty of hiding places in the cloister near the chapel," Sammy said.

"Let's go then; you lead the way," Kat said.

Sammy hurried to an arched opening in the wall, which led into the central quadrangle. He flattened himself against the brick and peered inside before beckoning for Kat to follow him. The archway was several metres deep, with doorways on the interior sides leading into the building. Flyers, advertising the next meetings of the school's clubs, were pinned to noticeboards on the wall. They flapped a little in the gentle breeze that blew through the opening.

Kat rushed to the far side of the archway and peered out into the darkened quadrangle. A covered stone walkway ringed the interior on all four sides at ground level, with openings leading into the courtyard at various intervals. Security lights embedded into the arched roof of the cloister bathed the building in soft light.

"The chapel should be open. We can hide in there," Sammy whispered behind her. "This way."

He turned right and started to jog along the walkway

but froze as his footsteps slapped and echoed against the flagstones underfoot. He turned to Kat, a look of terror in his eyes.

"It's okay," she whispered. "Let's tiptoe."

Keeping close to the inside wall, they hurried to the end of the cloister and turned onto a matching walkway. Halfway along stood two enormous wooden doors framed by a stone portico. Spotlights illuminated the words 'Sawyer's Hill Chapel' carved into the stonework above the door. Set into the right-hand door was a smaller entrance. Sammy turned the handle, and it sprang open.

"Quick," Kat said, glancing over her shoulder as the beam from a flashlight hit the end wall of the walkway.

Sammy and Kat hurried through the door into the vestry and were engulfed by the darkness of the chapel. Kat eased the door shut behind them, bending the handle so that it closed with a near-silent click. She looked around and gave a yelp as a figure loomed in the darkness.

"It's okay, that's just the Virgin Mary," Sammy said.

Kat put her hand to her chest and felt her heart thudding. "I thought someone was there."

"Over here," Sammy whispered as their eyes adjusted to the gloom. He drew back a red velvet curtain beside the door to reveal a curving set of narrow stone steps leading to the upper level of the chapel.

Heavy footsteps sounded outside on the walkway, and Kat put her fingers to her lips. They sat on the third step and let the curtain fall back into place, obscuring them.

"Nah, can't see them," a muffled voice said.

Sammy began to shake and clapped a hand over his mouth to stop any sound from escaping.

"Yeah, but the tracker suggests they should be around here somewhere."

Chapter 35

"What tracker?" Kat whispered.

"I dunno." Sammy's trembling intensified.

They heard the footsteps move away from the door and further along the cloister.

Kat squeezed his arm and stood up, slipping back out past the curtain. She crept across the vestry and picked up a wooden chair from beside a table of hymn books. She carried it across to the doorway, gently placing the back legs on the floor and wedging the back of the chair under the door handle. She tiptoed back to join Sammy.

"Check your pockets," she said, slipping a hand into her jeans' pockets.

Sammy stood up and patted the front pockets of his trousers and then the back before pausing. He slipped his hand into the back pocket and pulled out a small piece of square plastic.

"That's a Find Tile," Kat whispered. "I've got one of these in my wallet because I'm always losing it."

"That isn't mine," Sammy said. "How did it get into my pocket?"

"Wilson must have slipped it in when he was tying you up, in case we escaped," Kat said. "Give it to me."

Sammy placed the tile into her hand, and Kat rushed over

to the statue of the Virgin Mary and dropped it into her outstretched marble palm. She rechecked her own pockets in case they'd tagged her too, but they were empty.

The door to the chapel rattled, causing them to jump. Kat looked aghast at the door, willing the chair to hold.

"The tracker just moved," the man said. "Oh no, hang on, it's stationary again. I'm right outside the chapel, but the door's locked." There was a moment's silence. "Okay, I'll wait."

Kat and Sammy crept away from the entrance into the nave of the chapel. Muted light shone through three substantial stained-glass windows at the far end behind the pulpit, showering the choir stalls in soft coloured light.

"There's a side door over there that leads to the robing room," Sammy said, pointing.

"Great, there might be a phone," Kat said.

They skirted along a row of pews and behind another curtain into a small dark room with several chairs and a rack of clerical robes.

"Where does that door go?" Kat asked, pointing to the outline of a door on the opposite side of the room.

"That might take us outside," Sammy said. "Shouldn't we just hide in here until morning?"

"No, we should keep moving," Kat said. "We need to let the police know what's going on here."

Sammy didn't appear convinced.

The door had a key in the keyhole. Kat turned it and eased the door open, and peeked through the opening. The main entrance driveway to the school lay in front of them, edged on either side by vast swathes of mown parkland.

"We need to get to those trees," she said, pointing to the giant oaks framing the driveway.

"If we get to the main steps, there's a passageway beneath them that we could hide in if anyone comes, then it's only a short distance to the trees," Sammy said.

"Good idea, let's go."

Kat grabbed his hand, and they jogged along the side of the building until they reached the staircase, ducking their heads as they slipped into the narrow passageway beneath it. They crept to the far side and listened for any sounds.

"You're doing really well, Sammy," Kat said.

"I'm terrified," he said. "What if we get to the gate and the security guard is in on this? Even if he's not, I don't think he will let me leave with you in the middle of the night."

Kat thought for a moment. "We could say that you're sick," she said. "And besides, even if the guy operating the main gate is part of this, we are at least by the road, so someone driving past could see and help us."

"And I'll be able to tell you if it's one of the usual security guys or not," Sammy said.

"That'll be helpful," Kat said. "Now, are you ready to run?"

"As ready as I'll ever be," he said. "If I ever needed reminding that I needed to get fit, it's tonight."

They ran across the driveway, their feet crunching in the gravel, expecting to hear someone coming after them at any moment. But they made it to the first tree unseen, skirting around to the far side and leaning against its massive trunk. The beam of a powerful flashlight swung around the side of the main building. Sammy gasped, but the light disappeared again.

"We need to keep moving," Kat said, peering around the tree. "I wish we had a phone. This is the second time this week that I've had mine taken."

"There could be one in the caretaker's cottage, he's away," Sammy whispered. "And it's down a path on the way to the front gate."

"No, that's where Harry was hiding out, and if he's working with Wilson, that may not be a safe place for us."

"So that's where he was. I didn't know that," Sammy said.

"They can't have gone far. Get the rest of the security lights on and check the cameras," a deep voice spoke, not far from where Kat and Sammy cowered.

They stayed frozen in place long after the crunch of the man's feet faded.

'I don't know where he came from," Kat whispered. "I didn't even hear him approach."

"Me neither," Sammy said, his hand resting over his heart as if to slow it down.

"Come on, we can't stay here," Kat said. She rose and moved across the manicured lawn towards the next tree. Sammy followed, glancing behind them as he hurried after her.

"Kat, there's a camera on the end of the building up there, see," he said, pointing to the camera mounted on the brickwork.

"Okay, we just need to stay on this side of the tree line then," Kat said.

"But if they come around the end of the building again, they will see us," Sammy said. His teeth were starting to chatter.

"Even more reason to put some distance between them and us," Kat said. "Come on."

They ran to the next tree and slid around behind it, resting for a moment before Kat checked that they were clear, and they jogged to the next tree in the line. The driveway curved away from the main building the further they went. After another minute, it was out of sight, and the small wooden gatehouse came into view at the top of the driveway. A light shone in the window, illuminating a security guard leaning back in his chair. He laughed, and Kat realised that he was probably watching a TV show.

"We might be able to crawl under the barrier since he's distracted," she said.

"No, they have sensors," Sammy said. "To stop us kids sneaking out at night."

Kat opened her mouth to speak as two police cars with lights flashing, followed by a third car and an ambulance, pulled up across the entranceway.

Kat broke away from the cover of the tree and rushed towards the cars as the doors opened. Adam leapt from his car and ran to meet her.

"It's Andrew Wilson, he tied us up in the basement," Kat said as she reached him. Her words tumbled out in a breathless rush. "He's had the kids laundering stolen money for him."

"What were you even doing here?" Adam said.

"Harry arranged for me to meet Sammy here." She turned and signalled for Sammy to join her. "Harry wanted me to collect the evidence against Wilson that he and Marshall hid in the library."

"You should have called me," Adam said.

"I did, but you were busy, and I couldn't wait. I left a message." Kat sighed. "I suppose you're going to have another go at me?"

Adam's expression softened, and he shook his head before drawing her into his arms, holding her tight for several moments.

"Thank God you're okay," he murmured into her hair.

Kat pulled back and tilted her head to study his face. His eyes were shining with emotion that he didn't bother to disguise, and she realised in that instant that she was the sole source of his concern.

"Adam, I'm sorry. I should have told you where I was going."

"I'm sorry too. I kept pushing you away when what I really wanted to do was this." Adam dipped his head and kissed her, a gentle brush of her lips at first, then deeper. Kat moved her hands to hold his face and relaxed into his embrace. Adam eased back and gazed at her, reaching out to tuck a stray strand of hair behind her ear before she rose up on tiptoes to kiss him again.

A throat was cleared.

They sprang apart to see Sammy standing a little way away, hopping from one foot to another, his cheeks scarlet in the lights of the vehicles.

"Ah, sorry, hi." He gave an awkward wave. "I wasn't sure where to go. I'm a bit scared to go back into school in case he's still there."

"No, mate, you're to stay with us," Adam said, slipping his arm around Kat's waist. He rested his other hand on Sammy's shoulder. "You've had quite a night, by the sound of things. Are you alright?"

"Thanks to Kat, she's amazing. You should have seen her kick Wilson, then break out of the cable ties," Sammy said.

Adam looked back at Kat, taking in her flushed cheeks and dishevelled appearance. He smiled at her. "Somehow, that doesn't surprise me."

Kat's grin was sheepish.

"You both need to let the paramedic check you over."

"I'm fine," Kat said.

"It wasn't a suggestion," Adam said.

Kat resisted the urge to roll her eyes and instead reached beneath her top and retrieved the USB stick from her bra.

Sammy gave a gasp. "I wondered where you'd hidden it," he said. "I couldn't believe it when Wilson searched your pockets and didn't find it."

Adam's playful expression darkened.

"This is what I came here to get, but rather than drop it off to Harry, as he requested, I'm giving it to you," she said. "There should be some useful evidence on here of the operation that Wilson has been operating from the school." She dropped the USB drive into Adam's hand. "I believe we may find a link to the retirement home fraud that Connor was investigating."

"Thank you."

Adam dug his hand into the pocket of his jeans and retrieved his car keys. "Once the ambos have checked you over, you two can wait in my car." He handed Kat the keys.

"Where are you going?" Kat asked.

"To arrest Wilson," he said, giving her arm a squeeze before letting go.

"He's not alone. There were a couple of others searching for us when we escaped." Adam started to move towards his team. "And, Adam?" she called.

"Yeah?"

"Be careful."

Kat watched him as he walked away, unable to stop the smile that spread across her face.

"So you and DS Jackson, huh? I thought you didn't have a boyfriend?" Sammy said.

"I don't," Kat replied.

Samuel's eyebrows disappeared into his hair. "Didn't look

that way a moment ago."

Kat laughed and reached for his arm. "No, I supposed it didn't," she said. "Come on, let's go and see the paramedics."

PC Eloise Salter smiled as they approached. "Who's first?"

Kat pointed to Sammy, who shook his head. "You go."

Eloise directed Kat to the back of the waiting ambulance. "I'm Eloise," she said to Sammy. "You can wait right here with me." She reached into one of the many pockets on her jacket and pulled out a small bar of chocolate. "Are you hungry after all that excitement?"

Samuel nodded and gave her a shy smile.

* * *

"How many other vehicle exits are there from the school grounds?" Adam asked the security guard in the booth at the front gate.

"Just one other, leading into the park," the man answered. "I really should call the headmaster."

"No, let me do that," Adam said. "Can you bring up any images of the boarders' dorm?" Adam asked, looking past the man to the four security camera monitors.

"Only the front steps," the security guard said. "The security hub is in the main building."

"Stay with him and make sure he contacts no one," Adam murmured to the uniformed police officer standing in the corner of the security booth.

"Boss, backup is five minutes out," Julian said as Adam approached the car. Tony held an iPad with a map of the school grounds and buildings. Adam took it from him and set it on the bonnet.

"Wilson's rooms are here, on the ground floor of the boarding dorm. But Kat and Sammy were held in a basement room beneath the library in the main building, here," Adam said, pointing to the various locations on the map. The other uniformed officers leaned across and looked.

"I want this place locked down. No one leaves. We have at least three suspects," he said.

Adam's next call was to the headmaster.

"Mr Beauchamp, DS Jackson," Adam said. "Are you at the school this evening?"

"No, I'm at a charity dinner in central London tonight," Beauchamp replied. "Why? Is there a problem?"

"Yes. Andrew Wilson kidnapped a member of my team and one of your students tonight. Fortunately, they managed to escape and raise the alarm. Still, I'm now facing the prospect of raiding your school, unless you can help me locate Wilson and his companions."

"Companions?" Beauchamp spluttered. "Now wait a minute, you can't go guns blazing into my school."

"Which is why I need your help. Who can I trust to see if Wilson's around without raising suspicions?"

"Matron," Beauchamp said. "She's as straight as they come. She will be supervising the boys tonight. There was a movie marathon starting at 7 p.m. for the boys who remain at the weekend."

"I hadn't thought of it being Friday night," Adam said. "How many boarders have stayed for the weekend?"

"Off the top of my head, around fifty," Beauchamp said. "Matron should have them all rounded up in the cinema by now. I can call her."

"No, I'll call her."

Beauchamp obliged. "I'm on my way back. Please keep me in the loop."

Adam promised that he would and ended the call, immediately putting one through to the school's main number and selecting the Matron's extension, which diverted the call to her mobile.

"Sawyer's Hill, Matron speaking," she answered in a whisper.

"Matron, DS Jackson. We need to urgently know the whereabouts of Andrew Wilson. Have you seen him tonight?"

Adam heard a door close. "Yes, he and some friends left about fifteen minutes ago. It's his weekend off. What's this about?"

"You didn't happen to see which direction they went, did you?"

"Towards the park," she said.

"Is that usual?"

"Now that you mention it, it's not. And they were on foot, detective."

"How many?"

"Three, maybe four. I'm sorry, I'm a bit distracted. I can't locate one of my charges. I'm hoping he hasn't taken off without telling anyone. His aunt was here earlier, so he may have gone with her, but I can't find any mention of an aunt in his records."

"Do you mean Samuel Rowley?" Adam said.

"Yes?" Matron sounded surprised.

"He's here with us. He's safe."

"Oh."

"Matron, several police vehicles are about to enter the school. Can you please ensure the remaining students in your care stay with you?"

"Certainly, can I ask what's going on?"

"Mr Beauchamp will fill you in."

As Adam pocketed his phone, a dark police van pulled up behind the police cars. The commander climbed from the passenger seat and approached Adam and Julian as they lifted stab vests from the boot of one of the police cars and pulled them on.

"It appears that the suspects may have left on foot through the park," Adam said. "Tony, can you take two cars to the other entrance? We'll go in the front."

Chapter 36

"I can't believe they got away in that small window of time," Kat said when they arrived at the station two hours later. They followed Adam up the stairs from the parking garage, where he signed them in with the night sergeant behind the reception desk. He then ushered them along a corridor to a small interview room. Exhausted, Sammy dropped down onto a chair at the table.

"Tony's reviewing CCTV footage as we speak," Adam said. "They must have had a vehicle waiting. We'll know soon enough. Now, Sammy, you can't repeat anything you heard or saw tonight, which means no social media. Do you understand?"

Sammy nodded and yawned.

"How old are you?"

"Sixteen."

"I will need a support person with you before I take your statement," Adam said.

"Please don't call my grandmother yet," Samuel said. "It's the middle of the night, and a call like this could kill her. Could Kat stay with me while I make my statement?" Samuel asked.

Adam looked over at Kat.

"Fine with me," she said. "I gave my statement to Eloise

earlier."

"There's a social worker from child services on their way, so once they arrive I'll get the basics from you tonight, Sammy, and we'll talk more in the morning," Adam said. "Kat can sit in if that would make you more comfortable."

Sammy nodded.

A knock on the door a short while later announced the arrival of a smiling middle-aged woman from Child Protection Services.

"Hello, Sammy," she said. "I'm Laura, I hear you've had quite a night."

Sammy nodded.

"Are you okay to give your statement or would you like to talk to me in private first?" she asked, adjusting her glasses.

"No, I'm fine, thank you," Sammy said.

Kat and Laura sat either side of Sammy with Adam opposite. Adam switched on the recorder and introduced those present.

"Sammy, can you tell us what happened at Sawyer's Hill Grammar tonight?"

"Mr Wilson and another man took us from the library and tied us up in the basement of the main building," Sammy said. "He didn't believe that Kat was my aunt and kept asking how much she knew."

He turned to Kat, who gave him an encouraging smile.

"Knew about what?" Adam asked.

"About *Zombiegamez* and what he had some of us doing, I suppose," Sammy said.

"And what exactly was that?"

"He would give us each a page with the details of around twenty credit cards, and we would create twenty new email addresses. We'd then buy several *Zombiegamez* gift cards using one credit card and one email address. We had to copy the gift card redeem code to a Google doc and delete the email account. We'd repeat this for all credit cards." Sammy hung his head. "You'll think I'm stupid, but he said that he knew the *Zombiegamez* creators and that we were doing a special testing project for them and that none of this was real."

"Not stupid, Sammy. Men like Wilson can be compelling, especially when they're in positions of power, as he was with you," Adam said.

Sammy gave a weak smile. "We were rewarded with game merchandise, gift cards and extra privileges at school."

"How many of you were doing this, and how often?" Adam asked.

"About ten of us, a couple of times a week for the last two months or so."

"Including Harry and Marshall?" Adam said.

"Yes, but they were doing other things too."

There was a knock on the door, and a staff member slipped into the room carrying a tray with three mugs of tea and a hot chocolate. Adam passed mugs to Kat and Laura before handing the hot chocolate to Sammy. He waited while Sammy took a gulp.

"What other things were they doing?"

"Harry is a genius with coding and stuff. And he can hack anything. I think Wilson had him doing other things," Sammy said. "I think maybe he was writing a programme to automate the process, so Wilson wouldn't need us."

"Actually, if I can interrupt, that makes sense because the theft from Connor's grandfather's card was instant," Kat said.

Adam nodded. "What about Marshall?"

"I think he was just doing it for kicks," Sammy said.

"When did you realise it wasn't testing?" Adam asked.

"A couple of weeks ago," Sammy said. "I questioned what we were doing and found myself on detention with all privileges revoked. And I was shut out of the finance club, ostracised."

"Why didn't you tell someone?"

"Tell who? Mr Wilson is our housemaster. He always seems really friendly with Matron and the headmaster. And I had no proof. I should have made copies of the credit card lists, but I didn't, and Mr Wilson always took all the papers away when I'd finished," Sammy said, stifling a yawn.

"Okay, that's really helpful, Sammy," Adam said. "Let's leave it there for tonight."

"What happens to me now?" Sammy said. "I'm not going back to school, especially if Mr Wilson hasn't been caught. And Granny's retirement village is two hours away."

"You can stay with me for the rest of tonight, Sammy," Kat said. "If you'd like."

Sammy's gaze swung from Kat to Adam. "Can I?"

Adam looked across the table to Laura and raised his eyebrows in question.

"I'm not sure that I will be able to find a suitable placement at this hour," Laura said, almost to herself.

"Kat has been thoroughly police vetted, since she works for us as a forensic accounting expert on occasion," Adam said.

* * *

Sara was watching through the window when a police car dropped Kat and Sammy off at Kat's flat a little while later. She rushed to the door to greet them, throwing her arms around Kat and holding her tight.

"You gave me a hell of a scare," she said.

"I gave myself a hell of a scare," Kat said, untangling from her sister-in-law. "This is Sammy."

Sammy closed the front door behind him and gave Sara a tiny wave.

"Sammy's staying here tonight," Kat said, giving Sara a meaningful stare.

"Hi, Sammy," Sara said, smiling at the boy. "Are you hungry? We have some pizza left."

Sammy nodded and followed her through the entrance hall and into the living room.

"Why don't you sit there?" Sara said, pointing to a barstool at the kitchen island.

Kat hung her coat up and engaged the three locks on her front door. Even though Adam had assured her that a police car would remain outside all night, she knew from experience that it paid to be cautious. Kat joined Sammy at the counter and helped herself to a slice of pizza.

"Glass of wine?" Sara asked.

"Yes, please," Kat and Sammy replied in unison.

Kat turned to stare at him as he burst out laughing. "Actually, could I have a glass of water instead, please?"

Sara laughed. "Coming right up," she said.

"Sammy, you can sleep in my office. There's a rollaway bed made up in there already."

He smiled at her. "Thank you. I don't know what I would have done without you tonight."

"You probably would have been watching movies," Kat said.

"True, but I wouldn't have had this adventure."

Sara handed Kat a glass of red wine and a packet of frozen peas. "You might have a black eye tomorrow," she said, peering at Kat's face.

"Ugh, I hope not."

"I can't believe that man slapped you," Sammy said. "My grandma says that men who hit women are cowards."

"Your grandma sounds like a sensible woman," Sara said.

"I guess I did start it. I hit him first," Kat said.

"Where did you learn to do that?" Sammy asked.

"A friend at my gym teaches me."

"Cool."

Kat took a gulp of her wine before pressing the cold bag to her cheekbone. She winced. Sammy helped himself to another slice of pizza.

"Where's Zelda?" Kat asked, looking around.

"You've been usurped. George has her wrapped around his little finger," Sara said. "Come and see. You too, Sammy."

They crept along the passage to Kat's bedroom, where George was tucked up on one side of the bed, snoring softly. His fair hair fell across his forehead, and his mouth was open, his lips forming a little triangle. Zelda was lying on her back, curled into his side, purring with contentment.

* * *

Kat woke the following day to giggling. Light snuck into the living room around the edges of the blinds, and it took several moments for her to remember where she was. She pushed herself upright on the sofa as the duvet fell to the floor. The door to her office was open, and she could see George sitting on the end of the rollaway bed, chatting to Sammy.

"Hey, sleepyhead," Sara said, walking into the room from the kitchen. She placed a cup of coffee on the table in front of

Kat and sat down beside her. She reached up to touch Kat's cheek. "That doesn't look too bad. You'll be able to cover it with makeup."

"Thanks, Sara," Kat said, reaching for the coffee and taking a grateful sip. "I'm sorry that your weekend has been ruined."

"It hasn't been ruined," she said. "The weeks run into one another when Carl is deployed, so it's just nice to have a change of scenery. To be honest, if George is happy, I'm happy. It doesn't matter what we do."

Another peal of laugher sounded from Sammy's room.

"Those two are getting on like a house on fire," Sara said.

"Good, because if they don't find Wilson today, Sammy might need to stay here tonight too," Kat said.

"What happened yesterday?" Sara asked. "Adam said you'd been tied up in a cellar but had managed to escape."

"Yeah, some dodgy stuff has been going on at Sammy's school. But I think we've only scratched the surface. Nothing adds up right now."

The intercom buzzed, and Kat jumped up to answer it.

"Breakfast delivery." Adam's voice cut through the crackle of the intercom.

Kat felt an unwanted smile forming as she pressed the door release. "Sara, can you let him in while I freshen up?"

Sara gave a knowing grin. "Sure."

"Stop it." Kat glared at her, but Sara just laughed.

When Kat returned to the living room ten minutes later, Adam and Sara were leaning against the counter separating the room from the kitchen, chatting like old friends. Adam straightened and ran his eyes over Kat, coming to rest on her face. His eyes narrowed.

"It's only a tiny bruise, don't go all caveman on me," Kat

said, rolling her eyes and pushing past him into the kitchen.

"And a good morning to you," Adam said. "Is she always this grumpy, first thing?" he asked Sara in a loud aside.

"Yup," Sara said.

"Noted," he said. "I brought breakfast. I figured you could make the coffee, Kat."

The kitchen counter was covered with bags and boxes from Kat's local café, containing pastries and yoghurt fruit sundaes.

Kat turned to smile at him. "Sorry, I don't mean to be prickly."

"Hello, DS Jackson."

Sammy wandered into the living room holding George's hand.

George looked up at Adam. "Hello, this is my new friend, Sammy," he said.

"Hello, George," Adam said. "How are you this morning, Sammy?"

"I'm fine, thanks," Sammy said.

"Adam's brought breakfast. Grab a plate and help yourself," Kat said. Sammy helped George up onto a barstool at the kitchen counter and sat down beside him.

"This looks amazing," he said, passing George a croissant before getting one for himself.

"Mummy, can Sammy come and see the dinosaurs with us today?" George asked.

Sara looked over at Adam, with her eyebrows raised.

"No, sorry, buddy," Adam said. "Sammy needs to help me with a case today."

Chapter 37

Adam drove Kat and Sammy to the station. The weather was overcast, and the roads were quiet early on a Saturday.

"Harry and his parents are joining us this morning at 11:30," Adam said.

Kat turned to look over her shoulder at Sammy in the back seat, whose chatter had all of a sudden ceased.

"You okay, Sammy?" she asked.

"I hope Harry isn't mad at me," he mumbled.

"I think you're the least of Harry's problems right now," Adam said. "Kat, we've finally got access to Marshall and Harry's CryptoMania accounts. Can you work your magic before we meet with them?"

"I just need a computer."

"Sammy, I'm afraid you'll need to stay at the station today until I speak to Mr Beauchamp. And, as I said last night, stay off social media."

"Yeah, okay," Sammy said. "Safest place to be, right?"

Adam signed Kat and Sammy in at the front desk. He presented them with visitor passes on lanyards before leading them through a door and along a corridor to the incident room. He set Kat and Sammy up on desks beside one another in one corner. Julian was already working at his desk. After a brief conversation with Adam, he broke away from what he was doing to log Kat into her computer with a guest login.

"I've emailed you the details of the two CryptoMania accounts," Julian said. "Adam said you'll know what to do."

Kat began typing. "I've got some files that I sent to my email account to compare the transactional data against."

"Shout if you need anything," Julian said.

"I will," Kat said, already downloading the transactions from Harry's account into a spreadsheet. "Anything more from *Zombiegamez* yet?

"No," Adam said.

"Okay, mate," Julian said, moving along to Sammy. "Would you like to watch a movie? I'll get you some headphones."

"Alright," Sammy said, looking down at his hands.

"But first, come with me. I'm going to teach you one of the most important jobs that all trainee police officers have to learn – how to make a good cup of tea."

Kat smiled as Sammy jumped up and followed Julian from the room.

Harry, Rosie and Terry arrived just before 11:30 a.m.

"Kat, Sammy," Adam called. He beckoned to them to join him in the doorway of the incident room.

Adam intercepted the Comptons in the corridor as the duty officer was showing them to an interview room.

"Good morning," he said.

"Good morning," Terry said, shaking the offered hand. "We're still waiting for our solicitor to join us."

"Hi, Rosie," Kat said. "How are you doing?"

Rosie looked surprised to see Kat, but she reached out and hugged her. "Better now that Harry's home."

Harry took the opportunity to slip behind Kat and talk to Sammy.

"Did you find it?" Harry whispered. Sammy nodded and shuffled his feet, avoiding eye contact with Harry. "And you gave it to Kat?" Sammy nodded again.

Harry turned to eyeball Kat, who looked over at the mention of her name. "I thought I told you to bring it straight to me," he hissed.

Kat was taken aback by his tone. "Was that before Wilson detained and locked us in the basement or after we escaped and met up with the police?"

Harry's mouth dropped open. "You let Wilson catch you?" he said to Sammy. "I knew I should have gone myself."

"Yeah, you should have," Sammy snarled back. "You should stop getting other people to do your dirty work."

Harry took a step closer to Sammy, who straightened to his full height but still had to tip his head back to look Harry in the eye. Harry held his stare for a long moment before turning away with a snort of disgust.

"The interview room is just here," Adam said. "I'll be with you shortly."

Harry followed his parents, but not before catching Sammy with his shoulder as he passed, knocking him off balance. Sammy's foot shot out, tapping Harry's ankle. Harry stumbled, but he spun around and shoved Sammy backwards into the wall.

"Enough." Adam stepped between them.

"Harry," Terry said.

Harry's lip curled, and he followed his parents into the room.

Adam propelled Sammy back into the incident room.

"Good for you, sticking up for yourself," Kat whispered.

Sammy beamed, rubbing his shoulder. He returned to his seat and put the headphones back on, and continued watching the movie.

"Adam," Kat said, following him to his desk. "I forgot to ask if there was anything useful on the USB stick. Harry mentioned a video?"

"There's a piece of software that our techs are analysing. It's well encrypted, so it's going to take some time. There's also a file containing a list of credit card details along with some photos, but no videos," Adam said.

"Photos?"

"Yeah, of Andrew Wilson and a woman. We haven't identified her yet."

"Can I take a quick look?" Kat asked.

"Julian, can you show Kat the photos from the USB drive?" Adam said.

"Adam?" Kat rested her hand on his arm as he turned away.

"Yeah?" He glanced down at her hand before looking up and giving her a warm smile.

"Where are Sammy's parents?"

Adam looked across the room at Sammy, engrossed in the computer, headphones covering his ears. "Dead," he said. "Car accident when Sammy was little. His grandmother brought him up, but she's unwell, which is why he's at boarding school."

Kat sighed. "Poor kid."

Julian brought four photos up on his screen. "Here, Kat, the photos appear to have been taken on a phone at night, so the quality isn't great," he said.

The first two photos showed a man and a woman who appeared to be kissing, standing beside a car. In the third and fourth photos, they were standing further apart, talking. The man was Andrew Wilson, and the woman with long dark hair tumbling over her shoulders wore a pale coloured coat.

Kat's lips parted, and she leaned in for a closer look. She turned to Adam. "I know who that is."

"Who?"

"That's Deborah Sharp. She's one of my clients, the founder of the Digital Kids charity."

"Interesting," Adam said, stroking his chin. "I wonder how they know one another?"

"It could be innocent," Julian said. "She runs a computer charity for kids, and he's a school teacher. They could be working together."

"Mmm."

"Adam, with everything that's happened, I haven't had a chance to fill you in on Connor's investigation. And seeing that," Kat pointed at the images on Julian's screen. "I think it's relevant, at least some of it."

"Okay," Adam said, leaning back against an adjacent desk. Julian turned in his seat to listen.

"The night Connor was drugged, he left me a message saying that he'd found the link and cracked it. Connor's method of investigative journalism is to look for patterns, so I assumed he was referring to the ransomware crimes he'd been investigating. I took a look at all the UK firms who'd reported a malware attack in the last year to see if they had anything in common."

"And do they?"

"Have you heard of something called the Future Sustainable Business Initiative?" Adam shook his head. "It's a government sustainability programme which supports locally owned and operated businesses. Many of the companies on the ransomware attack list had been visited sometime in the previous few months by a member of the committee promoting the scheme."

"A coincidence, perhaps?" Adam said.

"I thought you didn't believe in those?" Kat said.

"I don't."

"Good, 'cos that's not the only coincidence," Kat said. "The committee is chaired by the Honourable Jeremy Sharp, Deborah Sharp's soon to be ex-husband."

Chapter 38

Ali Singh had joined his clients on the far side of the desk when Kat and Adam entered the interview room. He appeared to be a little flustered and was shuffling papers while talking in a low voice with Harry. He peered over the top of his glasses when Adam spoke.

"Thanks for coming in again today," Adam said. "We now have a lot more information on what's been going on at Sawyer's Hill Grammar, Harry."

"I wouldn't believe everything that Sammy tells you. He knows nothing," Harry interrupted.

"Harry," Rosie said, sounding shocked at Harry's rudeness.

"Interestingly, everything that Sammy has told us, we've been able to confirm with independent enquiries," Adam said. "We know that Wilson had a group of students buying *Zombiegamez* tokens and gift cards using stolen credit cards and single-use email addresses."

Rosie gasped.

"The students thought they were conducting testing for *Zombiegamez* and being rewarded with gift cards, wild card entries to e-game tournaments and *Zombiegamez* merchandise. We believe Wilson was selling the tokens at a discount via chatrooms and forums. So, in essence what was really happening was that the boys were assisting him to launder the stolen funds."

"As you said, we thought we were doing testing for the game manufacturers," Harry said.

"Maybe initially, but then you and Marshall worked out what was going on and decided to set up for yourselves. Am I correct?" Harry didn't reply. He started to shake his head from side to side. "The problem for you was obtaining enough credit card details until you landed on a rich source of unsecured credit cards. Your grandmother is taking a Senior Internet 101 class at her retirement village. So you targeted some of the most vulnerable people in society – the elderly."

"No," Rosie said, her hands pressed to her face.

"You searched for a list of villages offering similar classes and then hacked the education bodies providing the training to get the email addresses of the participants," Adam said.

"No, that was Wilson. He told us that it was just testing." Harry's voice rose.

"Then it was a simple case of sending an email to one or more email addresses purporting to be from someone they regularly received emails from. But there was a virus embedded either in a meme or a photo attachment which, once opened, would infect the device," Adam continued.

"Which is exactly what happened to Connor's grandfather," Kat said.

"Harry, you knew from talking to your grandmother that sending emails was something that the class taught. The residents usually practised by sending emails to one another. The virus lets you into the person's bank account the next time they logged in on that device and used an algorithm to harvest the credit card details. Initially, you employed

Wilson's approach and bought *Zombiegamez* gift cards and sold them at a discount, but then you got greedy and started making payments to various crypto exchanges using the credit cards, where the recipients, you and Marshall, were untraceable."

"No," Harry said. "You've got it all wrong."

"Have we, though?" Kat said. "We've tied the timing of crypto purchases made on several credit cards stolen from a handful of retirement villages to deposits into yours and Marshall's CryptoMania accounts. The timing of other credit card transactions ties in with deposits of unusual amounts from offshore exchanges, into the bank accounts of your various companies."

"We were trading some of the more obscure coins," Harry said. "I don't know anything about retirement villages. You have to believe me. If there are payments from stolen credit cards into my account, then Wilson must have done it to set me up."

"Can you show me the transactional data from your account at the exchange?" Kat asked. "To prove you were trading?"

"Yeah, I can."

"The USB drive, that Kat retrieved for you, contained a file of stolen credit card details, which haven't been used yet. We've contacted the banks concerned and compiled a list of owners, who all happen to be from a care home in Brighton," Adam said.

Harry sat back in his chair. "I told you, Wilson gave us those credit card details. That's the evidence that we were compiling against him."

Adam wasn't convinced. "Did Wilson discover that you were ripping off his scheme? Was he concerned that *Zombie-*

gamez would discover the scam if too many people were doing it and shut down his lucrative side hustle? What happened when he asked you to stop?"

Harry was silent, his eyes darting from Kat to Adam before he finally spoke. He seemed to be waging an internal battle.

"Wilson is working for these other people. He wasn't the big criminal player that he had us believe," he said. "We thought it was just him, but it turns out he's part of an organisation which specialises in different sorts of cybercrime. By the time we realised this, we'd started compiling evidence against what we had thought was his scam, and they found out. I think that's why Marshy's dead and why they trashed our house the other day."

Terry made an incoherent noise. Kat glanced at him. He looked as though he was about to be sick. Rosie had tears tracking down her cheeks.

"Do you know who Wilson was working with?" Adam said.

Harry shook his head. "That's what I think Marshy was trying to find out the night he died."

There was silence for a long moment, broken only by the scratch of Singh's pen on his legal pad.

"Now, what can you tell me about the photos on the USB stick?" Adam laid the four photos on the table in front of Harry.

"Marshy and I slipped out of school for a smoke one evening about six weeks ago. We saw two people sitting in Wilson's car on the road leading into the park; Wilson and a woman. They were making out like crazy, so we tried to see who she was. When they finally got out of the car, Marshy recognised her as someone who'd attended functions with his parents. He took a few photos before we slipped back into school, where we searched online for photos of his father and found her in several of them. She's the wife of an MP, going through a bitter divorce, if you believe social media."

"So you tried to blackmail her with the photos?" Adam said.

Harry hung his head. "It was Marshy's idea, and she paid well too, in crypto. But then Marshy was killed, and she stopped paying. I figured that they must have worked out that it was us, so I went into hiding. I was scared that they'd kill me too."

"Who was Marshall really going to meet the evening he died?" Adam asked.

"I don't know; that's the truth," Harry said. "He just told me to trust him. That he was off to get us a better paying gig."

"I figured that Wilson must have killed him and that I would be next. So I remotely uploaded some pornographic images that I found on the darknet to Wilson's computer to discredit him. I thought it would help me to come out of hiding and get protection. The thing is, I never wanted to do any of this; Wilson and Marshy manipulated me, and before I knew it, I was in too deep to get out."

Adam raised his eyebrows at Harry's last comment.

"Can I have some time alone with my client?" Singh said.

"Sure," Adam said. He and Kat rose to leave the room.

"Son, I think we need to have a long overdue talk," Kat heard Terry say as she reached the door.

"Not now, Dad," Harry said.

"Now." Terry's voice rose. "You are facing multiple charges. We need to work out what we're going to do and how you are going to repay all of the money you stole."

"Haven't you been listening? I didn't steal those old people's money." Harry's voice rose. "I've been set up."

Kat turned to look at Harry and his parents.

Harry's lip curled, and he gave his father a look of disdain. "I'm not going to prison if that's what you're thinking. This is all on Wilson."

Terry sighed. "No, Harry, it's time to come clean."

Harry stuck out his bottom lip and spoke in a childlike voice. "But, Daddy, I was so naïve that I believed Mr Wilson when he said we were doing testing work for *Zombiegamez*. And I was so in awe of Marshall and his money that I went along with him when he suggested we go out on our own so that he would continue to be my friend."

"But that's not true," Terry said.

"Says who?" Harry's voice turned defiant. "You know nothing. In fact, if it wasn't for you and your pathetic life, I wouldn't have needed to get involved with these people. You're the loser here, not me."

"Harry," Rosie said, shocked.

Kat pulled the door closed and followed Adam back along the corridor to the incident room.

* * *

Singh opened the door of the interview room and signalled to the duty officer. "We're ready to talk to DS Jackson," he said.

Adam and Kat joined them in the room once again.

"Harry is willing to co-operate with your investigation in exchange for some leniency in any charges against him," Singh began.

"I can't make any promises, but I will speak to the Crown Prosecutor," Adam said.

Singh looked to Harry, who shrugged.

"So, where do we find Wilson?" Adam said.

"I think the person you want to find is Deborah Sharp," Harry said. "I think she is involved in more than just a relationship with Wilson."

Kat sat forward and watched Harry. "Why do you say that?"

He shrugged. "Just a feeling," he said. "She seemed to have ready access to that crypto to pay to Marshy."

Kat flicked through her notes. "That would be the four Ethereum payments into his CryptoMania account each week over the last month?"

"Yeah," Harry said.

There was a knock on the door of the meeting room, and Tony stuck his head in. "Boss?"

Adam stood. "Interview paused at 1:05 p.m., DS Jackson leaving the room." He pressed pause on the recording. "Excuse me for a moment," he said before joining Tony in the corridor and closing the door.

"No sign of Wilson or his companions coming or going from Deborah Sharp's home," Tony said.

"And Wilson hasn't returned to the school?"

"No. We have an alert out on the car we saw on CCTV that picked them up from the edge of the park near the school last night, but no hits yet."

"Thanks," Adam said. He thought for a moment before returning to the interview room and restarting the recording.

"I need more than your hunch to bring Mrs Sharp in for questioning," he said. "We have no proof that the payments are from her or that she is guilty of anything."

Harry considered this for a moment. "You asked what Wilson had Marshy and me doing for him that differed from the other kids?" Adam remained silent. "Wilson had us selling Bitcoin and buying several other cryptocurrencies, including privacy coins like Monero. We initially thought we were learning how to trade, but when he started paying us a tiny fraction of a Bitcoin for our work, we realised that there must be more to it."

"Privacy coins, Kat?" Adam asked.

"They're just like other cryptocurrencies, except they have an additional layer of cryptography, which allows for private transactions hiding a user's identity. There's huge pressure on many exchanges not to host these types of coins," Kat explained.

"Just how much of a tiny fraction of a Bitcoin, Harry?" Adam asked. "Give me a rough value in pounds?"

"It varied," Harry said. "Between five hundred and a thousand."

"And that was the basis of your cryptocurrency trading?" Kat said.

Harry squirmed in his seat. "Not all of it."

"Why didn't you talk to an adult about your concerns?" Terry said.

Harry gave him a withering look. "No one would have believed us. Marshy and I hacked Wilson's email to see if we could find out exactly what he was up to. We, of course, found several notes from Deborah Sharp, so we used those to hop into her email and computer. We quickly realised that she has a complex network with lots of layers of security. We thought this seemed odd for a woman who ran a charity, so I began working my way through the various levels. It took several weeks as I had to go carefully and not trigger any alerts that she'd been hacked."

"And what did you find?" Adam asked.

"A piece of off-the-shelf malware," Harry said, sitting back and looking pleased with himself. "The sort that encrypts files and sends a ransom demand for a certain amount of Bitcoin. We knew then exactly what Wilson had us doing – we'd been unwittingly helping him to launder the proceeds of those ransoms."

Rosie made a garbled sound.

"It's called chain-hopping or tumbling. It's where the initial ransom payment is quickly obfuscated to avoid detection and tracking, by breaking it into smaller pieces and exchanging it for a number of other crypto-assets using multiple exchanges," Kat said.

"And what did you do once you'd discovered this piece of software?" Adam asked.

Harry grinned. "We stole it."

"So that's what got Marshall killed," Adam said.

Harry's grin vanished. "I think so. I stole it just because I could, but he wanted to ransom it. Ransom the ransomware, he said. She's got plenty of money and will pay to get it back. We argued about it the night he died, and he stormed off. I think he went to meet with her."

"Deborah Sharp? How did he get in touch with her?"

Harry shrugged.

Adam made a note to check the missing number from Marshall's noticeboard again.

"Perhaps I could arrange to meet her? Get her to admit to killing Marshy or to using malware?" Harry said.

"I've met Deborah Sharp," Kat said. "She's tiny. She doesn't strike me as the sort of person to get the better of a six-foot teenage boy."

"Yeah, but she has plenty of money to hire someone to do her dirty work. And she won't want those photos or the evidence of having malware coming out before her divorce is settled. Isn't she playing the betrayed wife?" Harry said. "I could offer to delete the photos in front of her."

"You're very well informed."

"What can I say? Marshy did his homework. How do you think he knew how much she'd pay to keep the photos off social media? I could get her to talk, I know I could."

Adam considered this. "Let me talk to the DCI."

"I don't like the idea of my son being used as bait to catch someone who may already have killed," Terry said.

Chapter 39

The café was situated on the ground floor of the Forsyth building, in a bright and airy atrium. White tables and chairs were scattered around the space, but most were empty at 9:30 a.m. on a Monday. A businessman sat alone reading a newspaper, and a young woman stood leaning against a tall table, messaging on her phone. A pair of wide winding staircases descended from the first floor on either side of the foyer.

All dressed casually, Eloise, Julian, and Tony entered through the main automatic glass doors and wandered up to the counter to order coffee from the café's barista. They took a table at one side of the café and started chatting about the weekend's football results.

"Comms check," Adam said.

They each nodded once as their earpieces registered the instruction. On the opposite side of the atrium, two older gentlemen engrossed in a chess game also gave a single nod each.

"I wish you'd have let me go in there too," Kat said, sitting on a stool between Adam and a surveillance specialist in the back of a dark coloured van with no rear windows. The van's interior had been stripped and replaced with electronic surveillance screens on a bench along one side. They were parked across the street, watching the café on a screen and listening to the conversations through headphones.

"No, if we are to believe Harry, Andrew Wilson and Deborah Sharp are working together. Either of them would recognise you. Besides, now that we've involved the National Crime Agency, we're lucky that they're letting us run this little operation. I'm not sure that would stretch to allowing you to participate any more than this."

Two men in navy blue overalls carrying white hard hats walked in moments later and ordered drinks and food to go before taking a table near the door. Kat pointed at them on the screen.

"A little too obvious, but then again, I'm not sure how sophisticated these people really are," Adam said.

They watched as a waiter delivered takeout coffees to the men, who stood up and left the building.

"You were right," Kat said.

"Maybe, maybe not," Adam said. "They may have been scouts."

"Do you believe Harry?" she asked.

"No, not entirely," Adam said. "He keeps amending his story, although I think we're getting closer to the truth. I can't help but wonder if there's something he's holding back. He sat with our forensic technology team yesterday afternoon and showed them how he hacked Deborah Sharp's computer network. They replicated what he'd done, and it was clean. There was nothing unusual, so either Harry made it up, or she's had time to remove the layers of encryption and any incriminating evidence."

"What about the malware he stole?"

"Yeah, that's what was hidden in a heavily secured directory on the USB stick that you recovered," Adam said. "The NCA techs are now looking into it. They should be able to come up with a way to break it, which could help any firms exposed to that particularly nasty little virus in the future."

A group of women dressed in active wear carrying rolled-up yoga mats arrived next. They sat chatting in front of the counter as several people dressed in business suits came and went, collecting takeaway drinks and food.

As planned, the side door of the café opened fifteen minutes later, and two uniformed officers strolled into the atrium. They greeted the waitress and wandered across the floor, exiting through a side door into a courtyard. They stood with their backs to the door as though enjoying the sunshine. Back in the café, the businessman put down the newspaper and hurried to a different exit. He passed by the tall table where the woman was busy texting and murmured something to her as he passed.

"Those two?" Kat was surprised.

"Watch." Adam pointed to a screen showing the side of the building, where a small garden hid the road from view. "The presence of uniforms always filters out the plants."

The man left the building by the side door and was detained by a police officer. Eloise jumped up and crossed the room, surprising the woman by snatching the phone from her hand.

"If you would be so kind as to come with me," Eloise said, flashing her warrant card.

The woman appeared flabbergasted for a moment before she complied and allowed herself to be escorted from the premises.

Kat looked back at the screen showing the main entrance

to the building as Harry strolled in. He purchased a water bottle at the counter and sat by the window near Julian and Tony. They ignored him and continued their conversation. Harry unscrewed the water and took a sip, slopping a little onto the table. He wiped his mouth with the back of his hand.

"Poor kid is nervous," Kat murmured.

"Poor kid? Really?" Adam said.

"Yeah, he's completely out of his depth."

"Here she comes," Adam said.

They watched the screen as a car pulled up on the forecourt, and an elegant and composed Deborah Sharp alighted from the back seat and strode into the atrium. She was dressed in a grey suit with a narrow pencil skirt and high stiletto heels. She stalked across the foyer straight to Harry's table and sat with her back to Tony and Julian.

"I'm so pleased that you called. You are either very brave or very foolish," Deborah said. "Do you know who I am?"

"Yes." Harry's voice was raspy. He cleared his throat. "Marshy recognised you with Mr Wilson."

A buzzing sound cut across the feed to the van outside, scrambling the signal so that the conversation was unintelligible, just fragments of words here and there. Adam and Kat leaned closer to the screen, trying to make out the conversation.

"But you weren't content to just blackmail us, were you?" Deborah whispered. "I know it was you who hacked my network."

"So I have your attention? You know I'm good. I could be a real asset to your organisation," Harry said.

Deborah looked around and registered Julian and Tony, trying to appear as though they weren't eavesdropping. She sat back and crossed her arms.

"Digital Kids? Delivering and setting up computers for underprivileged children?" Deborah said, louder this time. "It would be volunteer work."

"No," said Harry. "Not that, your other activity, instigating ransomware attacks on unsuspecting businesses."

Deborah's eyes turned hard, and she put a hand to her chest, feigning shock.

"I know what you do and how you distance yourself," Harry said. "You provide the software and use a host of contractors to carry out the attacks so that if any get caught, nothing comes back to you."

Deborah smoothed her hair, and her eyes widened. "I don't know what you're talking about."

"I'm looking for a job." Harry reached into his ear, removed the device Adam had placed there earlier and dropped it into his water glass.

The feed from Harry's earpiece to the van completely cut out, and Kat watched the screen as Julian turned to look over at Harry.

"What's he doing?" Kat asked.

"I don't know," Adam said. "I hope the other two can hear what he's up to."

Seconds later, the building's fire alarm rang out with an ear-splitting wail, and doors opened on either side of the café. Two men wearing hi-vis vests entered, and one called, "Evacuate now, please, quickly and orderly."

"Quick, Harry, this way with me." One of the yoga class women seated in front of the counter rushed over and grabbed Harry's arm, leading him towards a door at the rear of the atrium.

Adam swore as their view was obscured by people from the offices upstairs flooding into the foyer via the two staircases.

"The woman who grabbed Harry was one of yours, right?" Kat asked.

"Tony, Julian, can you hear me? Get after Harry," Adam spoke into his headset.

He cursed again. "They can't hear me. Our feed is being blocked. Come on, we have to find him, or we'll have another dead teenager on our hands."

Chapter 40

"Adam, wait, I know how to find him," Kat said, jumping down from the back of the van and running to catch up with Adam as he jogged across the forecourt to the café. Tony came running through the door to meet them.

"He's gone, sarge. The door at the rear leads down into the underground carpark, which we knew. What we didn't know was that there's another concealed door that leads to the parking garage of the next building."

"Where's Deborah Sharp?" Adam asked.

"She's over there, with the people we evacuated from the building after the fire alarm," Tony said. "I don't know what Harry was up to, but it sounded like he was asking her for a job."

Adam shook his head. "I knew I shouldn't have trusted him. Don't let her go anywhere. I will need to speak to her."

"Does Harry have his phone on him?" Tony asked. "Can we ping it?"

Adam shook his head.

"Adam," Kat repeated. "I can help."

Adam turned to her. "What do you mean?"

"Don't be mad, but I have a car finding tile, similar to the one that Wilson used on Sammy, in my wallet because I'm always losing it. I slipped it into Harry's pocket when you were helping him with his earpiece earlier."

"You mean…" Adam began.

"Yeah." Kat tapped an app on her phone, which opened with the image of a street map. "It looks like it's out of Bluetooth range, but the last place it registered is in the next block heading west."

"If it's out of range, how's that going to help us?" Tony said.

"We could try the community find function," Kat said, biting her lip as she followed the menu prompts. "If I select 'lost' on the app, then, in theory, everyone running the app will automatically and anonymously start scanning for my lost tile. If one of them comes within range, it will send me a mess—"

Kat's phone chimed.

"That was quick," Tony said, leaning over to look at the screen. "Nice one, Kat."

A blue dot flashed on Millbank.

"Come on," Adam said, turning and jogging back to the van, with Kat and Tony on his heels. He spoke to the driver while Tony relayed the situation on his phone.

They climbed into the van, which executed a U-turn and drove through the back streets and down onto Grosvenor Road.

"Has it moved, Kat?" Adam asked.

"Only a little. It looks to have stopped four blocks ahead."

The van continued through the next set of traffic lights.

"It's moving again," she said.

"Someone cut across our audio feed," Adam explained to Tony.

"I wondered," Tony said. "Our earpieces went silent."

"Oh no, I've lost it," Kat said.

"Let me see," Adam leaned across to look at her phone. The cursor was rotating, searching for a new signal.

"Maybe they moved out of range of your original contact," Tony said.

Kat studied the screen, willing it to reconnect. "Here we go, they've turned off. Go right at the next corner, then left."

"Is there any way of finding out the type of vehicle we're pursuing?" Adam asked.

Kat shook her head.

"It's dropped again. We can't lose him. I'll never be able to face Rosie," she said.

They all watched Kat's phone for a moment before Tony pointed at the screen.

"There, they're down on Millbank again," Tony said. "They're taking a circuitous route to wherever they're taking him."

"It's stopped," Kat said.

"They could be stuck at traffic lights, like us."

"True," she said. "Oh, it's gone again." She watched the screen for a full minute before looking up and giving Adam a desperate look. "I don't know what's happened. It must be out of range."

"Maybe something's blocking it. Let's go to the last known location."

"Okay, turn right, here," Kat called. "And stop around the corner."

When the van pulled over, they all got out.

"Oh, this is strange," Kat said, reading the name on the building they'd parked across from.

"What?"

"I know this address," she said.

"Yeah, it's one of the largest private residential complexes in London," Tony said.

"No, I've come across this recently. Perhaps we were wrong about Deborah? This is where her husband has a pied-à-terre, one that he forgot to mention on his asset disclosure for their divorce."

"What's the flat number?"

Kat closed her eyes and tried to visualise the documentation. "I can't remember, sorry."

"Tony, call Julian and have him ask Deborah the number of her husband's flat."

While they waited for Tony to speak to Julian, they watched a silver Audi drive up the ramp from the underground parking garage and merge with the traffic.

"I imagine a flat in there wouldn't be cheap," Adam said.

"Look, it's moving again," Kat said. "Away from us."

Adam narrowed his eyes and watched the Audi turn a corner and disappear from view. He looked at the screen of Kat's phone.

"Okay, if we borrow your phone, Kat?" he asked.

"Sure," she said, handing it to Adam, who leaned into the van and spoke with the driver. The van pulled away as Tony ended his call.

"It's number 536," Tony said, pocketing his phone.

"Where are they going?" Kat asked.

"They're following your tile while we check out the flat," Adam said.

They entered the red brick complex through a set of double glass doors from the side street. The foyer was well-lit and spacious, with comfortable cream sofas and side tables arranged in groups. Adam crossed the floor to the reception desk while Kat and Tony hung back and studied a floor plan on the wall beside the lift.

"Looks like we need to head towards the rear and take a lift to the fifth floor from there," Tony said, pointing at the map.

Adam returned from reception with a key card, and they hurried down a long carpeted corridor to the second set of lifts. The lift came and they rushed inside. Adam swiped the access card that he'd been given, and the elevator car rose.

"Okay, you're going to wait by the lift while we enter the apartment," Adam said.

"But—" Kat began.

"No buts."

The doors opened onto a corridor with cream walls, soft pale blue carpet and framed black and white images of iconic London scenes on the walls. Kat perched on the edge of an armchair in an alcove by the lift. She watched as Adam and Tony moved on silent feet along the passage. When they reached the door of Sharp's flat, they paused, listening for a long moment, before Kat saw Adam nod once to Tony and place the access card against the reader on the door.

"Police," Adam called as they entered. The sounds of a scuffle ensued, and Kat leapt to her feet. She heard Tony's voice.

"Andrew Wilson, I presume, so this is where you've been hiding."

Adam stuck his head out into the corridor and called to her.

"Kat, Harry's here."

Kat began walking towards him when the lift chimed behind her. She turned as a heavy-set man with a shaved head stepped into the corridor carrying a stack of takeaway food containers. They recognised each other at the exact same moment.

"What the...?" the man said as Kat broke into a run, but she wasn't quick enough. The man tossed the takeout to the ground and grabbed her, dragging her back towards the lift.

Chapter 41

Adam started along the carpeted passageway towards them, holding out his hands as though trying to placate a wild animal.

"Stop," the man said. "Or I snap her neck."

Adam slowed.

The man had his arm across Kat's chest and one hand on the side of her head. Kat stamped down hard on the man's foot and slammed her elbow back into his abdomen. The man grunted and loosened his hold on her. Kat spun and ducked out of his reach, aiming a knee to his groin. The man anticipated her move and side-stepped, pulling her against him once more before she could regain her balance.

"Kat," Adam shouted.

"Get back," the man growled at Adam. "I mean it."

Adam hesitated for a moment before he continued advancing towards them, placing one foot in front of the other as though he was walking in slow motion. The man frog-marched Kat backwards to the lift and punched the call button. Seconds later, the doors sprang open, and he dragged Kat into the lift with him.

Adam bolted for the stairs, taking the steps two at a time. He burst into the hallway on the next floor to see the lift continuing to descend. He cursed and re-entered the stairwell and ran down another flight. This time, when he entered the corridor, the lift doors were closing. He stuck his foot between them, forcing them to bounce open again, but the lift was empty. He heard a door close further along the passage. He raced towards it, reading the words 'Gym' on the door before he entered an empty reception area. Through a glass wall ahead of him he saw a four-lane indoor swimming pool. The pool was unoccupied, but halfway down one side, he saw Kat resisting her captor, struggling as he tried to hurry her along. Adam slipped through the door into the wet area, and a wave of warm, humid, chlorine heavy air hit him.

The man turned and locked eyes with him, pulling Kat in front of him like a shield.

"I thought I told you to…" he began.

Kat let her head fall forward for a moment before slamming it backwards at speed.

"Arrgh," the man cried, letting her go as his hands flew to his face.

Kat's kick landed this time, and the man stumbled backwards, teetering for a moment on the edge of the pool before falling and hitting the water with a loud slap. The water splashed up, drenching Kat from head to toe. Adam rushed to her side as the man surfaced, spluttering and cursing.

"There you go, I've isolated him. I'll leave it to you to arrest him," Kat said, shaking the water off.

Adam shook his head at her, bemused. "You're unbelievable. Does nothing intimidate you?"

The door that Adam had just come through crashed open, and four police officers rushed into the swimming pool area.

The man moved to the centre of the pool. "You don't think

I'm going to make this easy do you?" he jeered.

A look of resignation crossed the two youngest officers' faces, and they began removing their belts, boots, and jackets. They jumped in either side of the man, who swung his fist, missing the first officer, who dived below the surface and grabbed the man's ankles, tipping him off balance. After a minute of thrashing, he was in handcuffs, being hauled up the steps at the far end of the pool.

"That was a well-placed kick," Adam murmured. "Are you okay?"

Kat nodded.

"Take him up to the fifth floor," he instructed the two dry officers.

Adam slung his arm around Kat's shoulders and started to follow them from the pool area.

"Ew, you're all wet," he said.

Kat hugged him, laughing. "A bit of water never hurt anyone, Adam."

"I'm glad you can still laugh after that," he said, stopping and turning to her, becoming serious. "I'm sorry, Kat, I shouldn't have brought you along."

"Stop it," she said. "You know I can look after myself."

"Mmm, so you keep telling me."

Tony met them at the lift, amusement dancing in his eyes at their wet captive and Kat's bedraggled state. The doors of several other fifth-floor apartments were open, and curious residents had poked their heads out to see what the disturbance was.

"You got something to say, Tony?" Kat asked, trying to hide a grin.

"No, ma'am," he said, looking beyond them to the onlookers

gathering in the hallway. "Police," he called, flashing his warrant card. "Please wait inside your apartments until we give you the all-clear."

The doors slammed shut, and they followed their prisoner along the passage to Flat 536, where Wilson was seated, handcuffed to a chair at a two-seater kitchen table. The flat was small but well-proportioned with expensive furnishings. The kitchen area opened onto a sumptuous lounge with expansive windows overlooking a grassed courtyard with a tennis court and bowling green.

Kat surveyed the room. There were no personal touches anywhere to give any indication of the personality of the occupant. In fact, it was more like a hotel suite than someone's home. Opposite Wilson, rubbing his wrists, sat Harry Compton, with severed blue cable ties on the table in front of him. He glared at Wilson with a barely concealed look of hatred in his eyes.

"Harry, can we have the chair, please," Adam asked.

Harry stood and scooted out of the police officer's way. Adam directed their captive to the chair and reattached the handcuffs around the armrests. Water dripped from the man's clothes and pooled on the floor.

Kat leaned against the door jamb with a pool towel draped around her shoulders. She felt an ache in the back of her head where it had connected with the man's nose. Her hair felt sticky, and when she put her hand to it, it came away bloody.

"You've opened up that cut from the other night," Adam said, coming alongside and inspecting the injury.

Kat nodded. "And it was this man who gave me the original injury."

"You mean?"

"Yeah, this is the man who tried to kill Connor."

"Name?" Adam asked, looking across at the man.

The man sneered in reply. Adam glared until the man looked away.

"I've heard of keeping tabs on your students, but I'm sure you'll agree, kidnapping is a little extreme," Adam said, turning his attention to Wilson. "Care to explain?"

The man with the shaved head shook it at Wilson.

"Ah, come on, Anton, you know she'll throw you under the bus," Wilson said.

"Who?" Adam said.

"Deborah Sharp," Wilson said. "This was all her idea, to stop Harry exposing her cyber schemes."

"At this stage, it's just her word against yours," Adam said. "She says that Harry contacted her about a job at Digital Kids."

In the corner, Harry nodded.

"There are emails between us," Wilson said.

"There are," Adam agreed. "Discussing you helping with her charity work."

"No, there's more than that," Wilson said. "You can check my email and hers."

"We have," Tony said. "I'm not sure who you think you've been emailing with, but it's not Deborah Sharp."

"But it was her that arranged to have Marshall beaten as a warning to the lads to stop interfering. She was furious when she found out that the two boys were stealing from us," Wilson said.

"What do you mean?" Adam said.

"I discovered that Harry and Marshall were taking a small portion of every Bitcoin that passed through their accounts and passing it off as price variance. Deborah wanted to teach them a lesson."

"That's a lie; you gave them to us for helping launder your money for you," Harry said.

"You've told so many lies that no one believes anything you say anymore, Harry," Wilson's voice rose, and he looked wildly from one face to another. "You." He pointed at Kat. "She told me to detain you and Samuel."

There were voices in the corridor, and seconds later, Eloise entered the flat with both Deborah and Jeremy Sharp. Two uniformed police officers remained standing outside the door.

"Now, look here," Jeremy Sharp said. "What's the meaning of this? I've been called from an important select committee hearing."

"Jeremy Sharp?" Adam said. "DS Adam Jackson, DC Tony Dupont and Kat Munro. This is your flat?"

Jeremy nodded and adjusted the cuffs of his pale pink double cuff shirt beneath his navy-blue suit. He bore a passing resemblance to George Clooney, with his silver hair parted and slicked back.

"Do you know these men?"

Jeremy peered at the two men. "Never seen them before in my life."

"Mrs Sharp?"

Deborah looked at the men handcuffed at the table with a puzzled expression.

"Andrew?" she said.

Wilson narrowed his eyes at her and gave a slow shake of his head.

"Andrew Wilson and I are old friends from university. But I don't understand what he's doing here," she said, looping her hand through her husband's arm.

"Debs, come on," Wilson said.

"We met up recently to discuss a plan for expanding my school technology outreach work. Part of the social plan is to get the more elite schools helping those less well funded, and when I realised that Andrew was working at Sawyer's Hill Grammar, I got in touch."

Wilson's mouth fell open. "Liar."

"Mrs Sharp, were you being blackmailed?" Adam asked.

"Blackmailed?" Deborah gave a short laugh. "Who would want to blackmail me?"

"Someone who saw you kissing Mr Wilson."

Deborah scoffed. "I didn't kiss Andrew. Well, maybe as a greeting, but that would be all."

"So you haven't been paying off two of Wilson's students with cryptocurrency to keep compromising photos out of the media?"

Deborah laughed again. "I wouldn't even know where to begin. That sounds like something Andrew would know more about than me."

"So we would find nothing like that in your finances," Adam said.

Deborah shook her head, her eyes wide. "You're welcome to check, although I believe that she may have already done that as part of our divorce proceedings." She turned her cool gaze to Kat, acknowledging her presence for the first time. She ran her eyes over Kat's dishevelled appearance and pursed her lips.

Kat shook her head. "No, we were working for you, so we just analysed Mr Sharp's finances."

"It doesn't matter now, anyway," Jeremy said, patting the hand that Deborah had tucked through his arm. "We've decided to give our marriage another go."

Deborah beamed at him and snuggled closer. "So we won't be needing you any longer," she said to Kat.

"Why did you meet with Harry earlier today?" Adam asked.

"I thought he wanted to help with Digital Kids," Deborah said. "As I said, I thought Andrew was getting some of his students involved."

"And Harry just happened to be kidnapped under your nose?"

Deborah looked confused. "I rushed outside when I heard the fire alarm. I thought Harry was right behind me."

Across the room, Wilson snorted. "You conniving little cow," he said. "I have evidence that I was working with you and that we are more than just old friends."

"Andrew, we were only working on my charity," she said before gasping. "I hope you haven't used Digital Kids for nefarious purposes behind my back?" She stabbed an accusatory finger in Wilson's direction.

Wilson gave a bitter laugh. "Oh, you're good. But you will get yours."

Voices in the hallway indicated that further backup had arrived, and soon the tiny flat was filled with police officers.

Wilson and Anton were read their rights.

"Ask her about Snapp Software," Wilson called as he was led away.

Adam and Kat left the building with Harry. The surveillance van had returned and was parked behind an ambulance. Julian was leaning against the van, enjoying the sunshine that had broken through the clouds and chatting with the driver through the open passenger window.

"Hey, it looks like I missed all the fun," he said as they

approached. His gaze moved to Kat, and he pushed himself upright. "What happened to you?"

"She helped capture one of our suspects by kicking him into a swimming pool," Adam said.

Julian bumped knuckles with Kat. "Sweet."

"Did you follow the tile tracer?" Adam asked the van's driver.

"Yeah, we stopped and searched a silver Audi three blocks from here and found it on the floor. The woman driving admits to delivering Harry Compton to a man in the underground garage of this building."

"Good work," Adam said.

An ambulance officer reapplied steri-strips to the cut on the back of Kat's head and gave her some painkillers. He confirmed that Harry was no worse for his adventure.

"Are you okay?" Kat asked Harry as a police car drove them back to the station.

"Yeah," he said. "What's going to happen now?"

"That depends on how much you help us," Adam said. "Why did you remove your earpiece in the café?"

"You heard her; she was on to us," Harry said.

"Actually, we didn't hear anything," Kat said. "The sound feed was comprised."

Relief crossed Harry's face. "So you didn't hear anything I said?"

"We didn't, but the two officers at the next table did."

Harry's hopeful expression faded. "I was just trying to get her to trust me."

"Trust," Adam said. "I'm afraid that you haven't done very much that's made you trustworthy."

"Look, I can help you break Wilson's operation apart in

return for getting any charges against me dropped," Harry said.

"Harry, I don't really think you're in a position to bargain with me. You may have successfully traded cryptocurrency, but your source of funds was from your laundering services and blackmail receipts, all of which are highly illegal, last time I checked."

Chapter 42

Kat stopped by the reception desk in the spacious foyer of the gym after her shower. The lobby was busy with a changeover of classes, as some people were leaving, their faces glowing from exertion, and others arriving for their evening workout.

"When am I next rostered on to teach?" Kat asked the fit instructor clad in lycra, staffing the desk.

"Thursday at 7 p.m.," the young woman replied, looking at the schedule taped to the desk. "Oh, and Tommy over there wanted to talk to you." She indicated with a flick of her head towards the seating area where Tommy was reclining, flicking through his phone.

"Thanks," Kat said. "See you later in the week."

She hoisted her gym bag on her shoulder and approached the sofas.

"Hi, Tommy," she said, dropping down onto the seat next to him.

"Oh, hey, Kat," he said, putting his phone away and looking up at her. His cheeks were flushed, and his eyes bright. "I'm hoping you can do me a favour."

"If I can," she said.

"My mate who was going to drive me home has ended up

going out drinking. I would get a cab, except that I need to get the car home because the mechanic is coming first thing to take it to get modified so that I can operate it," he said. "Would you drive me, and I'll pay for you to get a taxi from my place."

"You don't need to pay for a taxi. I'll happily do it. Where do you live?"

"Out past Greenwich," Tommy said.

"Okay," Kat said. "Let's go, then. Where are you parked? Do you want me to bring the car around?"

"No, I'm just over the road," Tommy said, pushing himself to his feet and digging his keys out of his pocket. "Here you go." He grabbed his crutches and started towards the door.

Kat fell into step beside him.

"I saw you on the news," Tommy said.

"Really?" Kat said.

"Yeah, Adam was helping you into his car outside that posh school out in Mile End," Tommy said.

"I didn't realise we were being filmed," Kat said, colouring a little. "How soon before they fit your new leg?" she asked.

"It's been delayed again," Tommy said. "The swelling still hasn't completely gone down. I'm so frustrated if I'm honest."

"That's a shame," Kat said. "Don't these things always seem to take longer than you want?"

Tommy nodded. "I just want to get used to the basic one so that I can then get a blade. I want to run again."

"And you will," Kat said. "Marco says that you're making such great progress."

"Here we are," Tommy said, coming to a stop beside a blue VW Golf.

Kat pressed the unlock button on the key fob, and the lights flashed once as the doors unlocked. Tommy manoeuvred himself around to the passenger side as Kat opened the driver's door and got in. She adjusted the seat, moving it closer to the steering wheel.

"You've had someone tall driving," she said.

"Yeah."

"You must be looking forward to being able to drive yourself," Kat said.

"You have no idea," Tommy said, stowing his crutches as Kat pulled away from the curb.

"What's the best way?" she asked.

"Cross over Blackfriars Bridge and then basically follow the A2 to Blackheath, and I'll direct you from there," he said.

Kat turned onto New Bridge Street and crossed over the Thames, the pairs of old-fashioned streetlights on either side of the bridge lighting their way.

Tommy fell silent as they drove along the Old Kent Road past blocks of shops and then houses. Kat glanced across at him.

"What else is new with you, Tommy?" she asked.

He turned to look at her, a strange distant look in his eyes. "Nothing, absolutely nothing," he said.

"Well, hopefully that swelling will go down in the next couple of weeks, and you'll be ready for that new leg," she said.

"I'm not sure there's much point," Tommy said.

Kat frowned. "What do you mean?"

"Even with a false leg, I can't go back in the army," he said.

"Tommy, there are plenty of other things you can do," Kat said.

"I'm not like you, I'm not cut out for a desk job," he said. "I need to be outside."

"Have you talked through your options with the rehab people?" she asked.

"Not really."

"You should," she said. "They will have all sorts of ideas for you."

Tony gave a bitter laugh. "I was about to say, what would you know, but you would, wouldn't you?"

Kat nodded. "If it's any consolation, it does eventually get easier."

"Yeah, well, a hand is easier to replace than a leg," Tommy said.

"I wasn't aware it was a competition."

Tommy glared at her. "Turn here onto Charlton Way," he said. "And then left onto Blackheath Avenue."

* * *

Adam returned to the incident room after a long day dealing with the arrests of Andrew Wilson and Anton Grange, whose fingerprints were already in the system from previous convictions for aggravated robbery and assault. Julian and Eloise were still at their desks typing up reports.

"Sarge," Julian said, looking up as Adam entered the room.

"You two should go home, finish those up tomorrow," Adam said.

"I'll go after this one," Julian said.

"I'm almost done," Eloise agreed.

"I can't believe that we can't pin anything on Deborah Sharp," Julian said.

"At this stage, there's just no evidence. She's either incredibly clever or very naive – I can't decide which," Adam said.

"If you believe Harry, then she's behind all of the local ransomware attacks over the last eighteen months."

"Again, no evidence of that," Adam said. "But it will be interesting to see what the NCA's technical forensic team finds."

"She was pretty open about them searching her computer," Julian said. "What about her husband? It was his apartment that Harry was taken to, and there's some sort of link between him and the ransomware victims. You don't think he used the sustainability initiative to target vulnerable firms?"

"I think he was set up," Adam said. "Including the use of his flat. His alibis are tight for Harry's abduction and the attacks on Connor O'Malley."

"He could have orchestrated it but not have gotten his hands dirty, I guess, "Julian said, leaning back in his chair. "But we're back to that evidence thing. You don't suppose Wilson really set it up to look like Jeremy Sharp was behind it all? If he was in a relationship with Deborah Sharp, perhaps he wanted him out of the way."

"It's possible, although Andrew Wilson doesn't strike me as a great criminal mastermind," Adam said. "Did forensics find anything at the Snapp Software premises?"

Julian shook his head. "Nah, it was scrubbed clean, commercially. Nothing to tie it to Jeremy, Deborah or Wilson, not even a fingerprint."

"That would have been too easy."

"Is the conclusion that Deborah Sharp is running a complex cybercrime network who are stealing credit cards and laundering the proceeds with gaming currency and cryptocurrencies? And also infecting vulnerable businesses with malware to extract ransoms?" Eloise asked.

"In a nutshell, yes," Adam said. "But suspicion is one thing; building a watertight case is another thing entirely. The NCA have their work cut out."

"At least we have Marshall Tyler's killer," Julian said. He leaned forward and, using his mouse, clicked on an image and dragged it to add it to the digital incident screen on the wall at the end of the room. "There was enough DNA under Marshall's fingernails that forensics were able to match it to Anton Grange."

"Although, he's claiming that it was accidental. He pushed Tyler, who fell and hit his head, which does fit with evidence at the crime scene."

"It's closure for Tyler's family, at least. What's Grange saying about the attempted murder of O'Malley?"

"Claims it wasn't him," Adam said. "That Kat was mistaken. Unfortunately, the security cameras were conveniently not working at the hospital for an hour either side of the attack on Connor."

"And is Harry co-operating?" Julian said.

"Yes, I think he was completely out of his depth," Adam said. "His father explained to me that Harry was desperate to be accepted by the wealthy kids at the school and that he would have done anything to have the things that they had, and he didn't."

"That's a tough lesson."

"Yeah. Kat thinks he genuinely did make quite a lot of money by cryptocurrency trading. Still, the problem is the source of his original funds. It's going to take some time to unravel it all. We're still not sure whether he and Marshall were paid in Bitcoin for their laundering services or whether they just helped themselves. Either way, he's facing several charges."

Adam sat down in his chair and ran his hands through his hair. A courier envelope was sitting on his desk.

"When did this arrive?"

"A courier dropped it off at the front desk a short while ago," Julian said.

Adam opened the courier packet and dropped it in the wastepaper bin beside his desk. He drew out a white envelope and frowned. Apart from the two unsigned notes, he received so little physical post that he had become paranoid. This letter was different from those notes though; the address was handwritten. He peeled the flap open and pulled out a message, which read:

'You can't be there to save her every time. Soon you too will know the pain of losing someone you love.'

Adam gave a sharp intake of breath and re-read the note. The writing was scrawled as though it had been written in a hurry. His first thought was Kat. But that made no sense, as no one knew the extent of his feelings for her. Except… Adam jumped up and retrieved the courier envelope. The pick-up address was in Wandsworth. He swore.

"Okay, sarge?" Julian asked, looking over at Adam.

"Webster is messing with me," Adam said.

"You mean your old army mate, who's in prison awaiting trial?" Eloise said.

"This note," Adam said, waving the piece of paper in the air. "It's a definite escalation. He's just threatened Kat. Eloise, can you call Wandsworth Prison and get me his visitor log for the past three days? He's got someone on the outside sending these for him." He grabbed his phone and car keys and bolted from the room with Julian close behind.

Chapter 43

Kat eased the car to a stop at the end of Blackheath Avenue alongside the imposing General Wolff statue, gifted to the British by the Canadian government in the 1930s to commemorate his victory against the French at Quebec. The Royal Observatory of Greenwich was in darkness to the left; the last visitors had left for the day. Below them, past the gloom of the park, beyond the colourful illumination of Queen Anne's house and the floodlit buildings of the Royal Naval College, the lights of the skyscrapers at Canary Wharf twinkled.

"This is one of my favourite places in London. I have always loved this view," Tommy said. "I like being on a hill, looking down over everything. I try to imagine all the different lives going on in the streets below. We're all just tiny little insignificant cogs in the wheels of life."

"It is beautiful," Kat agreed. "Do you live near here, Tommy?"

"No." The tone of his voice made her look across at him. Tommy leaned against the passenger door with a handgun pointed at her.

Kat gasped. "What are you doing?"

"I'm sorry, Kat, but he has to pay. He has to feel the pain

that I'm feeling."

"Who?" Kat said, looking from Tommy to the gun.

Kat's phone rang in her bag.

Tommy smiled. "Right on time. Get it out and put it on speaker."

Kat complied and pulled her phone from her bag. Glancing at the screen, she felt a wave of relief to see that the caller was Adam. She tapped the speaker icon.

"Hello."

"Kat, are you okay?"

"Not really." She turned to Tommy, who nodded and motioned with the gun for her to continue. "I'm here with Tommy."

"Tommy?"

"Hello, Adam."

"What's going on, mate?"

"Kat and I have gone for a drive."

They could hear Adam's footsteps, followed by a door opening and closing, then an engine starting.

"Where to?"

Tommy laughed. "I wouldn't want to make it too easy for you."

"Adam, he has a gun."

Tommy lashed out and struck Kat on her cheek with his free hand.

She cried out, tasting blood in her mouth.

"Tommy, calm down," Adam said. "You don't want to hurt her."

"Ah, but you see, I think I do," Tommy said.

Kat's stomach dropped, and she held her hand to her cheek as the stinging sensation caused her eyes to water.

"No, I think the person that you really want to hurt is me," Adam said. "Do you want to tell me why?"

"Because your life is perfect, you're good-looking, whole, you have everything, and I have nothing."

"My life is far from perfect, as you well know," Adam said.

"Well, it certainly won't be by the time I finish with it," Tommy said. "Your best mate's missing, probably dead. Your wife is having someone else's baby, although you probably haven't worked out whose yet. And your lover is about to die because you couldn't save her."

"It doesn't have to be like this, Tommy. Tell me what you need," Adam said.

"First of all, I'd like to know why my brother died in that ambush and not you or Jake?"

"Ah, Tommy, we were at war."

"Yes, but who made Jonno sit upfront while you guys got the extra protection in the back? I heard that Jake insisted that you two sit in the back. Did he know something was going down? He was military intelligence, after all. In fact, why was he even there?"

Kat slid her hand down the side of her seat, feeling for the seatbelt release.

"Don't even think about it, Kat," Tommy said, smashing the gun down on top of the knuckles of her left hand. Kat felt her prosthesis spasm as the internal wiring bent. She tried moving her fingers and found that she couldn't.

"Kat, just do what he says," Adam said, his voice calm. "Tommy, have you been sending me anonymous notes?"

"Oh, you got those did you?" Tommy sneered. "Did they make you think Jake was still alive?"

"I knew they weren't from him, Tommy."

"Oh well, at least the last one finally got your attention."

"Tommy, Kat has nothing to do with this. Why don't I meet you, then you can let her go, and we can talk face to face."

Tommy was silent for a moment. "I was going to do it over video, but having you here to see your lover die, would be an added bonus."

"I'm not his lover," Kat said.

"Adam mate, you disappoint me," Tommy said, starting to laugh. "What? He never told you how he feels about you? You mean you two haven't done the deed? Perhaps I will beat you to it? First Nancy, then Kat."

Adam was silent, and Kat could picture him controlling his temper. She anchored herself with an image of him racing to get them. But what then? Tommy could kill them both.

"Adam, did you hear what I said?"

"I don't know what you think is going on, but Kat and I are only work colleagues," Adam said.

In the light from the streetlamp, Kat saw Tommy's expression falter for a moment. "That's not true," he said. "Donny said that you leapt in to save her when he threatened her."

"I was the only police officer there, Tommy. Just doing my job, right, Kat?"

Kat nodded. "Yeah, that's right."

"But Donny said that you two were together."

"Donny doesn't know everything, and besides, he is a cheat and a liar," Adam said.

"No, he's not." Tommy's voice had become high pitched. "He's my mate. He was the only one who was there for me when this happened." He thumped his fist on his thigh. "And then you took him away and put him in prison."

"I don't think that's entirely true, Tommy. Nev, Pete, Noah,

and I have all been trying to support you, one way or another."
Tommy was silent. "And Donny did this to himself. Tom mate,
what he was doing was affecting thousands of lives. He had
to be stopped," Adam said. "What else is bothering you?"

Tommy looked across at Kat, keeping the gun trained on
her. She eyed it.

"If Jonno hadn't died, I wouldn't have stayed in the army
this long, and I would still have two legs," he said. "No one
wants a cripple, especially a hideously disfigured one."

"It doesn't have to be like that," Kat said. "Losing a limb
doesn't change who you are. Believe me, being bitter and
closed off is no way to live. It eats you up inside. Don't put
limits on yourself and what you can do."

"It's easy for you," Tommy spat. "You're still pretty."

"No, actually, it's not easy," Kat said. "It took me a long time
to overcome the limited view of how I thought my life would
be after the accident and to shake off my self-pity. I didn't
feel attractive, and any thoughts of ever having a relationship
again seemed an impossibility. Who would want someone
who wasn't whole?"

"Exactly," Tommy agreed.

"But I started working again, which has helped my self-
esteem, because my job is something that I'm good at, and I
started rehab with Marco. I volunteered for the experimental
prosthesis programme, and now I have the next best thing to
a real hand. Basically, I made myself get out of bed each day
and keep moving forward. I'm not saying it's easy, Tommy,
but it can be done."

"But you have lots of people supporting you."

"So do you," she said. "You just have to let them. But you
have to do some of the work too. I met up with an old school

friend by chance the other day who has become homeless through bad business deals. I mean, he was at rock bottom, in a worse situation than either you or me. He had nothing and no one. He was living on the streets, but he's managed to pick himself up and ask for help at a shelter. Last I heard, he had a job, working nights stacking supermarket shelves. It's not much, but it's something. It's a start. No situation is ever completely hopeless."

Tommy shuddered, and a single tear ran down his cheek.

In the rear-view mirror, Kat saw a flash of car headlights before they were extinguished.

"Tommy," Adam said. "Let us help you. We're not the enemy here."

Tommy began to shake his head from side to side as more tears fell. He moved the gun so that it was pressed under his chin.

"No," Kat cried, lunging across the centre console and grabbing his hand. The weapon fired, and the passenger window shattered, showering them both in a waterfall of splintered glass. The door was wrenched open, and Adam prised the gun from their entwined hands. Tommy's hands fell into his lap, and he started sobbing. Kat pressed the seatbelt release with her right hand and leaned across to pull him to her. Tommy rested his head on her chest and cried.

"I'm sorry," he said. "I'm so sorry."

"Ssh, it's going to be okay."

The sirens of two police cars and an ambulance wailed as they pulled to a stop behind Tommy's car. Adam made Tommy's gun safe and handed it to Julian, who'd accompanied him on the high speed drive to Greenwich. Kat held Tommy until his tears were spent and the heaving sobs racking his body subsided.

"It's going to be okay," she murmured over and over.

"I'm so sorry, Kat," Tommy mumbled as Adam finally assisted him from the car and retrieved his crutches from the back seat. Julian led Tommy to the waiting ambulance. Kat climbed from Tommy's car and fell into Adam's arms. He kissed her head and held her tight for a long time.

"What will happen to him?" Kat asked when she eventually eased away from him.

They watched the ambulance turn and drive back along Blackheath Avenue.

"I'll make some calls. We should be able to get him into one of the rehab centres. He needs help, not punishment," Adam said. "More importantly, are you okay?

"I think so," Kat said. "Although, my hand is broken." She held out her prosthesis to show him. There was a significant dent in the centre, just behind her knuckles.

"I'm really sorry," Adam said, gathering her back into his arms.

"It's not your fault. You didn't know Tommy was going to do that," Kat said, pulling back and looking up into his face.

"I shouldn't have been so quick to ignore the notes I'd been receiving, especially when you got one," he said. "I found out tonight that Tommy has been a regular visitor to Webster in prison, who has been fuelling his hatred by filling his head with lies about me. Tommy was vulnerable, and Webster exploited that."

"What about what he said about Nancy?" Kat asked, starting to shake a little.

"I don't know, and I don't want to know," Adam said. "Come on, let me take you home."

"Will you stay?"

Adam gave her a sweet smile. "If you want me to."

Chapter 44

The frosted glass doors sprang open, and Kat emerged with the strap of her gym bag over one shoulder, laughing at a comment from her companion. The breeze caught her hair, whipping it around her face. She grabbed it with her new prosthetic hand and tucked the strands of hair behind her ear. Adam climbed from his car to greet her.

"How was it?" he asked.

"Great," she said. "Sammy did really well."

"It was awesome," Sammy said, flicking his still-wet hair from his eyes. "Marco is so cool. He's set me up with a workout programme that I can do in the gym at school."

"Fantastic," Adam said.

"And Sammy is going to come and stay with me one weekend a month, so we can go to the gym and get his progress measured," Kat said, grinning at the boy.

Sammy beamed.

"Are you ready to go and visit your grandmother?" Adam asked.

Sammy's smile lost some of its luminescence. "Yeah, I guess."

Kat dropped her bag on the ground beside the car and rested her hand on his shoulder. "It'll be fine, Sammy. We'll come in with you at the start to help explain everything that's happened."

He gave a resigned nod before doing a double-take at Adam's car. "No way," he said. "Is this a 1976 Ford Capri?" Adam nodded. "Just like in *The Professionals*? Granny and I used to watch old shows."

"Yeah," Adam said, opening the door and tilting the driver's seat forward. "Jump in."

Sammy dived into the back seat. "Just when I thought today couldn't get any better."

Kat laughed and passed her bag to him. "Can you put that beside you, please?"

"Sure."

Kat started to move around to the passenger side, but Adam snaked his arm around her waist. "Not so fast," he said. "We haven't said hello properly."

Kat grinned against his lips. "Hello," she murmured.

"Ew," Sammy called.

"Shut up in the cheap seats," Adam called, kissing Kat once more before releasing her.

"Adam, what's going to happen to Harry?" Kat asked.

"He's been charged and will appear in court," Adam said.

"Is he likely to go to jail?"

"No, he'll probably be given a rehabilitation order of some kind and have his computer hard drives and phone confiscated for a while. It depends on the judge," Adam said.

"And Deborah Sharp?"

Adam shook his head.

"What? Nothing?"

"There's no solid evidence linking her to either the credit card fraud or the ransomware attacks," Adam said.

"So Andrew Wilson will take the fall?"

Adam nodded. "There's a mountain of evidence against him. Anyway, what's the latest on Connor?"

"He's out of ICU and is recovering," Kat said, opening the passenger door. "Unfortunately, he can't remember anything from the day he was drugged."

"At least he's getting better, that's the main thing," Adam said, climbing into the driver's seat. "Does he know?" Adam indicated between them with a flick on his hand.

"Yes, and he's cool. He's got more important things to contend with right now," Kat said as she pulled her door closed. "Besides, he'd guessed after talking to Tommy that you and I had unfinished business."

Adam turned to look into the back seat. "I hope you like 90s rock anthems, Sammy," he said. "We've got a two-hour drive ahead of us."

"I knew it was too good to be true," Sammy said, putting his hands over his ears and laughing.

The End

Acknowledgement

A huge thank you once again to my editor, Gary Smailes, for his valuable advice and guidance. Many thanks to Julia Gibbs for copyediting and to my beta readers Sarah and Craig whose time and effort I hugely appreciate. The gorgeous cover is by Warren Designs. Thanks also to Lawrie for letting me pick his brain on all things crypto currency related and all the helpful people in the Cops & Writers group who patiently answered my police procedure questions. Special thanks to Deborah who, as a thank you for answering a number of law enforcement questions for *Death Count*, has had a villain named after her. (I hope you enjoy your namesake's escapades!)

My advance reader team has once again been massively supportive with their early reads and reviews and for getting in behind Kat and Adam. A big shout-out to Shannon, Michaela, Melanie, Judy, Eveie, Roger, Karen, Graham, Eileen, Suzanne, Kathryn, Jackie, Milena and Carol. And a huge thank-you to the book bloggers and reviewers who help to share their excitement for my books. Congratulations to Eloise from my Reader's Group, who won the 'name a character competition' and lent her name to PC Eloise Salter.

Lots of love to my family. I couldn't keep all the balls juggling in the air without your love and encouragement.

And finally, a big thank-you to you, my readers. Thank you

for your emails! Your messages are the encouragement I need on those days when I'm buried deep in a plot hole.

If you would like further information about me or my books you can check out my website, www.slbeaumont.com or join my Reader's Group to be kept up to date about up-coming book launches, exclusive giveaways and competitions and receive a FREE copy of *The Reluctant Witness* novella.